Emily Gives Miriam a Better Future: An Adoption Story

This is a work of fiction. Names, characters, places, and incidents either are products of the author's imagination or are used fictitiously. Any resemblance to actual events or locales or persons, living or dead, is entirely coincidental. Though this is a work of fiction, stories like this play out all the time when a family or individual welcomes a child(ren) into their home and adopt them.

Dedication

This book is dedicated to the countless individuals that have welcomed children into their homes, who were not biologically theirs. By welcoming these children into their homes, they have given the kids hope, hope for a better future.

Emily Gardner is a successful real estate developer living in, Tulsa, Oklahoma. She has the ability to look at a property, and not see it as it looks today, but how it can look. She loves taking a rundown, former rental house and transforming it into a dream first home for a couple. Though it can be a physically demanding job, she doesn't do the physical transformation herself, she has teams that do the work. It gives her the ability to focus on finding new properties.

Emily stands five foot six, although most would say she was 2-3 inches taller, as she is rarely seen without heels on. She averages about 115 pounds, though she doesn't frequently work out, she likes to stay active. Her caramel-colored hair flows to just below her shoulders. Around the office and town, she is usually seen with a knee-length dress, or dress shirt and pants, though she prefers the dresses.

Though she is petite and of average height, when she enters a room, there is something about her that commands respect. Though most men will initially pay attention to her, as they find her attractive, when she speaks, they know to listen as she has this no-nonsense attitude about her. She is intelligent, well-spoken, and knows how to reach her audience. She is a favorite speaker at many groups, including at the university, where she often speaks to college women and shares her story. She is so fond of this group, that she would often hire one or two each semester as interns, where they would work alongside her.

If there is one area that Emily has not been successful, it is in a dating relationship. She is quite attractive, and men want to go out with her, but most are either interested in her body, or they know she is successful and want her to be their sugar mommy. The few that do not fall into either of the two camps, want to be dominant in the relationship, whereas Emily wants someone to be an equal partner, who will share in things. She is still in her early thirties, so she holds out hope that she will meet that special guy someday, though she felt something was missing.

One Friday after work, she stops at her favorite restaurant for dinner and a glass of wine. While there she runs into Laura, a classmate from her graduate school days, who she had not seen since shortly after graduation.

"Hey, Laura! How have you been?"

"I've been great Emily. I've been following your career and am impressed with how successful you have become."

"Well thanks! I've worked hard, and as a result, I have been quite successful when it comes to my career. If only I was successful in other areas as well."

"I know that feeling. Relationship issues?"

"Unfortunately, I've been in a dry spell since graduate school. I had been with Keith for almost two years when I decided to go pursue my master's degree. He saw no need for an advanced degree when my job was to get married to him and start pushing out kids."

"What a loser. Don't know if you knew but soon after you left him, he found someone new, they married a year later and she pushed out six kids for him before he left her for someone younger."

"That could have easily been me! I'm glad I dumped his pathetic self when I did."

"I'm glad you did Emily. He was a complete loser. Any regrets?"

"Not about dumping him. I had thought I would have some kids by now. I know I still have time; I just hope I don't spend so much time and focus on my career that I completely miss out on children."

"Have you considered adopting a child?"

"I don't want to raise a baby by myself right now."

"It doesn't have to be a baby. Many people adopt older kids. As much time as you spend speaking to college girls and giving them internships, adopting a teen girl would be perfect for you."

"I had no idea that it was even a possibility. That sounds exactly like what I have been looking for. How should I proceed?"

"My cousin is a caseworker in Tulsa County. I will give you her contact information and you can contact her to get more information."

"Thank you so much, Laura! I'm glad I ran into you today." They hug before Laura leaves. Emily gives the caseworker a call and sets up an appointment for the following week to discuss adoption. As she is finishing her pint, she gets a text from Kelli, her commercial real estate broker, that a new property has hit the market and she might want to look check it out ASAP.

Emily rushes home and gets on her laptop to see what this property is. Much to her surprise, it is an abandoned office building that had been on the market just a few months ago. She planned to redevelop it into an upscale hotel, but she was outbid by someone who thought it could be converted to condos. She quickly calls her broker to see what the story was with the property. It turns out that the company that outbid her, ran into a variety of issues. They had issues with financing as the banks didn't think there was enough interest, and the potential buyers did not want to commit until they thought it was a serious project. After a few months, everything fell through and it was back on the market. Luckily for Emily, she still had the original proposal that she had created, so she let her broker know to resubmit everything and see if their offer would be accepted this time.

    It was quite a day for Emily. A project that she thought she had lost out on, was back in the picture. More importantly, the prospect of having a child in her life just moved closer to becoming a reality. She was excited, but she didn't want to get her hopes up until she spoke with the caseworker in a few days. Until then she will just imagine what it will be like to have a young lady in the house with her.

These had been a few exciting days for Emily. Her proposal had been submitted and things were looking good. She was finally on the way to speak to the caseworker about adopting a child. She had so many questions. Adoption was not something that she had considered before, so there had not been much research on her part for how this would work.

After a few minutes of waiting, Rachel, the caseworker, came out to take her back to the office. After exchanging pleasantries, Rachel decided to find out what brought Emily to see her today.

"So, tell me about why you are considering adopting."

"Well, honestly, it was not something that I had thought about before I spoke to Laura the other day. I've always wanted children, just have not had much luck with finding that significant other in order to have kids biologically.

"I see. Tell me about your work."

"Well, I am a real estate developer. I work on my own, so I do have some flexibility in when and where I work."

"Well, that will be a help in assisting the transition for a child. I've seen many couples that are so busy with work that they do not have adequate time to help the child transition, and that is a big disservice to the child. They need that time to help them become accustomed to their new surroundings. It can be traumatic for them, so the more you can do to help with this transition the better. What did you have in mind for what type of child you were looking for?"

"I don't want a younger child, like a baby, though I know many do. When I was talking to Laura, she mentioned maybe a teen girl, as I do a lot of volunteer work with college-aged girls, giving them internships and speaking to them about college and careers."

"I think that would be a wonderful idea. Instead of an internship lasting for a few months, think of this as an internship that will last for a few years, and you will be a role model for them through the teen years and beyond."

"I like that idea and it sounds perfect for me. Where do we go from here?"

"Well, the first step is a background check, just to make sure you're not a homicidal killer or something. Once that has been completed, we will come out to your house a complete a home study. It just allows us to see what your house looks like and make sure it is an appropriate environment. Once that has been approved, then we can look at placing a child with you and finding a good fit."

"That sounds great. I can assure you that I am not a homicidal killer so there will be no issue with the background check." Both ladies laugh.

"Well before you go, here is the application packet to take home and fill out. Just bring it back when you are done, and we can go from there."

"Well thank you for your time Rachel. You answered so many questions. I will bring this back soon, as I can't wait to get started!"

"Thanks for coming in Emily. I'm looking forward to working with you as well."

As it was late in the afternoon, and Emily was too excited to do any more work for the day, she called it an early day and headed home to fill out the application. She poured a glass of wine and began to work through the application. The first part of the application was the standard get to know the applicant stuff that was to be expected. The second part of the application was more troubling. It was asking about what type of child she was looking for and what was she willing to accept. Would she take a child that had been molested? What about physically abused? Sexually active? Learning disabilities? Emily began to realize that things may not be as simple as she had thought.

  She decided to think it through overnight and decide what type of child she would like and what features she was going to be OK with. She cooked dinner and sat by the fireplace contemplating what she was willing to accept. As she sat there watching the fire die, it came to her that if she had a biological child, she would have little say in what features it would have. Sure, she wouldn't have to worry about it having a history of abuse or neglect, but it could have mental or physical disabilities and she would still love that child. Why should an adopted child be any different? She wanted to be a parent to a young lady that needed her, just as much as Emily needed the young lady. She quickly filled out the remainder of the application, and went to bed, knowing that soon she would change a young lady's world around. Little did she realize how much the young lady would also change her world around.

The next morning Emily dropped off the application, before heading to the office. As she arrived in the office, Kelli called with news of the project.

"Emily, I just heard from the seller. They like your idea for an upscale hotel, and they think it is in the perfect location. They do have a few concerns though."

"Anything serious Kelli?"

"After the last project fell through, they want to make sure this is a serious project, so they do not waste several months on something that has zero chance of becoming a reality. They would like to see some assurances that your plan is more serious than a dream. I think they are wanting to see something from the bank that the financing can be arranged. They do not doubt that you could redevelop the building, but they want to know what the plans are once the building is finished. Will the hotel be an independent hotel, or will it be part of a chain? I think they want to make sure that there is a good plan in place and the building will not end up abandoned in a few years."

"I understand Kelli. I'm glad that they like my idea. It sounds like I need to do a little more work to make sure everything is in place before they are ready to proceed."

"That is what I am thinking as well, Emily. I think the financing part will be easy to put in place, as that should not be a problem for you, as you are well known and have successfully completed many projects locally. The issue will be deciding what to do once the building is completed. I know you had mentioned starting on the project then begin to market it, but we might have to reverse those."

"That is what it is begging to sound like. I will speak with a few people and get back to you. Let me know if you hear anything else, Kelli."

"Will do Emily. Have a great one."

"Thanks, Kelli. You as well."

Emily sat down at the computer to send out a few emails to see what she could accomplish in gathering more information for her plan. She sent an email to her banker letting her know what was going on, and she attached a copy of her plan for the building to see if there would be any issues. Before she could get started on any more emails, she got a call from Rachel.

"Hey Emily, this is Rachel. I was looking over your application, and everyone looks good. It will take a couple of days to get the background check back, but we want to go ahead and schedule your home study. Normally we would wait till everything was back, but you have a solid reputation in the community. I spoke with my supervisor, and she also feels we can go ahead and schedule the home study."

"Wow! That's great news! I thought it would take a lot longer. Well, my house is pretty much ready, so whenever you are available."

"I know it is quick, but how about this evening? Your house is on the way home for me, and I know you'd like to get this over with."

"Wow, yeah that would be great. I'll be home after four, so any time after that would be great."

"Sounds great Emily. See you later this afternoon."

Emily could hardly believe the day that she has been having, and it was not even lunchtime yet. Her project had a good chance of being accepted and it seems like she was on the fast track to adopt, when only last week she had not even contemplated adoption before. Trying to keep her mind on work, she decided to pull up the real estate listings to see if any residential properties looked appealing. Try as she may, she couldn't focus on the listings and instead began to dream about her future daughter. After a few hours of minimal work accomplished, and lots of dreaming, Emily decided to head home and make sure the house was as clean as she was hoping it was.

Emily arrived home a few minutes before four, and fortunately for her, little needed to be done. She lived by herself, and she was pretty good at keeping the place looking good. In her mind, it was easier to do a little bit of cleaning every day, instead of waiting till the work piled up in the sink. She walked through the house and was glad that there was little that needed attention. She was just about through the house when the doorbell rang.

Emily opened the door and was not surprised that it was Rachel.

"Hello, Rachel. Come on in."

"Thanks, Emily. Is this still a good time?"

"Of course."

"Good. Well tell me about the place and show me around."

"Well, it is relatively new, as it was built five years ago. There are officially four bedrooms, though as you will see, some have been converted to other uses. Each bedroom has its own bathroom. Clearly, the front door leads to the living room. There is plenty of seating for about a dozen people. Off to the right is the kitchen. The fridge is large enough for a small army, though it is just me. Feel free to take a look around."

Rachel opens the fridge and sees it is relatively empty. She checks the walk-in pantry and sees plenty of food.

"Everything looks good so far. I see lots of good food and plenty of space. Let's see the bedrooms."

"If you'll follow me. This first room is mine." She stops so Rachel can take a quick peek inside. "This next room is my home office. I could do all my work out of here if I wanted to, but like keeping a traditional office, so I can get out of the house. I also don't like meeting with work people at the house."

"So, would you work here for a while after placement?"

"That would not be a problem. Since I am my own boss, I can work as much or as little as I want to. I am willing to do what is needed to help with the transition period."

"That's good to hear."

"This next room is the primary guest room." Emily opens the door revealing a nice size room with a queen-sized bed, large dresser, large flatscreen, and a large closet. "I don't' have as much furniture in here, as I don't use it often. Once someone is placed, they would be free to add more items to make it their room. Through this door would be their bathroom. It is pretty standard but would give someone a place for their toiletries and makeup. It would also give them lots of privacy and their own shower."

"It all looks wonderful. I know I would have loved this when I was a teenager."

"I hope my future daughter feels the same way. If you come with me, I will show you the last room. I haven't done much with it. I feel like I need to do something with it, I'm just not sure what. With a possible placement, I think I will keep it open for now." Emily opens the door revealing a similar-sized room as the guest room, but pretty much bare.

"That's not a bad idea to keep this room open for now. You never know what you might need it to be. I must say I am greatly impressed with the house. Everything looks wonderful. I've been taking notes as you have been showing me around, and I have a few things to finish up tomorrow at the office, but you can consider the home study passed. I see no reason why someone could not be placed here."

"I'm so excited to hear that! I can't wait to have a daughter of my own!"

"Well, I am glad to hear that. Once everything is formally approved, which shouldn't take long, then we can begin to discuss particular kids that you might be interested in. Until then, try not to get too excited."

"Thank you so much, Rachel! I look forward to hearing from you soon! Have a great evening."

"Thank you so much for having me over, and I hope you have a great evening as well."

Emily couldn't believe it. Just a few weeks ago, she had never considered adoption, she barely knew anything about it. She had thought that without being married, that she may not have kids, at least for a while. The next few weeks could be extremely long. How was she supposed to keep herself occupied when she was this close to having a child of her own?

The next morning shortly after she arrived at the office, Emily received a call from Kelli.

"Hey, Kelli. What's going on?"

"Well, I hope you are ready for some good news. I just got off the phone with the broker for the property that you were wanting to convert to an upscale hotel. The owners loved the ideas that you submitted! As long as you can arrange the financing, they will sell it to you!"

"OH MY! I don't know what to say!"

"Well, congrats! That is quite an accomplishment! Now comes the fun part, arranging the financing. Have you talked with your banker?"

"I sent her an email a few weeks ago, and she didn't see any problems. I've been so busy that I haven't been able to sit down with her and discuss the details."

"Well, you better sit down with her soon! I don't want to see this opportunity pass you by."

"I will call her as soon as I finish with you."

"Well, I better get off so you can get to work! Congrats Emily! The hard work is just getting started!"

"Thanks, Kelli! Don't remind me about the hard work. Talk to you soon!"

Emily takes a moment to regain her composure and take a breath or two. She gives her banker, Brooke, a call.

"Hey, Emily. What's going on?"

"Hey, Brooke. Do you know a bank where I can apply for a loan to purchase an abandoned building and convert it to an upscale hotel?"

"Emily! They accepted your offer?!?!?"

"I just found out a few minutes ago."

"That is wonderful to hear. You better come in soon so we can finalize everything. I did pass on the information that you gave me a few weeks ago, and the VP sees no reason that we can't do the deal. We've done many deals with you, and the bank has made money every time and we have had no issues with you in the past."

"I am so glad to hear that Brooke. You are always so easy to work with. I'm glad to hear that financing shouldn't be a problem. I will stop by after lunch and get started with the paperwork if that will work for you?"

"Sounds great Emily. Looking forward to seeing you this afternoon and getting started on this project."

"See you then Brooke."

Emily could tell it was going to be one of those days and it had just started. It was time for a coffee run, before tackling this day. A few minutes later Emily returned, and her phone rang. She looked at the phone, and it was Rachel.

"Hey, Rachel. What's going on?"

"Hello, Emily. Well, I thought I would give you an update and some potentially good news."

"I love good news!"

"Well, first of all, everything is looking great. Everything is pretty much done on the approval side. We just need one more person to sign off on everything, and it will be official."

"Well, that is good news. So, what is the potentially good news?"

"I was about to get to that. I don't want to say too much until we can meet in person, but we have a young lady that we feel could be a good fit for you."

"Really?"

"Yeah. It is an unusual situation, and well, many of us think it could be an ideal situation for both of you."

"Now that you have me intrigued, when can we meet to discuss her?"

"How soon can you be available?"

"I am free for the next hour or so."

"Sounds good. I will be over in a few minutes."

"Can't wait to hear about her."

Emily was glad that she got that extra cup of coffee. She was going to need it to get through this day. How was she supposed to get to work when she was constantly meeting with people or talking to them over the phone? If this keeps up, she will need to hire an employee just to ensure that work gets done.

A few minutes later Rachel was at the office to go over some of the details that she wanted to do in person.

"Hey, Rachel. Come on in and let's get this started."

"Hey, Emily. I like the office. I can see why you have it when you also have the home office."

"Thanks. It's nice being able to get out of the house regularly, but also have the ability to work at home when needed."

"Well before we get started, I do need you to sign this form. It states that I am sharing confidential information with you, and you are not to share it with anyone."

"That won't be a problem. Let me sign that quickly and we can get started."

"Good. The young lady is named Miriam and she is 13. She came to this country, with her family, when she was 3. They were originally from Guatemala. Three years ago, there was a tragic car accident and every passed except for Miriam."

"That's terrible."

"Yes, it is. There was no other family in the US, and the few distant relatives that could be located in Guatemala did not want her sent back, so she has been in foster care since then."

"How has she been doing since?"

"She has made some improvements, but still has a way to go. The issue and this is where you come in, is she's spent most of that time in large settings. Her therapist feels that she would do better in a smaller setting, where she could be given lots of one-on-one time."

"I see. How is she doing academically?"

"Not too bad. She is in 8th grade and is average grade-wise. Since she has been in the US since she started school, she is fluent in English, but learned plenty of Spanish at home."

"That's good to know."

"So, what do you think?"

"I can't wait to meet her! That's what I think."

"Wonderful. How does Saturday sound?"

"That would be fantastic."

"Wonderful. We will keep it simple, so she is not overwhelmed. I want the two of you to be able to talk, but I do not want it to seem like an interrogation. We can do the meet at Woodward Park to give the two of you a few minutes to walk around and talk. Afterward, we can head down the street to Utica Square to shop and eat dinner."

"That sounds fantastic!"

"Wonderful. I will work on the arrangements. I will leave some of this file with you. It has a lot of her information that you can read through. Lots of notes from doctors and therapists from past visits. It will help you have a better understanding of her for Saturday. I will let you know that it is not an engaging thriller, and parts of it are incredibly sad."

"Thanks for the warning. I will save it for the evenings when I am alone and can better process it."

"Well, I will leave you to start working on the details. Hopefully, things will work out for the two of you. She has had a rough life and could use lots of love and attention."

"I can understand that. Hopefully, I am the right person to give it to her."

Rachel heads out and looks at her watch. By the time she grabs lunch, it will be time to head over to the bank and work with Brooke on arranging the financing for her new project. It has already been quite the day. It started with her finding out that she successfully bid on her dream project. She has dreamed of doing such a project. Now she finds out that she gets to meet Miriam in a few days, and this could lead to her adopting Miriam. She hasn't met her yet and only has one picture of her, but already wants to take her home. Saturday cannot come soon enough. With nothing left to do at the office for the day, Emily closes up so she can get lunch and head to the bank to meet with Brooke.

A few hours later, Emily is back home after a very eventful day. Her meeting with Brooke went well but was filled with lots of paperwork, copying and sending files, and lots of financial disclosure. Emily also met with the VP, who seemed quite interested in being involved with this project. She should know something in a few days.

After dinner, she decides to pour a glass of wine and take a look at the file that Rachel had given her earlier in the day. The first thing she notices is how much of the information has been blacked out. It looks like something the CIA would put out. From the first few pages, she wasn't able to learn much, except that her name is Miriam, she has a November birthday, so she will be 14 soon, and she is average height and weight for her age. She reads through and finds some notes from a caseworker. "Miriam is feeling extremely anxious and overwhelmed. She has been responding to therapy but is finding that there is too much going on at her foster home for her to feel at ease. The therapist feels that she would benefit from being in a smaller home, where she is potentially the only child and could receive the undivided love and attention that she needs to help her cope. We have attempted to find such a home but have been unsuccessful. Hopefully, soon we can find a permanent placement for Miriam. She is a sweet girl, with potential, if she can get the help she needs." After reading the note, Emily just cried. She knew she could give Miriam the undivided love and attention that she needed.

The next few days seemed like an eternity to Emily. She couldn't wait till Saturday to finally meet Miriam. As much as she tried to focus on work, she kept finding herself thinking about Miriam and what life would be like with her. Brooke did call her, and let her know that things were looking good, and they were just finalizing the terms of the financing before making it official.

It was finally Saturday morning, and in just a few hours, Emily would finally meet Miriam. She knew she needed to stay busy, or the next few hours would be torture. She went out to get some coffee, and she thought she should pick Miriam up something as a gift, but was unsure of what to get her, as she hadn't met her yet. She was browsing through a store when she saw something that she thought would be perfect. She purchased it along with a gift bag to place it in. Emily decided to head to Woodward Park to wait till it was time to meet Miriam.

After walking around for a few minutes, Emily saw a car park that she thought looked like Rachel's. She started to walk towards it when she saw Rachel get out of the driver's side and walk over to the passenger's side. Rachel opened the door and let Miriam out. She was exactly as Rachel described her. Miriam was dressed in a knee-length floral dress with silver flats. Her long black hair was pulled back, and she had a beautiful red bow in her hair. Rachel spotted Emily and started walking over to her, with Miriam following behind her.

When they walked over to Emily, Rachel formally introduced everyone.

"Miriam, this is Ms. Gardner. Emily, this is Miriam." Emily extended her hand, and Miriam decided to instead give Emily a big hug. Emily was quite surprised but was not going to complain, so she placed her arms around Miriam and held her close. After a few moments, Miriam finally let go, and when she pulled away, Emily could see a few tears. Not wanting to embarrass Miriam, Emily decided not to say anything.

"It is so nice to finally meet you, Miriam! I have been looking forward to meeting you since I first heard about you." Miriam just blushed. "I picked up something for you. I hope you like it." Emily handed Miriam the gift bag, and Miriam got a big smile on her face and said thank you. Miriam dug into the bag and had an excited look on her face. She pulled out a pink hoodie, and when she opened it, the word "HOPE" was written across it.

"I love it!" Miriam exclaimed. "I am usually cold, so I love hoodies, and pink is my favorite color. I especially love what is written on it."

"I am so glad to hear it, Miriam. I wanted to get you something, and I am thrilled that you love it. Would you like to walk with me as we walk around the park?"

"I'd love to". Miriam walked up next to Emily and placed her hand in Emily's, who graciously held onto it tightly. The two of them walked through the park, while Rachel followed.

"Tell me more about yourself, Ms. Gardner."

"I'd love to Miriam. I am a real estate developer. What that means is that I find buildings or houses that need to be fixed up, and I fix them up to make them look good again, so people can enjoy them again."

"Oh, that sounds wonderful!"

"It is Miriam. I enjoy taking those that look ugly and make them beautiful again. I like taking something that is damaged and bringing out the best in it." Emily gave Miriam's hand a squeeze when she said that, and Miriam smiled some more and leaned over, so Emily took her arm and placed it around Miriam as the two continued to walk around the park, neither speaking for a few minutes, just enjoying each other's company.

After a few minutes, Emily asked Miriam, "Miriam I am enjoying our time together. Would you like to head over to Utica Square for some shopping, and get some food?"

"I'd love to!"

"Great. Let's discuss the arrangements with Rachel."

Miriam runs to Rachel. "Ms. Gardner is going to take me shopping and get some food!"

"Well, that sounds like fun Miriam. We will follow Ms. Gardner. Does that work Emily?"

"That sounds great."

Five minutes later they had both parked at the center of Utica Square. Miriam barely let the vehicle come to a stop before she was trying to get out and be close to Emily again. As soon as she could, Miriam was by Emily's side, with her hand firmly in Emily's hand, ready to spend a few hours by her side.

"What should we go see first Miriam?" Emily asked her.

"I don't care, as long as I can stay with you."

"You are so sweet, Miriam. This store right here looks like it sells clothes for girls your age. Let's start here, and you can let me know what you like."

"That sounds wonderful."

They enter the store and Miriam heads over to some dresses that caught her eye. She picks up a couple to see how they would look on her.

"Those are very pretty Miriam. I noticed you were wearing a pretty dress today. Do you prefer dresses?"

"Oh yes, I do. I feel so pretty in them."

"Well, you look very pretty today Miriam, and I am sure you look pretty all the time." Miriam just blushed. "If you noticed, I am wearing a dress today as well, and I do most days." Miriam's eyes got big when she heard this. "I usually wear heels as well, though today I wore my wedge sandals, as I knew we would be walking a bit more than I usually do. Do you want to try one of those on?"

Miriam picked a pink one and headed off to the dressing room to try it on, as Emily and Rachel headed over to wait for her.

"Things seem to be going well, Emily."

"I couldn't agree more Rachel. Miriam is so sweet, and I love spending time with her. It's crazy how alike we seem to be."

"I won't even ask if we should move on to the next step."

"I wish we could just jump to the end, but I know we need to do what is best for Miriam."

"The whole way here from the park, she talked about nothing but you, so I know she feels the same way about you. We can talk more after I drop her off later and plan from there."

"Sounds good."

"What sounds good?" Miriam asked as she came out of the dressing room.

"Planning more time for me to spend with you, that's what sounds good." Miriam smiled at the thought of more time with Emily. "That dress looks so pretty on you Miriam. Would you like me to get that for you?"

"Yes, please."

"Well, then I will." The two of them walk over to the register to buy the dress. After purchasing the dress, the two of them head out of the store, holding hands.

"How about we head over to the Pottery Barn Kids over there and you can show me what things you like."

"I don't think I have ever been in that store before. What do they sell there?"

"They sell lots of furniture for younger people. They usually have lots of pretty things to look at."

"That sounds like a nice place. I'd love to go with you and look around."

"Well let's go then."

They enter the store and Miriam is shocked at all the pretty furniture. She had never seen such beautiful furniture before. One of the sales associates recognizes Emily and comes over to greet them.

"Hey, Emily. What brings you to Pottery Barn Kids?"

"Hey, Lily. This is my new friend Miriam. We were just checking out some of the pretty furniture here."

"Nice to meet you, Miriam. We have lots of pretty things here that I am sure you'd love."

Miriam runs off to look at the first display and Rachel follows.

"Nice to see you, Emily. I'm sort of surprised to see you here."

"Nice to see you as well. Well, I am hoping to eventually adopt Miriam. Today is our first meeting and I was showing her around. If things work out, she will need lots of stuff. My guest room is minimally furnished."

"That is exciting to hear! I will help you out as much as I can."

"Thanks. Now let's go see what she has found."

They head over to find Miriam and she has indeed found a set that she loves, and she is laying on the bed.

"Well, I think Miriam found something she loves."

"I love it! It is so pretty. I have never had anything this pretty before."

"Well Miriam, I will make sure that our friend Lily makes a note of how much you love this set." Emily glances over at Lily and makes a motion to write it down then motions talking on the phone. Lily smiles and gives a thumbs up. The three of them head out of the store. When she gets outside, Emily glances at her watch.

"I can't believe how much time has passed. It seems like we just got here, but it has been a few hours already. I am having so much fun, no wonder that time is flying by so quickly! I hope you are having as much fun as I am Miriam."

"I have not had this much fun in a long time. I enjoy spending time with you." Miriam gives Emily a big hug.

Rachel asks the group, "Does anyone else feel like dinner?"

"That sounds great Rachel. What about you Miriam? What type of food sounds good to you?"

"I love Italian food."

"Me too Miriam. Italian is one of my favorites. There is an Olive Garden around the corner. We can go there for dinner."

"That sounds great!"

The three of them head over to the Olive Garden, are quickly seated, and glancing at the menus.

"What looks good to you Miriam?"

"I love the spaghetti and meatballs."

"That sounds good to me as well. I think that's what I will have also."

Everyone places their orders and Emily decides to get to know more about Miriam, while they await their food.

"So, Miriam. What kind of things do you like to do for fun?"

"Well, I like shopping. I like to travel and see different things."

"Well, I am sure you can tell that I love shopping as well. I also love to travel as well. Have you been anywhere exciting Miriam?"

"Well, not really. When we were in Guatemala we didn't get to see much. When we moved to the US, we took a train through Mexico, and we saw some of Texas, but I haven't seen much else."

"Well, I am sorry to hear that Miriam. I have seen quite a bit of the US. I'd love to be able to show you more of the US, Miriam. I have the feeling that we will get along well together!"

Miriam smiled at the thought of spending more time with Emily. It was at this time that their food arrived. It was relatively quiet at dinner, as they could tell that Miriam was enjoying her food, and they didn't want to bother her with more questions. Once they had finished, they headed out.

"What should we do now, Miriam?"

"I don't know I'm feeling a little tired. Can we just sit on that bench over there for a few minutes?"

"That would be a great idea."

They head over to the bench and Emily sits down. Miriam sits down close to Emily and leans against her, so Emily places her arm around her and just holds her. After a few minutes, Miriam decides to ask Emily something.

"Ms. Gardner, can I ask you a question?"

"You can ask me anything you would like Miriam."

"Why are you wanting to adopt me?"

"Well Miriam, I have always wanted kids. When I heard about you, I had a feeling that we would be perfect for each other. One of the reasons that I gave you that hoodie that had "HOPE" written on it, is I didn't want you to ever lose hope. I know we have been through a lot, and I feel like our meeting was meant to be."

"I feel that way as well. I have been hoping to find someone one day who would love me and be there for me and would treat me like I was their own."

"You have nothing to worry about Miriam. I am choosing you, and I want to make you my own child."

After a few minutes of lying there, Rachel could tell that Miriam was getting tired.

"Well, I hate to break up the party, but I can tell Miriam is getting tired. I know it has been a busy day for all of us."

"I hate to go. I want to spend more time with Ms. Gardner."

"Don't worry Miriam. We will have lots of time to spend together. I will work out a schedule with Rachel, so we can be together soon. I promise."

"That sounds wonderful, as I had the best time today that I have had in a long time!" Miriam turns around and hugs Emily with all she can. After a moment she gets up and heads out with Rachel.

"I will see you soon Miriam!"

As Miriam walks away, Emily can't help but feel like a part of her is leaving. A couple of days ago, she didn't know Miriam existed but now can't imagine Miriam, not in her life. She has so much on her mind right now that she decides to walk around for a few before heading home. After a few minutes, her phone rings, and she sees that it is Rachel.

"Hey, Rachel. How's Miriam?"

"She's doing great. You will never guess what the only thing she talked about was the ENTIRE ride home."

"She's such a sweet girl. I couldn't have imagined that today could have gone better."

"I feel the same way. Normally we would either schedule a 2nd visit or an entire weekend, depending on how it went, but I know I don't even have to ask."

"I'd love to spend the weekend with her."

"I figured as much. I will call her and let her know. I can drop her off Friday after school and pick her up Sunday evening."

"That would be wonderful. I am already looking forward to it."

"Great. Well, have a good evening."

"You too Rachel."

Emily was excited, but now she needed to plan a weekend of things for Miriam. It was at this time that she noticed that she was outside the furniture store, so she headed back in to talk to Lily.

"Hey, Emily. Nice seeing you again. Can I help you with something?"

"Yes, I will go ahead and purchase that furniture set that we looked at. Miriam is staying over next weekend, and I would like to have it ready for her."

"That is so great to hear! I already wrote up everything, so I just need you to check it over, sign it, and swipe your card."

"That's great. Here's my card and let me sign this so we can have it ready for her."

After a few minutes, Emily had purchased the full set for Miriam and arranged for it to be delivered on Wednesday so that she would have plenty of time to make sure it was ready by Friday. She felt ready to head home, grab a quick drink, and go to bed.

The next morning Emily had only one thing on her mind, and it was Miriam. How could she miss someone so much that she had just met, and only spent a few hours with? She never felt like this when she was dating. While she had a good time with many of the men she had dated, she did not have this longing in her soul to be with them when they were not around, yet that is exactly how she felt about Miriam.

Emily knew she needed to keep occupied, so after pouring a cup of coffee, she headed back to the bedrooms to take a look around. She needed a bedroom to put Miriam's new furniture in, but she had some decisions to make. She liked the room that she used as a guest bedroom, and she felt it was the better of the two rooms, especially the bathroom. There was not much furniture, so she figured it would not be hard to move it to the fourth bedroom. She always felt weird having a vacant room with nothing in it, especially since she was a real estate developer. Why could she develop multi-million-dollar properties, but not a bedroom?

It did not take long for her to get the few pieces of furniture moved from one bedroom to another. She would save setting them up for later, so she headed back to what would be Miriam's room, and something didn't look right. While she knew part of it was because the room was empty, she felt the room didn't look very girly to her. The walls were painted a beige color with a darker colored carpet. While it was a fine choice for a generic room, it would not suffice for Miriam.

She decided to give her primary contractor a call to see what he thought. He had worked with her for many years on many different projects. When she told him what was going on, he was excited for her and thought the room could use some work. He said he would speak to his wife and daughter for a color recommendation, and he would come by later in the afternoon for her. Since she had been so good to him over the years, this would be his present for Miriam. Emily was so happy to hear it.

Now that she felt like the room was more worthy of Miriam, she could relax some, or so she thought. Miriam would be here in a few days, and she needed to plan some activities. What about food? Did she want to stay at the house and eat, or dine out? Maybe she should just not plan a bunch of things and see what Miriam wanted to do? What if Miriam felt bored if they just stayed at the house, and never wanted to visit again? These questions were going to drive her nuts if she spent all her time dwelling on them. She decided to give Rachel a call in the morning and see if she had a few suggestions. In an effort to keep her sanity for a little longer, Emily decided to set up the other bedroom, and possibly head to the store to purchase a few more items for the room.

The next morning, Emily was anxious to get to work and try and stay busy. She would finally see Miriam in a few days, and needed to keep her mind occupied, or else she would only think of the worst things that could happen. Once she was at the office, she decided to give Rachel a call to get some advice on the weekend.

"Hey Rachel, It's Emily."

"Hello, Emily. How are things going?"

"Things are great. I'm very anxious to spend some time with Miriam, which is why I am calling. I wanted to get your opinion on activities for this weekend, specifically, should we stay at the house and spend more time here, or should we stay busy outside doing lots of activities?"

"I'm glad that you are giving this weekend much thought, but I don't want you to spend so much time thinking about it that you lose it. I would have some activities for the house planned and some outside activities planned. Same thing with food. Do some meals at the house where you can work together on something and then plan either doing take-out or dining in. You could give Miriam a choice and let her decide. I will let you know, and you likely picked up on it the other day, but she is not a very social person. She much prefers a more intimate setting, instead of large crowds. Does this help at all?"

"Thanks, Rachel. That is exactly what I wanted to hear. I did notice that she seemed less social, and she seemed happy just spending time with the two of us."

"She would have been happier had it just been the two of you."

"You think so?"

"I know so, Emily. She told her foster mom that she didn't feel she could get as close to you as she wanted to, as I was around. She will likely be at your side the entire weekend."

"That makes me feel so wonderful to know that is what she thinks of me. I can't wait till this weekend. You've been most helpful Rachel."

"Thanks, Emily. Feel free to ask any questions that come up, and I will contact you later in the week to arrange the times."

"Sounds wonderful! Have a great day!"

"You too Emily."

Emily was now as anxious as before. She had a better idea of how much Miriam wanted to be with her, and it made her feel like she had to make the weekend perfect for her, but she knew that she did not need to overdo it. She needed to plan a few key activities, and not worry about every detail. Before her brain could go chase another rabbit down the hole, her phone rang, and it was Brooke.

"Hey, Brooke.

"Hello, Emily. Have I got some news for you! I hope you are sitting down for this."

"I hope it is good news, Brooke."

"Well, here is the abbreviated version. The VP that you met with when you applied for financing was at a party over the weekend, and also in attendance at the party was one of the major hotel owners in town. Well, they got to talking and the VP mentioned that you had applied for financing for a new property that you were planning to develop. He even showed the owner some of the drawings that you had submitted. Well, the owner loves the concept.

They had looked at adding a location in the vicinity of where this building was located but had not found the perfect property, that is until they saw your proposal. The owner told the VP that they had better approve the financing because they were serious about taking over the property when it was finished. Well, long story short Emily, but I wanted to formally let you know that your loan application has been formally approved by the bank!"

"That is so exciting to hear! I can't believe it!"

"Well believe it! The hotel owner wants to speak to you before things get started, but not to worry. It is just to let you know that they love what you have submitted, and as long as you don't make major changes, they are interested in purchasing the finished project."

"Well, I can't believe the good news, Brooke! I am so excited that I am finally able to work on this project. You have no idea how long I have wanted to work on something like this!"

"I am so excited for you Emily! I know this will be a successful project for you, and one that will be highly profitable!"

"Thank you so much, Brooke!"

"You are quite welcome! Stop by sometime tomorrow morning and we can finalize all the details, and get you started."

"That sounds like a great plan. I will stop by in the morning, so we can get this thing finalized, and I can finally get started on this project. This has been a dream of mine, and it can finally become a reality. Hope you have a great day Brooke! See you in the morning."

"Same to you Emily. See you in the morning."

It had already been quite a morning, and it was still early. Emily was a little over four days from having Miriam stay for the weekend, and she felt like she had so much work to do to make the weekend perfect for Miriam. She had the feeling that she was going to over plan for the weekend, and it was driving her nuts. She needed to find a way to relax, but that was not going to happen now that her project had finally been approved. Once she met with Brooke in the morning, it would be full steam ahead for her. Normally when she was working on a larger scale project, it would consume her for weeks at a time. Now that Miriam was poised to enter her life, was she taking on too much? While she was excited about this new project, she did not want to interfere with her time with Miriam. Is this what normal mothers go through trying to balance a career and family?

Miriam hadn't even stayed a night, and she was already feeling overwhelmed. She felt like she needed to talk to someone, but she was unsure who. She knew Rachel would not be much help, and she didn't want Rachel to know how she was feeling. She had a lot of professional contacts, but not many that she felt she could be personal with. If she had thought about getting Laura's contact information when she ran into her a few weeks ago, that would have been ideal. Somehow, she felt like that if she wanted this adoption to be successful, it was time to expand her network beyond professional contacts and include people she felt she could open up to when she had questions or concerns.

Her meeting the next morning with Brooke consumed most of the morning, which was not surprising considering the scale of the project. Funds were placed into an escrow account, which would allow her to purchase the building when the formal closing was held in a few days. Another set of funds were placed into a second account, which is what she would use to pay expenses as the project was being developed.

She had a few days until she could officially start the project. She made some calls to make sure her teams were in place to begin. Normally one construction crew would suffice, but this time she decided to start with two, but both teams would report to the same manager to make sure everyone was doing what they were supposed to be doing.

Later in the afternoon, Emily receives a call from Andy, the hotel owner who had spoken with the VP at the bank about the property she was wanting to develop.

"Hello, Emily. This is Andy from Tulsa Hotels, Ltd. I had spoken with one of the VPs at your bank about your property that you were going to develop."

Hello Andy. Nice to finally get a chance to talk to you. So, you are interested in my property?"

"I am quite interested in it. I had been looking for a nice property downtown that was a little more upscale but had not found what I was looking for, that is until I heard about what you had planned."

"Thanks, Andy. I am honored that you think so highly of my project. Is there anything in particular that I can help you with today about the property?"

"As a matter of fact, that is why I was contacting you. I already have a hotel brand that would like their name attached to it once it is finished. I am not asking for significant changes, but they do have a color scheme that they would like to see. If the color scheme and other minor things are already up to their standard, then that is money I do not need to spend to change things, which means I do not need to discount the purchase price of the property to take into account making those changes myself."

"That makes a lot of sense to me, and I'd be happy to help in any way that I can, especially if it means a higher selling price for myself. I will give you my contact information and you can send me all the details about color and other information for furniture that may or may not need to be changed."

"That would be wonderful. This will be such a time and money saver for me, and that means we can get the hotel occupied that much sooner."

"If you are this interested in it, I will let you contact my broker Kelli to start negotiating to purchase the property once it is finished, with obvious stipulations that it is finished and meets the qualifications that you are looking for in the finished building."

"I appreciate this Emily. Normally I have to either spend a lot of time and money to make changes to a property once it is finished, or I need to do a lot of the work myself, which I would rather not do, as it is not a strength for me."

"I am really glad that I can assist you and that we can both benefit from this. I look forward to working with you more in the future on this project. Hope you have a great day Andy."

"Same to you Emily. Looking forward to working with you as well."

The next few days were unusually calm for Emily. The closing had been scheduled for the following Monday. She received the information from Andy that would help her in meeting the color standards of the new franchisor. This would also save her and Andy much time and money and Andy's time savings would translate to more profit for her when the property was finally sold. She now had a few days to look over everything to make sure it was what she wanted, so once she closed on the property, she could get started right away.

Rachel had called and set up some tentative times for the weekend with Miriam. Miriam would be dropped off around dinner time on Friday, and she would be picked up around the same time on Sunday. This would give Emily about 48 hours with Miriam, which she felt was not enough, but it would do for now. The furniture that Emily had ordered, was delivered and set up on Thursday, and she felt the room looked so much better with new color and furniture.

When Emily woke up on Friday morning, she couldn't believe that the day finally arrived. She was set to finally see Miriam again in just a few hours. She planned to spend Friday evening at the house, and just relax. They would have two full days to be more active. She had the feeling that Miriam would like some quiet time with just the two of them, especially that first night. Having some plans, at least for the first night, was a relief for her, and it allowed her to relax some.

With the closing set for Monday, and Miriam scheduled to visit in a few hours, Emily headed off to the office to do a last-minute check to make sure all her plans were set for the following week. She also wanted to make sure that her teams were ready to start on Tuesday, and that all the supplies were ready to begin work on that day. By lunchtime, Emily felt good that everything was taken care of for the following week. She decided to head home and make sure that the house was ready to receive Miriam in a matter of hours. On the way home, she stopped at the grocery store and bought a few snack foods and drinks that she knew Miriam would like, based on information that she had supplied for some of the reports, which Emily had read through a few weeks ago.

  By 1 PM, Emily was home with a few hours to go till Miriam was to come. She needed something to distract her for a few hours, or she would spend the next four hours worrying about what could go wrong. She realized that she had not looked through the residential real estate listings in a while to see what might be available to purchase and flip. She had been so busy with her large project that all of her professional time had been devoted to it. She did find two that looked like they would be a good opportunity for her. Worst case scenario is she rented them out for a while until she was ready for them, so she called the agents to set up a time to look at them, and one was available Monday afternoon, which would work with her schedule. The other one sounded like an offer had already been submitted, so the agent would call if it were still available. Before she knew it, Rachel was texting to let her know that she was picking up Miriam, and they would be there shortly.

  Emily decided to wait out on the porch for Miriam to arrive, as it was a nice day, and she was anxious to see Miriam. Somehow, she felt that this weekend would be life-changing for her, as well as Miriam. It was one thing to spend a few hours with someone in public, but another to spend an entire weekend with just the two of them. As much as she was looking forward to Miriam coming, she was dreading having to send her back for a few days. Rachel had mentioned a transition but never specified a time frame. Maybe she wanted to see how things went, and go from there?

Before Emily could finish her thought, Rachel's car pulled into the driveway. She swore that Miriam opened the door, before the car came to a complete stop, and was running her way as fast as she could.

"Ms. Gardner!" was all that Miriam said before running into Emily, and almost knocking her off her feet. Emily quickly embraced her, and at least one of them was crying tears of joy.

"I'm so glad to see you too, Miriam. I have been looking forward to this weekend with you!"

"You're all that she talked about on the car ride over. I think she's a tad excited to spend the weekend with you." Rachel opened up the trunk of the car and retrieved a suitcase and walked it over to Miriam. "Well, I hope you two have a great weekend! If you need anything, don't hesitate to call me."

"Thanks, Rachel. I know we will have fun." The two of them wave to Rachel as she heads out, leaving them to enjoy their weekend together.

"How about I grab your suitcase, we head in and I show you around?"

"That would be great!"

When Emily opened the door, Miriam was surprised at the size of the living room and the openness of it all. She was used to more enclosed and tighter spaces. She looked over at the kitchen, and it was far larger than she had ever seen. The fridge was at least two times larger than what she had with her family.

"This is the living room. Over here in the kitchen, I picked up a few things for you." She opened the fridge to let Miriam see some of her favorite drinks, then she walked over to the pantry, opened it and Miriam saw many of her favorite snacks. Emily could tell that Miriam was impressed and grateful. "All those drinks are yours, so feel free to help yourself." Miriam walked over to the fridge and grabbed an orange soda, before following Emily to continue the tour.

"This first room is mine." She opened the door and let Miriam take a peek inside. "This next room is my home office. I can do all my work here, or I can do it at my regular office." Miriam could never have imagined such a nice room before. The most she had before was one computer with one small screen. This computer had multiple large flat screens, instead of an old wooden chair to sit on, this was one of the most comfortable-looking chairs that she had seen.

"This next room will be your room." When Emily opened the door, she could see Miriam's eyes light up. It was the most beautiful thing that Miriam had ever seen. The room was filled with pink, purple, and bright green colors. She could tell the furniture was the set that she had looked at last weekend.

"I absolutely love it! It is so beautiful!"

"I'm so glad that you like it. I'll put your suitcase here next to the dresser and you can unpack some of the clothes if you would like. Through this door is your bathroom."

"I get my own bathroom?" This was unheard of for Miriam. She was used to sharing one bathroom with at least four or five other people.

"Yes, you do." Emily opened the door, and the bathroom was also filled with her favorite colors, including the towels and bathmats.

"It is all so beautiful! I can't believe all of this is for me!"

"I'm glad you approve. I wanted everything to be perfect for you."

"It is perfect!"

"I'm glad. There is one more room, and it is just a guest room if it is ever needed. You can take a look at it if you want later. How about some dinner?"

"That would be great. I normally have a snack when I get home from school, but my foster mom wasn't feeling well."

"Well, I was thinking we could spend the evening here and order dinner. How does that sound?"

"That sounds wonderful! Can we order Chinese?"

"Absolutely." Emily places an order for food. "While we are waiting, feel free to change into something more comfortable like your pajamas. It will also give you a few minutes to unpack."

"Sounds good. Oh, I brought the dress that you bought me last weekend, and I was hoping we can wear it to dinner tomorrow night if that is OK with you?"

"I would love to take you out tomorrow night for more shopping and dinner. It makes me so happy that you loved your dress and want to wear it out."

Miriam gave Emily a big smile before heading off to her room to unpack and get changed. Emily took the opportunity to also change into something a little more comfortable, and then head back to the living room. She was so glad that Miriam loved the room and everything in it. It was a relief for her, though she kind of suspected that she would appreciate it. Everything seemed to be going well, but how long would this last? Before she knew it, Miriam was back and dressed in a cute nightgown.

"Well don't you look adorable! Why don't you take a seat in the living room, and as soon as the food comes, I'll join you."

"That sounds wonderful."

Not long after Miriam got situated in the living room, the doorbell rang. Emily answered the door and after paying for the food, grabbed the bags and headed to the living room. She opens the bag and pulls out a tray labeled "orange chicken". "This must be your orange chicken to go with your orange soda." Miriam just smiles when Emily hands her the food. "Do you mind if we talk for a bit while we ear, even though it may not be proper manners?"

"I don't mind at all."

"Great. Well, I thought I would give you a rundown for the weekend. Tonight, we are staying here. I know you had mentioned tomorrow evening going out to dinner, which will be wonderful. The rest of the day we can do what you would like."

"Can we do pancakes for breakfast?"

"You bet we can. Do you have a favorite place?"

"I don't get out very often to eat, so I don't have a favorite place."

"Well, I know a place that has great food, and they have trains running around the place."

"That sounds like fun. I'd love to go with you."

"Great. We will have so much fun together!"

"Ms. Gardener?

"What is it, Miriam?"

"I just wanted to let you know how glad I am to have you in my life. I hope you get to adopt me."

"I am so glad to hear that Miriam! I want to adopt you as well. You already mean so much to me!" Miriam gives her a big hug. "Well, how about we put on a movie and finish eating our dinner. I will let you pick one out. The DVDs are over there."

Miriam walks over and glances through the DVD's and comes back with her selection *The Blind Side*. "I like this movie since the guy doesn't have a family, and at the end, he gets a family, who loves him."

Emily is trying not to cry at this point. She takes the DVD and while she is putting it in, she wipes her face to make sure she has no visible tears. She had no idea that Miriam would be this sweet. Why couldn't she just adopt her now? That seems like it would be ideal for both of them. She headed back to Miriam and the couch. When she sat down, Miriam moved next to her, so she could lean against her while she ate and watched the movie. Once Emily had finished eating, she placed her arm around Miriam and the two of them enjoyed the movie cuddled up with each other, and neither could have been happier.

Once the movie was finished, Emily could tell that Miriam was getting tired. It was now well after eight, and she had a busy day. "Why don't I take our trash, and then I can walk you to your room?"

"I would like that. I am getting tired, and I need rest for our busy day tomorrow." Emily took the trash then came back and took Miriam by her hand and led her to her room. She gave Miriam a big hug and wished her a good's night sleep, then helped her to bed. Miriam just smiled at her as she turned off the light and headed out. Before heading to her room, she grabbed a glass of wine.

It had been quite a day. Things with Miriam couldn't be better. Miriam seemed to like a lot of the same things, including eating out, and she volunteered to dress up. That was something that Emily did often and always enjoyed looking nice when she was out. She was excited about the prospect of having a daughter that enjoyed many of the same things that she did. She finished her glass of wine and decided to head to bed early. Before she went to sleep, she wondered what else the two of them had in common?

The next morning, Emily was up at six. She made herself a cup of coffee and headed to the living room with her laptop. She would use this time to get caught up on what had happened for the past few hours and get caught up on emails. She had turned off her email notifications on her phone last night when Miriam had come over, so they would not be disturbed. There was not much excitement in either her personal or professional email inboxes. She was glad she turned off her notifications, as she would have been interrupted to save money on clothing shopping. Somehow Miriam seemed more important.

Shortly after seven, Miriam came out of her room and sat next to Emily. "Did you sleep well?"

"Yes, I did. I slept better than I have in a while."

"I'm glad to hear it. Any particular reason?"

"Well, the bed was very comfortable and warm. I don't think I have slept in a more comfortable bed before. Also knowing that there was someone who cared so much about me to buy me that bed and stuff helped me get to sleep quickly."

"Miriam you are too sweet. How about we get dressed and head out for breakfast?"

"Sounds good."

The two of them got dressed and headed to the restaurant that Emily had told Miriam about. Sure enough, there were trains all over the place, including some that were driving around the restaurant. Needless to say, Miriam had never seen anything like this. The server seated them and gave them a minute to look over the menu.

"What looks good to you Miriam?"

"It all looks good. I think I will go with the pancakes and sausage."

"That sounds good." She orders two pancakes with sausage.

"This place is so wonderful. I love trains, though I have never been on trains this nice. When we traveled from Guatemala to the US, we took a few trains, but they weren't very nice."

"You mentioned last week that you had taken some trains to get here. Once we can travel, we will need to do that. Since you grew up in a warm climate, I think it will be fun to go somewhere colder."

"I would like that, as it was very warm where I grew up, and we didn't have much relief from the heat."

"How would you feel about flying on a plane?"

"That sounds like fun, but I would be so nervous."

"I love to fly on a plane, but it can be a hassle at times getting to the plane. Don't worry when the time comes, I will be at your side to help you."

"I'm glad. I want to travel with you and just spend time with you."

"I'm glad to hear that. Looks like our breakfast is here." The server arrives with two plates of pancakes and sausage and passes them out. The two enjoy their pancake breakfast with little interruption, except for the occasional train whistle as the train circled overhead. Miriam had mentioned that they were the best pancakes she had ever had and quickly finished her plate. With nothing left on their plates, they paid their bill and headed home to decide on what to do next.

When they arrived home, Emily was heading to grab her laptop, so she could look up some ideas when the phone rang. "Let me see who that is." She glanced at the phone and it was Rachel. "It's Rachel. She's likely wanting to see how things are going. Hey Rachel."

"Hello, Emily. How are things going there?"

"Well, they couldn't be better. We just got back from pancakes and were about to decide what we wanted to do for the rest of the day."

"I'm glad to hear that. Can you go somewhere where Miriam cannot hear us?"

"Sure. Just a minute. Hey Miriam, I'll be just a minute. I'm going to get cleaned up some, while I finish with Rachel then we can have the rest of the day together." She heads to her room and shuts the door. "OK, I am in my room with the door shut. What's going on?"

"Well, we had an issue come up since I dropped Miriam off."

"OK. Anything serious?"

"You could say that. When I picked up Miriam yesterday, her foster mom had mentioned that she was not feeling that great and was looking forward to relaxing some with Miriam gone."

"Miriam had mentioned that she was not feeling well, and the foster mom didn't give her a snack when she got home."

"Well sometime last night things got worse, and she had a stroke."

"Oh no! That's terrible."

"She will need a few weeks to recover. We are in the process of moving the other kids to other homes."

"What about Miriam? You said other kids."

"Well, I talked it over with my supervisor and she said as long as things had been going well so far, that we would just move her into your custody permanently and skip the normal process of several weekend visits. Are you OK with that?"

"That is quite a shock, but I would love to keep her. She's been the sweetest girl, and we have been having so much fun."

"I am glad to hear it. I will let you tell her sometime this weekend when you think it is appropriate."

"OK. What about the stuff that she has at her foster mom's house?"

"She doesn't have much there. The foster mom gave me a key. I can meet you there when you are ready. I will be in and out almost all weekend working with the other kids."

"Well, thanks for letting me know Rachel."

"You're welcome. Oh, it will take a day or two to make changes at her school, so plan on keeping her home with you on Monday. I don't want her there until we can get you listed as her legal guardian."

"OK. Monday was going to be a busy day, but we will manage."

"Glad to hear it. I will let you get back to Miriam." After you've told her and want to get what's left of her stuff, let me know and I will be there."

"Thanks, Rachel."

"Enjoy your time with Miriam. I will meet with you in the coming days to go over some information that might be helpful."

"Sounds good Rachel."

Well, Emily didn't have to worry about saying goodbye to Miriam at the end of the weekend, which was good, but this was not the way she wanted it to be. She needed to let Miriam know that she would not be going back to her foster mom's house, and instead would be staying with her for the next couple of years, till she moved out as an adult. Emily needed a moment to think that one over before heading out to talk to Miriam. After a moment to gather her thoughts, Emily headed back to be with Miriam.

"Hey, Miriam. We need to talk for a minute before heading out, is that OK?"

"I guess. Is something wrong? You look worried."

"Well, you know how you mentioned that your foster mom was not feeling well?"

"Yeah. Is she OK?"

"Well, she got a little worse after you left and had a stroke."

"Will she be OK?"

"Yeah, they are pretty sure, but it will take a few weeks to recover, so she can't foster anyone for the time being. All the other children are being sent to other homes for the time being."

"What about me?"

"Well, Rachel and her supervisor decided that if we were OK with it, that you would just move in with me, and live with me."

"Really?!?! I would love to live with you today!"

"Well OK then. I'm glad that you were OK with it."

"My foster mom was great, but there were too many people there. She never had much time to spend with just me, and I missed that. She was a nice lady, but I like you way more."

"Well, I guess I am glad to hear that! Rachel said that we can go over there to get the rest of your stuff when you are ready."

"Can we go now, so I can get it over with?"

"I suppose so. Let me text Rachel and see what she says." Emily sends Rachel a text and she quickly responds that now would work and she also sends the address. "Well, I guess we are off."

They head off to the foster mom's house. Emily is disappointed at the lack of clothing that Miriam has. There is also a lack of personal effects. She knew she needed to take Miriam out and get her more things beyond what she would need for school. After a few minutes of packing, they head back to their home. Emily helps her move all the stuff to her room and lets her know that she can unpack later.

"Miriam, how about we go shopping now since it is still early? We can still dress up later this afternoon, do some more shopping, and have our nice dinner?"

"That would be wonderful."

"Great. It looks like you have plenty of clothes for school. We can work on some clothes for around the house, and for days when you do not have school. We can also get things to decorate your room."

"That sounds like fun. Can I also get some stuff to go with my dress for tonight?"

"You better believe you can. What did you need to get for tonight, so I know what stores we need to go to?"

"Well, I could use some tights to go with it, and the only dress shoes I have are the silver flats, so I would like to get some more."

"Not a problem. I love shoe shopping, and I always wanted a daughter to go shoe shopping with me." Miriam smiled at the thought of being Emily's daughter and grabbed Emily's hand as they headed out the door.

They headed to Target since it was one of Emily's favorite stores and they headed to the shoe department.

"Well, what kind of shoes would you like to wear with your dress?"

"I'd love a pair of heels like what you are wearing, but I have not worn heels before."

"Well let me see what I can find for you. What size do you wear?"

"I am just starting to fit into a six."

"Perfect. Let me see. These black ankle boots have a stacked heel, so that should be easier to walk in for you, and they will look so adorable with your dress. Oh, I love these heels over here. They also have a wider heel on them. Those look so professional. Try those as well."

Miriam tried on the ankle boots first. She wobbled a little when she first stood up but quickly was able to walk around with no problem. She then tried the heels on and was walking around like she had been wearing heels for years.

"Those look so cute on you. Are you sure you haven't worn heels before because you are a natural? You walk just like I do in heels. I say we get both. I was going to wear a red dress, black tights, and my black ankle boots. We need to get you a pair of black tights to go with your boots, and we will look so alike."

"I really like that idea."

"I'm so glad to hear that!"

"Thanks for the shoes. I love them." Miriam gives Emily a long hug.

"You are so sweet, Miriam. Let's go find those tights and see what else you need for your room."

Miriam saw a few more casual clothes that she liked, so they picked those up along with the tights to help her match Emily. Afterward, they stopped in the home department and Miriam saw a lamp that she liked and a decorative pillow that matches her bedding and the color of the room. After leaving the store, they stopped for some lunch. While they are eating, Miriam decides to ask some questions.

"Would it be OK if I trimmed my hair some? I don't want it short, just trim it up a bit so it is about the middle of my back, kind of like how yours is."

"I don't have a problem with it but let me check with Rachel. I don't want to get in trouble for something like trimming your hair." She sends Rachel a text letting her know what she was wanting to do. A few seconds later she responds that a trim would be fine, as long as it is not drastic.

"She says it will be fine. Let me make a call and see if someone is available. Hey, this is Emily. I know it is last minute, but I wanted to see if someone was available for a trim this afternoon. Really? I will take it! Well, I hope you are ready because we are not only trimming your hair but facials and manicures as well! There was a cancellation, and they had a whole package booked, so I took it. You better hurry, as we have to be there in 15 minutes!"

"That sounds like so much fun! I can't wait."

A few minutes later they arrived at the salon. They walked in and everyone greeted Emily. Emily explained to the stylist that it was Miriam that was getting the trim, and why Emily was bringing her. The stylist was excited to hear the news and made sure Miriam looked as beautiful as ever when she was done. Emily and Miriam had very similar-looking hair when she was done, and they would have looked identical if it were not for a difference in hair color. They both had fun with the facials and getting their nails done. When they were heading out, Miriam commented that she felt so beautiful.

"You were so beautiful before anyone did anything to you. I don't want you to ever forget that Miriam. They just brought out the beauty that was always there, now it is easier for others to see. It's almost time for us to get dressed for tonight. I hope you are ready."

"I've been looking forward to this all week!"

Moments later they arrive at the house and head to their rooms to get dressed. When they were done getting ready, they headed to the living room to wait. They ended up getting done about the same time.

"Well don't you look absolutely beautiful Miriam!"

"Thank you. You look pretty wonderful as well. I like the fact that we look so much alike."

"Let's take a picture before we head out." Emily set her phone so that it would take a full picture of the two of them. She checked the picture and thought it was perfect.

She sent a copy to Rachel, and she quickly responded that they both looked wonderful and hoped they had a great time tonight.

As they were heading out, Emily forgot to mention something to Miriam. "When I spoke to Rachel earlier, she let me know that it might be a day or two to update the information at school, and until it was updated, she mentioned that you should stay home with me."

"So, I get to spend Monday with you as well?"

"Yes, but I have a few meetings, but you can come so you have a better idea of what I do, but we need to find you some professional clothes sometime tonight. The heels I got you will be perfect."

"That sounds so exciting! I want to learn everything I can about you! Can we shop first and then eat?"

"You bet we can!"

They pulled into the shopping center where they first met last week and headed to the store where Emily bought much of her work clothes. When they entered, Emily was immediately recognized, and the clerk asked if she was needing something new for work.

"It is for my soon-to-be daughter. She is needing a suit for Monday. I am thinking of a skirt, a matching jacket, and a dress shirt. We already picked up heels earlier."

"That is wonderful to hear Emily! We will get her fixed up." The clerk escorted Miriam to the back, where she was measured and within moments, had a new business suit on her that made her look like she was heading off to college. When Emily saw her in it, she began to cry.

"You look so beautiful and professional, but you look like you're off to college and I'm not ready for that yet. We will most definitely take it!"

"I look so much like you in it! I can't wait to wear it Monday!"

"You two will look so much alike, everyone will think that you already are mother and daughter."

The clerk rang up the purchase and they headed off to the restaurant for their long-awaited dinner date. Emily had picked one of the nicest restaurants in Tulsa to take Miriam for their first of what will be many dates together. They walked into the restaurant holding hands, and they were greeted by the server.

"Well look at you two! Don't you look like twins?"

"Well thanks! I'm pretty fond of my twin."

"Wonderful! Let me show you to your table." As she walks them to their table, Miriam is quite impressed with the restaurant. She sees almost everyone is dressed up, and for once she doesn't feel out of place, as she and Emily walk to their table. "My name is Becky, and I will be your server for tonight. Here are your menus. I will be back in a moment to see if you are ready to order."

"This place is so wonderful! I love being dressed up and going someplace nice. I love that I don't feel out of place. I feel so pretty and special."

"Miriam, you are so beautiful, and you are so incredibly special that I want to make you my daughter. I don't want you to ever forget that! I also don't want you to ever forget how much I love you, Miriam!"

"You mean that?"

"More than anything!"

"I don't know what to say, but I love you so much too, Mom."

By this point, both ladies are in tears, but so happy to be together. Their server is watching from a distance, and she was about to see if they were ready to order, but instead decided to give them a few minutes. After a moment, they realize they need to look over the menu to see what looks good.

"Well Miriam, what looks good to you?"

"It all looks so good. How about you?"

"Well, they have a roast duck that comes with sweet potatoes. It's the best."

"I've never had duck before, though I do love sweet potatoes. I think the roast chicken with the mashed potatoes sounds wonderful."

"That does sound good. Let me signal to our server that we are ready."

"Are you ready to order?"

"I will take the roast chicken with the mashed potatoes, with root beer to drink."

"Great choice. And for you?"

"I will take the roast duck with the sweet potatoes, along with the house red wine to drink."

"Another great choice. I will get these orders placed and be back with your drinks."

"I'm so surprised that you called me Mom. I'm not complaining, I just wasn't expecting it."

"This whole weekend you have been treating me better than anyone has since my Mom. I do miss her a lot but having you around has helped."

"I'm so glad that have me around has helped some. I want you to know that I never want to replace your mom. She sounded like a wonderful person, and she did a great job of raising you to be the sweet, wonderful person that you are today. I had hoped that someday you would see me as a mom and might call me that someday. I had no idea it would be this soon. I'm so happy right now!"

The server stops by with their drinks and lets them know the food will be out shortly.

"Mom, when do you think we will be able to travel?"

"Well, it depends. Until the adoption is final, I need permission to leave the state. I will need to ask what is involved. If we want to stay in the state, then we can travel anytime."

"I hope we get to travel soon. There is so little of this country that I have seen, and I want to see it all, with my new Mom of course."

"I will talk to Rachel in the coming days to see what is involved."

"Do you have a lot of family members?"

"Well, I do, but not many in the area. I was born and raised in New Jersey. Most of my family is back there. I do visit them regularly. My parents do know about you, and they can't wait to meet you. I also have two sisters that live there."

"So how did you end up in Tulsa?"

"I came out here to visit a friend, and I fell in love with the place. I have my undergraduate and graduate degrees from the University of Tulsa."

"I've been past the campus, and it is such a pretty campus. I can see why you went there."

"It's a great school. I will have to take you there sometime and show you around. Looks like our dinner is here."

The server passes out their dinners, and they start to eat.

"How's your chicken?"

"It's very good. Your duck looks good."

"It is quite good. Would you like to try a piece?"

"Sure."

Emily cuts off a piece and puts it on her fork and gives it to Miriam.

"That is very good. I will have to have some duck sometime."

"I'm glad you liked it. Duck is one of my favorite meats, so I will have to prepare it some time for dinner for the two of us."

"I'd enjoy that."

The two of them finish off their meals and decide to walk around Utica Square for a bit before heading home, as it is a nice evening and they both looked great. They were having a wonderful evening together, and they did not want it to end.

"Well Miriam, is there anywhere in particular that we should head?"

"Not really. I just enjoy walking with you and spending time with you."

"I enjoy spending time with you as well. Well, we don't need more furniture so we can skip those stores over there. This store over here sells jewelry, let's go take a look."

When they enter, they are warmly greeted by a sales associate, who asks if there is anything in particular, they are looking for today.

"I am looking for something for my beautiful soon-to-be daughter." Emily smiles as she holds up Miriam's hand so that the sales associate knows who she is referring to.

"Well, congrats! She is beautiful. Did you have something in mind?"

"I was thinking perhaps a necklace with some ice that will sparkle just like her eyes."

"That is an excellent choice. I think I have what you may be looking for." She walks behind the counter and opens the case to pull out a necklace, which she places around Miriam's neck. It is a beautiful white gold necklace with a matching gold charm at the end, with a diamond at the center of it.

"I love it! That is exactly what I had in mind for her. Do you like it, Miriam?"

"I absolutely love it. Are you sure this is for me?"

"I am more than sure it is for you. We will take it, and I am sure she will want to wear it."

"I had that feeling when I saw the look in her eyes. I will just grab the case for later, and I will ring you up when you are ready."

The sales associate rings them up and they head out of the store.

"Thank you for the necklace and dinner and everything else we did today, Mom."

"You are more than welcome, my daughter. Do you want to do anything else or are you ready to head home?"

"Can we grab some ice cream then head home."

"Sure."

On the way home, they stop for an ice cream cone with a scoop of their favorites ice cream. They sit side by side enjoying their ice cream until Emily leans over and licks Miriam's, then Miriam's decides to lean over and give Emily's a taste. They just laugh as they finish off their cones.

Once they get home, they head off to their rooms to change out of their clothes and into something more comfortable. Once they are done, they head off to the couch to relax a bit, before heading to bed. Emily is seated first, and as soon as she is settled, Miriam is by her side, leaning against her. Emily had the feeling that Miriam would sleep like this if she were allowed to.

"How about tomorrow we do something quieter and relax a little bit more?"

"That sounds great. I had the best time today, but I am getting tired, but I don't want to go to bed yet. I like being close to you."

"I enjoy being close to you as well. For breakfast, I will just pick up something and bring it back here. I do think at some point we will need to buy some groceries since you live here now." As she said this, she rubbed Miriam on the back.

"That sounds good. I'm tired now. Mom, can you walk me to my room?"

"Absolutely."

After walking Miriam to her room, and tucking her in, Emily headed to the kitchen for a glass of wine. As she drank it, she couldn't help but feel like her life was wonderful right now. The best part is this feeling was not due to a guy, and she felt like this feeling would last, unlike in the past.

The next morning Emily was up at six, which was pretty typical for her. She loved the early mornings. It was just her, her coffee, and her thoughts. Yesterday was one of those days that she will never forget. It started with the two of them having breakfast, and then finding out that Miriam would be permanently moving in. They topped it off with one of the greatest mother-daughter dates in the history of the world. Emily knew she had longed for a daughter with who she could do those things and enjoy spending time with. She had no idea it would be this soon.

After yesterday, she could use a down day, especially with a busy day at work tomorrow with Miriam coming along. It was going to be a nice day today, so she didn't want to spend it in the house all day. After a few more sips of coffee, she had the best idea and something she had the feeling that Miriam would love.

It was almost 8 before Miriam finally made her appearance.

"Well good morning sleepy-head. I hope you slept well last night."

"I did. I must have been really tired from yesterday."

"How about I go grab breakfast. What would you like?"

"I love biscuits and gravy."

"Well, that is what I was going to get, so I'll make it for two, plus some hash browns."

A few minutes later Emily returned with breakfast, and she saw Miriam at the table with a can of orange soda.

"Biscuits and gravy with orange soda is an interesting combination. It's a good thing that I love you so much!" She hands Miriam her breakfast and the two of them enjoy their biscuits and gravy, while just being close to each other.

"So, what is the plan for today?"

"Well, once you get dressed, we can go get some groceries. I have something special planned for lunch. After that, we can do whatever. I will let you decide on how you feel."

"Do I need to dress up again for lunch?"

"Not like yesterday! I'm just wearing a more casual dress with my heeled sandals, and that is what I am wearing for lunch."

"OK. Let me go get dressed."

A few minutes later Miriam returns and is dressed similarly in a casual dress that they picked up yesterday, along with her silver flats, and of course her new necklace.

"Don't you look beautiful!"

They head off for groceries. It is a new store that Miriam had never been to. They were based out of the Tulsa area and were throughout the region. Miriam was quite surprised how nice the store looked inside. It was much nicer than where she was used to shopping. As they head through the aisles, Emily asks about some of her likes and dislikes, to help her know what to buy. It was not much of a surprise that she enjoyed much of the food from the Hispanic aisle, but she also enjoyed many things from the Asian section, and of course the Italian.

Emily found herself in somewhat of a quandary. Some of the initial food she had bought for Miriam was not exactly the healthiest, but it was only supposed to be initially for the weekends. Now that she had her full time, she wanted her to eat a little healthier. She didn't mind the snacking, but she didn't want her to live off of orange sodas either. Luckily for her, the next aisle had the canned veggies and fruits, along with the fruit juices.

"Well, since you are living with me permanently, I need to do something about making sure you are eating healthy. I know a bought you a lot of sodas and stuff. You can drink them, but you need to pick out some other healthy drinks as well."

"OK. I love orange juice, especially with other fruits like pineapple put in it."

"Why doesn't that surprise me!" OK, we will pick up some. How about some other fruit juices?"

"Well, this one looks good, and it is a blend of many fruits and veggies."

"Somehow I thought this would be harder. What about veggies for dinner?"

"Sweet potatoes are my favorite. I also like carrots, broccoli, and cauliflower."

"Aren't you supposed to be yelling and screaming about not eating veggies?"

"My mom always cooked veggies and wanted me to eat them, as they would help me grow and make me smart."

"That's a smart mom. She did a good job with you. We can get some of those veggies since they are my favorites as well."

Surely this would be harder than this. For some reason, she was expecting a tantrum or lots of yelling and screaming from Miriam. She picked out some great juices to go with her meals. She thought a soda a day would be reasonable, especially for days when they were together.

When Miriam picked up some snacks, they were healthier choices than cookies. With enough food to last for at least a couple of days, they finished their hunt for food, and headed to check out, then on to the house, where Miriam volunteered to help unpack and put up the food. By the time everything was put up, it was about time for Miriam's surprise lunch.

"You ready for lunch?"

"That sounds great!"

"Great. Let's head out."

Emily stopped for fried chicken, mashed potatoes, coleslaw, and biscuits. She drove a few minutes more till they arrived at the University of Tulsa campus. Emily grabbed the food and walked to the back of the SUV, where she placed the box of food into a picnic basket that she had loaded when Miriam was not paying attention. They found a nice green area of the campus by a tree and Emily set up a blanket and they sat down for a picnic lunch at one of Emily's favorite places.

"This was such a wonderful surprise!"

"I'm glad you liked it. I had the feeling you would. I wanted you to see how wonderful this place was. Maybe you'll come here someday!"

"I hadn't thought much about college, especially since I lost, you know."

"It's OK Miriam. It's nothing to feel bad about. You still have a few years to think it over. I just wanted to show you something that meant a lot to me, and let you experience it for yourself."

"This does look like a great place. I would love to go to class in many of these buildings. They look so beautiful!"

"Once we finish eating, and put everything up, I will walk you around and show you many of the buildings, at least from the outside. Since this is a small campus, you can see a lot of it from here. That large building right behind you is the library. It is supposed to be haunted."

"Really!?!"

"That was the store when I was going here, though I never did see anything, I tended to avoid the library. That large building to your right is where the business classes are taught. I spent most of my time there."

"What made you want to be in business classes?"

"I don't know. I was always interested in business, even when I was a little girl. The first time I went here, I was a finance major, with an economics minor."

"Wow. You must have been smart!"

"Thanks. It was a struggle at times. After I graduated, I felt like I wanted to do my own thing, and not work for a company, so I went back and got my master's in business administration. It helped me in learning all the different areas that I needed to know to run my own business."

"You must be really smart!"

"You are so sweet. I've done well in business, but I had to work hard, especially in the early days. Once people saw the hard work and effort I put into things, it helped get my business going. Now I am well known in the business community, at least in the Tulsa area. If you are done, we can head walk around for a bit, and I will tell you more about this place."

"That sounds wonderful, Mom. I love learning about you!"

The two of them spent over an hour walking around the campus, with Emily showing her everything she could, and telling her all she knew about the university. Miriam was so excited to learn so much about her mom. She also really loved the university, especially seeing some of the dining options that were available to the students. They bought a snack and headed home to spend a quiet evening together watching movies and enjoying being with each other before their busy professional day the next day. Emily made sure that Miriam was in bed at a decent time, so she would be ready for a busy day of seeing what her mom does.

The next morning Emily was u at 5:30. She had so much on her mind, and she needed her coffee to help process it all. The big item on the agenda was the closing. She has been to dozens of them, but none for such a large project. It was not the meeting that had her worried, it was getting started on the project as soon as the meeting was done, assuming there were no issues. She also had an appointment to look at a house, which was a typical meeting for her. Why was she so nervous today? Could it be the teenager that was accompanying her today?

She looked at the clock and it was nearing six. She had enough time to get in the shower and get dressed, before making sure that Miriam was up and starting to get ready. A few days ago, she only had to worry about one person, and that kept her busy at times, or at least it seemed that way. Now, she had someone else to worry about. Would this be what every weekday morning was going to be like, except Miriam would be heading off to school, but the times would be similar? Hopefully, Miriam was easy to get up and get going, much like she was as a teen.

By 6:30 Emily was dressed and heading to Miriam's room to see how she was doing. She could tell the light was on when she got to the door, so she knocked and took a peek inside when Miriam didn't respond. She was relieved to hear the shower running, and she could see that Miriam had already laid out her clothes for today. She was about to head out when the shower stopped and a moment later Miriam appeared.

"Good morning Miriam. I was just checking to see if you were up and getting ready, but I can see that you are almost done."

"Good morning, Mom. You look so nice today. I am so excited to come with you to work today. I did have a question about the suit. Should I wear my black tights with it?"

"Well, that is up to you. I usually wear something, but it is more for appearances. You can do what you would like."

"OK I will wear them, so I don't get cold."

"Great. Now finish getting ready, and I will have breakfast ready in a few."

Emily heads out to leave Miriam to finish getting ready and so that she can prepare breakfast. Now, what did she pick up for breakfast? She opens the freezer and sees some French toast sticks, which sound great but not enough time to cook them. She sees some healthier breakfast sandwiches, which can be cooked very quickly, so she pulls two and cooks them while pouring a glass of OJ for Miriam and herself.

A few minutes later Miriam appears and sits down to eat her breakfast.

"This looks good. What's the plan for today?"

"Well, the first thing is we need to head to the office for a few. It feels like it has been forever since I have been there. Our big appointment is at nine. There will be lots of people there. That will likely take up most of the morning. Once that is done, we will likely head to an early lunch. The afternoon will be a little quieter, as we will head back to the office for a few then we will go look at a house. After that, we will likely head home. How does that sound?"

"That sounds like it is more fun than going to school!"

"I'm sure it does. Just remember if I had not spent all that time in school, I wouldn't be able to do this today, and would likely spending forty hours a week doing something I did not enjoy."

"OK I will still go to school, but not today,"

"Oh, Miriam!" Emily gives her a hug and kiss on the cheek before grabbing more coffee and putting it into an insulated cup, to get her through the morning. Miriam is done with breakfast and is placing her dishes into the sink. Miriam says she's ready to go, so the two of them head off to the office for a busy day together.

Miriam is quite impressed with the office, as it is more than one room. The outer room resembles a living room, and this is where Emily can meet in person if needed and is great for more informal meetings. The main area where Emily works is in the next room. It has all the technology that she needs to work, along with places for files and to store information. This room also contains a small fridge, which usually contains drinks. Off to the side is the bathroom. There is a third room off to the other side, which resembles a small dining room, and there is a table with chairs around it for larger groups or more formal meetings.

Emily sits down at the computer to get caught up on a few things when the phone rings, and she sees that it is Rachel, likely to see how the weekend went.

"Hey, Rachel."

"Hello, Emily. How have things been?"

"They have been beyond wonderful. Here, talk to Miriam and she will fill you in."

"Hello, Rachel. This weekend has been the best. Friday night we watched a movie. Saturday, we went out for breakfast, went shopping, got my haircut, facials, manicures. Then we got dressed up and went out to eat, and we had the best time ever! Sunday, we had a picnic lunch at the University of Tulsa and Mom showed me around the campus."

"That is wonderful to hear Miriam! Do you mind if I talk to Ms. Gardner again?"

"Well, it sounds like she had a lot of fun! I bet you did as well."

"I did. I never thought I would have so much fun with a teen. It has been amazing!"

"That's wonderful. Would it be possible for just the two of us to talk for a minute?"

"Sure. Hey Miriam. Why don't you go sit out in the outer room for a minute? Let me get you a snack."

Miriam heads out with the snack and is eager to check out the office.

"OK. It's just the two of us. What's going on?"

"Was it my imagination or did I hear her refer to you as "mom"?"

"Yeah, you heard that. She started that on Saturday evening. I was quite surprised."

"I'm so thrilled to hear that. She had been languishing at her foster mom's house, and we were hoping that some one-on-one time would change that, and it sounds like it has."

"She has really opened up over the weekend. Now that she has someone who can give her the attention and time that she needs."

"I'm so glad to hear that. You have no idea how worried we were about her. Any questions or concerns before I let you two go?"

"We had talked about travel, and I just wanted to see what was involved in that."

"If you want to travel within Oklahoma, and it is more than say two hours, just shoot me a text ahead of time, just so I know. A day trip to OKC is fine. If you want to leave the state. I need to know in advance the dates and states you will be visiting. I can type up a paper that you can take with you, just in case there are any issues. It also lists any medical information that might be needed in an emergency like allergies and insurance information. Were you wanting to travel?"

"Yeah. Thanksgiving is in a few weeks, and they are off that whole week. I was wanting to go somewhere with just the two of us, for our first holiday together."

"That sounds like fun. Did you have something in mind?"

"I was thinking of flying to Denver. We could spend a few days there, and depending on the weather, we could visit some of the other areas of the state."

"So, this would just be Colorado?"

"Yes."

"That won't be an issue. Once you know the dates, send me a text, and I can get started on the paperwork."

"Thanks, Rachel. Miriam will love to hear it."

"Go ahead and check out the dates and go ahead and purchase the airfare once you find something. I will leave the two of you to enjoy your day. Hope you have a great one, Emily."

"Same to you Rachel."

Emily heads out to the sitting room to see how Miriam is doing. When she opens the door, Miriam has just finished her snack and was about to see if she could wash up. Emily lets her wash up and they head out to the first meeting of the day.

They arrive at the closing a few minutes early, which gives Emily enough time to introduce Miriam to Brooke and Kelli. They are both excited to meet Miriam and are excited that Emily is expanding her family. They also assure Emily that everything is good to go in their areas and there should be no surprises. Kelli also talks with her about the negotiations between Andy and herself. They have agreed on a purchase price, assuming that the building is renovated according to the submitted plans, along with some of the color changes that Andy requested. Emily is surprised at the price, and if that is the final price, she is due to make a very hefty profit.

A few minutes after nine, the final members arrive, and things get started. The paperwork transferring the property is signed and the funds are transferred. It feels like all day to Emily, especially since she keeps signing and dating what seems like an entire forest. Surely Miriam is bored, but when she glances over, she is taking it all in. At the end of the meeting, Emily is given the keys to the property and she shakes a bunch of hands and has her picture taken with Miriam, who everyone thinks looks adorable in her business suit, which looks a lot like what Emily is wearing.

When they head out, Emily glances at her watch, and it is after 11. Looks like that early lunch won't be quite as early as she thought it would be. The head off and Emily says they need to celebrate, by heading to the Olive Garden. Miriam has no objections, as that is where she had her first meal with Emily, her new mom. Over lunch, Miriam asks what seems like a thousand questions about everything that happened at the closing. She was paying attention and wanted to know more about what her mom did.

After lunch, they head back to the office for a few. Emily is anxious to check out airfare, but she doesn't want Miriam to see what she is doing. She needs to distract her somehow, but how to do it, without making it obvious? She will let Miriam know that she needs to respond to a few emails, and if Miriam lets her work on them, she will look through some houses together online.

The plan works perfectly. It took her five minutes to find and book the airfare. They will leave the first day of break, a Saturday in the morning, and fly back the following Saturday, which will give them a day of rest before heading back to school and work. She also booked non-stop and first-class, though it cost a bit more, she felt Miriam was worth it. Feeling good, she pulled up the residential listing, and Miriam and she look through some of the houses, to see what looks good. They find a few, and Emily sends out an email for more information, and to see if she could visit them.

They head off to check out the house that Emily had arranged the previous week. While they are heading there, Emily decides to surprise Miriam with the news.

"Miriam, Thanksgiving is only three weeks away. I know I have a lot to be thankful for this year. I want this Thanksgiving to be extra special for you, so I talked to Rachel this morning, and she gave the OK, so we will be spending our Thanksgiving together in Colorado!"

"Really!?! That is so exciting! I can't wait! I know this will be the best Thanksgiving, especially since I will be spending it with my new Mom!"

"I'm glad you are excited since I already bought the tickets to fly there. We will have a week together, with just the two of us!"

"You're the best Mom! We will have so much, and I am already so thankful that I have you in my life!"

A few minutes later, they arrived at the property. From the outside, Emily could see that it required some work. The house was in a nice part of town, so she knew there would be a demand for it once it was fixed up. The listing said it was a three-bedroom and two baths. It would be an ideal first home for a couple with a child or two.

"Well, what do you think Miriam?"

"It needs some work, but I like it."

"I like it as well. Let's go take a look inside."

The seller's realtor was waiting for them on the porch. She had worked with Emily before on some other residential properties.

"Well hello, Emily. It is nice to see you again."

"Same here, Jordan. This is Miriam. She is my assistant for the day, and my daughter the rest of the time."

"Nice to meet you, Miriam. You look so much like your Mom, especially in your suit."

"Thanks!"

"So, tell me about the property. Looks like it would be a good first home for a couple."

"Well, funny that you mention that because that is what it was. A couple purchased it thirty-five years ago and raised three kids in it. They are getting up in age, and as you can tell, they have been unable to keep up with the maintenance. They would love to see someone fix it up and become another first home purchase. I will let the two of you take a look, and I will stay on the porch for now, if you have any questions. I know you know what you are doing, so I don't need to follow you around."

"Sounds good. Well, let's go Miriam, and take a look."

As soon as they enter, Emily could tell why Jordan was willing to stay on the porch. There was a strong odor, but she wasn't sure what it was. The living room was in decent shape, but the carpet had to go, and it needed a paint job. When she got to the kitchen, she found the source of the smell or at least part of it. There had been a water leak and there was a good deal of mold growing. The kitchen would have to be gutted for sure, which was not an issue, as most people weren't fond of 1970's kitchen décor and style.

The rest of the house was in much better shape. The bedrooms simply needed a refresh to bring them into the 21st century, the bathrooms, on the other hand, might have to be rebuilt. All together it looked like a very doable project. If she could get it for the right price, it should be a relatively quick flip, and while she was busy with her hotel redevelopment, she had a company that specialized in kitchen and bathroom work, and they would be ideal for this project. They headed out to talk with Jordan.

"Well, what did you think?"

"I can see why you stayed out here, while we looked around."

"It did not smell very pretty at all."

"I guess I should have warned you."

"That's OK. I can see the potential, and I am very interested in it. I just want to have someone check out the foundation and look under the house to make sure there are no surprises, and to check out the mold damage. If all that checks out, then I will take it."

"That's wonderful to hear. I have had a few people look at it, and they simply want to tear down ad build something new. This is such a nice neighborhood, and I would hate to see that happen, as would the owners. When I told the owners that you had expressed interest in the property, they told me to do what it takes to get you to purchase it!"

"That's nice to hear. I will see when my guy can get out here to look at it, and we will go from there."

"Wonderful. Nice to see you again Emily, and it was nice meeting you, Miriam."

The two of them head off for home after a busy day. Miriam was so curious about what she had seen today and was filled with questions about buying and selling real estate. Emily was glad that Miriam had been paying attention and wanted to learn more.

It was about three when they arrived home. Miriam loved wearing her new suit, especially since it closely resembled what her mother had been wearing. She also loved the compliments, but she was glad to change out of it. Emily had let her know that they were likely done for the day, so she could put on something casual for walking around the house. Before they could get situated, the phone was ringing, and it was Rachel again.

"Hey, Rachel. What's up?"

"Hey, Emily. How did today go?"

"It went well. Miriam paid attention and was asking lots of questions. She seemed to enjoy herself. I had a pic taken of the two of us at the closing this morning. Let me send it to you."

"Oh, she looks adorable in her suit. I will have to show it to my supervisor when I get a chance. She will love it. The reason I am calling besides seeing how today went, is to let you know that I just finished at the school and updated Miriam's information. She is good to go back tomorrow."

"Will there be any issues since I am in a different part of town than she was living in?"

"Normally there might be, but she goes to Rogers. They serve all of Tulsa, and she was selected to go there, so it won't be an issue."

"Well, I am glad to hear that. I would hate for her to have to change schools, especially two months in. I will let her know that she can go back tomorrow. Oh, I did let her know about Colorado and she is already so excited. We will have so much fun spending the next three weeks planning our trip."

"That is wonderful to hear. You have no idea how thrilled I am to see that she is finally thriving. It's been a journey for her. Hope you two enjoy the rest of your evening, and I will talk with you soon."

"Same here. Bye."

"Well Miriam, it is back to school for you tomorrow."

Miriam just gives a pouty face.

"I know. In less than three weeks, we will be in Colorado with a week of no school!"

"OK. I guess I will be happy for that."

"Let me go get my laptop and we can plan some for our trip."

"That sounds like fun."

"Well, we will be there for a week, and we will need a vehicle unless we want to walk everywhere, so we should get that first. Let me put in our dates and see what is available. Hmm. If we were going to be there in the summer, I'd go for the convertible or at least a sports car, but don't need one if it could snow."

"I hope it does snow. I've never really seen much snow before."

"Well, in that case, we should likely get an SUV. That way we are prepared for it to snow. Oh look, they have pickup trucks available. We could ride around as cowgirls!"

"That sounds like fun."

"OK then. Cowgirls it is! That means we need to do some shopping before we head there!"

"I love shopping with you Mom!"

"I love shopping with you too! Well, we have a vehicle, we just need to decide where to take it. We should spend a few days in Denver. Colorado Springs is an easy day trip. We could spend a couple of days in Aspen, especially if there will be snow. We could learn to ski."

"I so want to ski!"

"Well then. We get there on a Saturday morning. Should we pick up the truck and drive to Aspen for a few days, then head back to Denver?"

"That sounds good to me."

"That sounds good to me as well. This lodge looks nice, and they offer ski rentals, so we don't have to worry about buying all that stuff and flying with it. We can stay there for three nights, then head to Denver. You will love Denver. I know the perfect hotel for us. Well now that I have the hotels booked, how about I go start dinner?"

"That sounds good. I was getting hungry."

"I'm starting to think that you are always hungry. How about I grill a chicken breast and we steam some veggies with it?"

"That sounds good to me."

Emily heads off to cook dinner while Miriam looks at the pictures of the resort in Aspen. It is right next to a mountain, where she can ski. In the time she has lived in Tulsa, she has only seen a dusting of snow. She also loves the mountains. They look so beautiful, especially when they are covered with snow. They have mountains in Guatemala, but her family never climbed or skied on them. She just saw them from a distance.

A few minutes later Emily has finished cooking dinner and calls Miriam to the table. The food looks and smells so good. She loves the way the veggies taste. Her new mom must cook them differently, and she is glad.

"I love the way these veggies taste. They are really good!"

"Thanks. I cook them differently than most people do. It is a combination of fried in olive oil and steamed. I'm glad you like them. Saturday we will have to do some shopping for our trip. I know a place in town where we can get cowgirl hats and boots. I bet they even have dresses that you could wear with your boots. You will look so pretty!"

"You know I love wearing dresses, just like you like to wear them a lot."

"One of many things we have in common."

They finish their dinner and head back to the living room to relax a little before bed. There is not much on TV, so Emily lets Miriam pick something to watch, while she catches up on some emails. A few of the houses that she emailed for information, wrote back. She picks a few that look interesting and sets an appointment to see the properties. She also got a text from her primary contractor that work had started on the hotel, and that he will stop by and look at the house in the morning before he heads to the hotel. She lets the realtor know and cuddles up with Miriam to spend some time with just her, and no distractions.

After a few shows, it is time for bed, especially with school in the morning. Emily gives Miriam a hug and kiss goodnight and tells her sweet dreams. She heads off to bed, leaving Emily alone for the first time since early this morning. Emily had always considered herself to be a strong independent woman, who didn't need anyone else in her life, yet she didn't mind that Miriam spent so much time with her. She had a feeling that she was going to miss Miriam tomorrow when she was at school. The workday would not be the same without her adorable little assistant by her side. After some time thinking about how much her life had changed over the past few days, Emily decided to head to bed.

Emily awoke the next morning and checked the clock, and it was 5:30. Once again her internal clock gets her up when she needs to be up. She sets an alarm as a backup, but rarely uses it. Time to make the coffee, followed by one of her favorite times of the day, drinking the coffee. There was something about being alone with her thoughts and her coffee to start the day. She would need to drop Miriam off at 8, then off to the office for a bit, before heading to the hotel to see it for the first time in a few months.

She was finished with her shower and dressed at 6:15. Should she check to see if Miriam was up? They had never discussed what time she needed to be up in the morning. She took a peek in the hallway and was surprised to see Miriam's light on. This would be a good morning for those French toast sticks, since she was up earlier and Miriam was already up, so she headed to the kitchen to make them, along with some sausage.

Breakfast was just about done when Miriam wandered into the kitchen, dressed in another dress, but this time with the canvas shoes that they had picked up the other day at the store.

"Do you have an alarm that goes off when a meal is just about done? You look great this morning, like always."

"Oh, Mom! Breakfast does smell good though."

"Well, you are just in time. Here you go, and I already poured you a glass of juice to go with it."

"Thanks. This looks good."

"Did you set an alarm for this morning, or just happen to wake up?"

"I usually wake up around six, at least on school days, but I set my alarm for 6:15, just in case. I want to have enough time to shower and enjoy this good breakfast, before heading to school. I don't like to be rushed."

"I'm glad to hear that. I'm the same way. If I am rushed in the morning, it makes the whole day seem rushed."

They finish their breakfast and out the door at 7:40. Emily drops her off at Rogers, with plenty of time to get to her first class. She always thought the school had an interesting look to it, and she is glad that Miriam is going there. She heads off to the office to get started on her day.

Shortly after she gets to the office, she hears from her contractor. He checked over the house, and the foundation is solid as is the structure. The mold damage is only on things that would be replaced anyway. He did find another source of the smell and a raccoon had died in the crawlspace, which he had removed. He thought she should buy it, and it would look great when it was done, and would likely be very profitable.

When she was done talking with him, she called the realtor to let her know that she was going to take it. She was so excited that she lowered the asking price to show her appreciation for taking on this project. Emily let the realtor know that she would not need to wait for financing approval, as she had enough reserve cash set aside for smaller projects like this, so she could close on the property much sooner. The realtor is excited to hear that, so she lets the owners know, and see when they could to sign the paperwork.

After a relatively quiet morning at the office, she heads to the hotel to see how things are going there. Her contractor greets her to show her around and jokes that she owes him hazard pay for removing the raccoon. The first team is already starting on what will be the lobby and has already torn down many of the walls. He lets her know that the other team is on the top floor, which is the 10th floor. They will work on that floor first and then make their way down, while the other team finishes the lobby, along with the meeting rooms, and then heads up. With so much of the prep work done ahead of time, they can get right to work. He lets her know that in about three months there will be enough done that she can begin to show it to the prospective new owner, and they will have a good idea of what the finished product looks like.

She thanks him for the great work already and tells him to keep her updated. If things turn out like she thinks they will, she will need to reward him with a nice bonus. He has helped her so much over the years. Much of her success is due to his hard work, and she has rewarded him greatly over the years, which is one reason why they continue to work well together. She looks at her watch and has enough time to get back to the office for a few, before picking up Miriam and heading home for the day.

After a relatively relaxing afternoon, Miriam head to the school to wait for Miriam. She could have her ride the bus home, but most of the time she is either done for the day or can swing by and pick her up. One of the many advantages she has being her own boss. She finds a place to park around the corner from the school and decides to walk over and wait for Miriam. She realizes that she doesn't know where her last class is, and Miriam does not have a cell phone. Perhaps she should have had better communication with Miriam when she dropped her off?

After a few minutes, the final bell rings, and students begin to file out. While she is looking for Miriam, Emily realizes that she likely looks like a teacher that is on duty to keep an eye on students. Luckily, Miriam is on her way out the door, so she heads over to greet her.

"Hey, Mom!"

"How was school?"

"It was OK. Glad it's over. How was your day?"

"It was good. The house we looked at yesterday was checked out, and everything looks good. They found an additional source of the smell, and got it taken care of, just don't ask what caused it"?

"Ewwwww."

"Yeah. Took a visit to the hotel and they have already gotten started on it. I will have to take you to see it in a few weeks after they have made some progress."

"I'd like that. Are we heading home?"

"We need to make a stop to pick up something for you. Something that I have the feeling that you will love."

"What is it?"

"Well, when I was waiting for you, I realized that we need a way to communicate, so you know when I am picking you up and stuff."

"I'm getting a cell phone!!"

"Oh, I suppose, if you think you need one."

"Oh, Mom!"

"Don't roll your eyes at me, or it will be a flip phone for you!"

"What's a flip phone?"

"OK. I am not THAT old now. It's a good thing we are pulling into the store now."

They head in and look around. Miriam is drawn to a pink one that happens to be on sale. She is thrilled that she finally gets one, and they even had a matching case for it. On the way home, Emily establishes some rules for the phone and lets her know that she will be able to see what's going on, so she needs to be honest with her. It seems like yesterday her mom was having these talks with her.

After a quick dinner, Emily spends a few minutes going over each of her classes and what she has been working on in each of her classes, as well as what her grades have been, and what areas she has been doing well in, and what areas she has been struggling in. She is enjoying this time with Miriam and loves getting to know her better. Overall, Miriam seems to be doing well in school, which is a relief.

Once the schoolwork has been completed, Emily and Miriam spend a little time talking about some of what they would like to see and do in Colorado. Miriam has never been, so she is not familiar with what is there. Emily has been there a few times for business and leisure. It has become one of her favorite vacation destinations recently. She loves the mountains and the air up there. She is hoping that Miriam loves it as much as she does.

She booked the hotel for Denver, but she won't give Miriam the details. Emily stayed there before for a conference and loved it. Each floor has its own theme and is decorated according to that theme. She booked the 13th floor, which needless to say is horror-themed and has scenes from some of the great classic horror movies in the hallway. Miriam will absolutely love it. With some more plans made, it is time to head to bed.

After Miriam heads to bed, Emily grabs a glass of wine and checks her email. A few of the realtors had emailed her back about seeing the properties she had looked at online with Miriam on Monday. One had emailed her that if she could look at the property, it would be worth her while. She didn't have much else planned for tomorrow, so she writes back that she would be available. She agrees to meet after she drops Miriam off after school. With her glass empty, along with her inbox, she decides it is time to head to bed as well.

The next morning Emily awakens at 5:00, which is a tad earlier than normal, but that just gives her more time to think some things through. She grabs her cup of coffee and heads to the couch to think some things through. She is intrigued by her first meeting. What could the realtor mean that it would be worth her while to see this house ASAP? It was rather cryptic, but she was intrigued, to say the least. By the time she finishes her cup of coffee, she is just as clueless as to what is going on. She will find out soon enough, so she heads back to her room to shower and get dressed.

At about 6:15, she is ready and heading to the kitchen to work on her breakfast. She looks through the freezer to decide on what to make and sees some biscuits, so she figures she will surprise Miriam with biscuits and gravy. The sausage gravy is one of the things that she learned to make when she moved to Oklahoma. She is just finishing everything up when Miriam walks into the kitchen.

"Something smells really good, Mom."

"Just some biscuits and gravy."

"You're the best! Biscuits and gravy are one of my favorite meals."

"I know. Just wanted to surprise you this morning."

Miriam gives her mom a big hug, then grabs a plate, puts two biscuits on it, and pours the majority of the gravy over them. She quickly digs in.

"Oh, Mom. These are awesome!"

"Glad you approve and left me a little bit to eat."

"Any plans for today?"

"I am looking at one of the houses that we had looked through online the other day. I had mentioned that it was in a nice neighborhood, and I thought it was at a really good price for that."

"I remember that one. It looked nice on the outside, but there were no pictures on the inside."

"That's the one. She said it be worthwhile to see it ASAP but didn't say why."

"Maybe it is haunted!"

"You'd like it if it was."

"Yes, I would!"

"Oh, Miriam! You're something special and that is why I'm making you my daughter!"

"Oh, Mom! Only you could turn ghosts into something mushy!" Miriam gets up from the table and kisses her mom on the cheek. "It's stuff like that mushy stuff that makes me glad you're going to be my mom."

Miriam finishes getting ready for school and she's dropped off a few minutes early so that Emily can head to her appointment to see what is going on. She pulls up at the house, and it looks just as nice on the outside as the pictures showed. As she gets out of her car, the realtor is getting out of hers and is heading over to her.

"Hey, Emily. I'm Jazmen."

"Nice to meet you Jazmen."

"Well, I am sure that you are curious as to what I mean in the email about worth your while."

"You could definitely say that."

"Well, here is the situation, and I will try to keep it short. The owners of the property are a couple that has seen better times. I have been friends with the wife for years, and I could see the end coming, but not like this. Her husband had a history of affairs. The wife gave him an ultimatum, and he went out and had another affair. She found out the other day, and went on a rampage inside the house, which is why there are no pictures."

"Oh, Wow!"

"Yeah. The house is just in the wife's name. She called me as soon as she calmed down and said to put the house on the market ASAP, and sell it just as quickly, as she needs money to go after her soon-to-be ex-husband, with the best lawyer she can afford. Apparently, he has a good chunk of money, so that is where we are. She doesn't mind not selling it for the full value, as long as she can get cash ASAP."

"OK. That makes a lot of sense."

"When I saw you had expressed interest, I knew you'd be perfect for it. I also wanted to give you the first shot at it, as you had mentored my daughter, Lori when she was a student at the University of Tulsa. It made a huge difference in her life, and I would like to use this opportunity to thank you."

"I'm glad to hear that. Lori was such a sweet girl, and I saw so much promise in her. I'm glad to hear that I was able to help bring out the best in her."

"Well, let's go take a look."

The damage inside the property was pretty bad, and Emily could see why she didn't want to take pictures. Luckily, the damage was mostly drywall, which was easy enough to replace. When the realtor lets Emily know what the seller is willing to seek today for the property, she realizes that she could make a rather large profit, relatively quickly. Luckily, she has enough in reserves to pay cash quickly. Arrangements are made to meet on Friday morning to close on the property. This will be her 2nd residential closing this week, and her third closing. While it is nice to acquire new properties, it also nice to sell them and make a profit.

After leaving the meeting, Emily heads to her office to gather the things she will need for her closing of the residential property, which she saw with Miriam, later in the day. Once she gets to the office, she contacts the company that will be renovating the first property and lets them know about her latest acquisition. They think she would do best to simply repair the damage, and not try a full renovation. That would also bring it to market sooner, enabling her to recoup her money faster. Once she closes, they will send some people to start replacing drywall and painting it to match what was already there. They don't think it will take all that long to do, so she wants it to be a priority.

Before she knows it, it is time to pick up Miriam from school. Now that she has a phone, Miriam can simply send a text when she is out of the building and heading to the street, so Emily can simply pull up and pick her up. This is far easier and more convenient. So far getting her a phone has been making their lives easier, hopefully, that continues to be the case. Miriam gets in, and they head home.

"How was your day, Miriam?"

"It was OK. Just the usual boring school day."

"I'm sorry. Anything I can do to help?"

"I don't know. Just don't feel like talking about it right now."

"OK. Well, I am here for you when you do want to talk."

"Thanks, Mom."

The two of them head home, and Emily can tell that something is wrong, but she doesn't want to push the issue right now, but she doesn't want to ignore it either. After dinner, she will make another effort to find out what is bothering Miriam. It bothers her that Miriam doesn't want to talk, but she remembers when she was younger, and she would do the same with her mom. It always drove her mom crazy, and now Miriam is returning the favor. Her mom is going to love hearing that.

When they arrive home, Emily asks Miriam if she needs any help with homework, and she just replies that she's heading to her room for a bit, and she'll be down for dinner. Though she hasn't known Miriam for long, clearly something is troubling her. It upsets her that something is bothering her. In an effort to get her mind off of it, Emily decides to start cooking dinner. She prepares a grilled pork tenderloin, with some steamed veggies and applesauce. She was about to text Miriam that dinner was ready when she appeared in the kitchen.

"Something was smelling really good, so I came out to see if dinner was about ready."

"I was just about to text you that it was ready."

"Well, it looks and smells good, and I'm hungry."

"Now that's a shocker."

"I love the way the grill marks on the pork look, and those veggies look perfectly steamed."

"Are we a food critic now?"

"Oh, Mom! Always so dramatic."

"Well, I at least hope the food tastes good, and that you like it."

"It's wonderful! I love it!"

"I'm glad."

The two of them finish off diner and then Emily heads to the couch to sit for a few. After Miriam puts up her dishes, she joins her mom on the couch and cuddles up next to her, and has her mom place her arm around her, while she lays close to her. Emily always enjoys these cuddle times and hopes it is a way for Miriam to feel safe, so she feels able to talk. After a few minutes, Miriam decides to open up to her mom.

"Mom, in school we have been talking and writing about families. Most of the kids live with at least one of their parents and most have multiple siblings. I feel somewhat left out since I am so different. I came from another country, lost my family, and ended up in foster care. Some of the kids have even said some things about me, which hurt. We are supposed to give a presentation on Friday on what we have written, and I don't know what to do."

"Oh, Miriam. I am so sorry to hear that is what was bothering you. I know kids can be mean, but you are looking at it all wrong. Yes, you lost some things, but choices were made in your case, that are so important and didn't happen in the case of the other kids."

"Like what?"

"Well, many of them were likely born in the area and live with their parents. Their parents didn't choose them. Many of them grew up here because that's where they happened to be. In your case, your parents made a conscious decision to come to the US, as they wanted a better opportunity for the family. Yes, they died, but someone made a conscious choice to adopt you. She didn't have to, but she chose to pick you and love you like she gave birth to you. You were chosen and the rest of them were not, so that makes you pretty special!"

"Thanks, Mom! That makes me feel better."

"I'm glad that I could help. Anything else I can help with?"

"You could tell me what you did today. I know I wasn't in a good mood earlier, but I do want to hear about your day."

"You're sweet when you want to be."

"I try."

"Well, I officially own the house that we looked at the other day. I was thinking of keeping it as a place to send you when you get into trouble."

"I hope you at least get rid of the smell first."

"I'll think about it. I did look at the other house that we saw online, and you were right about it."

"It's haunted!"

"I'm starting to think that you're haunted!"

"That would be cool!"

"I meant that you were right that something happened in the house and they were wanting to sell it quickly. It was nothing like what you are thinking about. Basically, a couple had reached a point where they could no longer live together, so they are splitting and want the house sold quickly."

"Oh, that's sad."

"Yes, it is."

"Can we watch some TV together before bed?"

"Absolutely."

The two of them enjoy a few shows before Miriam heads off to bed. While Emily enjoys her time with Miriam, she also loves that time in the evening after she's gone to bed. It gives her some time to think about the day and what tomorrow could bring. The only difference is she usually drinks a glass of wine, instead of coffee. Today, she is glad that Miriam was able to open up to her and let her know what was wrong. Bullies were an issue back when she was that age, and it sounds like not much has changed. She never honestly thought about what Miriam had gone through. Yes, she had empathy for her and her situation, but never thought about how it must have felt for her. She has been through so much, but it still so strong.

On the business front, she will purchase two houses this week using cash reserves. When she became successful, she intentionally set aside money for this purpose. Sometimes a property becomes available and by paying cash, she can move quickly and often get it a little cheaper, like in the case of the property that she looked at today. This cash reserve is set up explicitly for this purpose, and it is separate from her checking account that she uses to pay bills and other expenses. In that account, she likes to keep a few months of cash on hand, as income can be very irregular. She normally only receives income when she sells a property, and some like this hotel will take many months if she's lucky.

While she is in no danger of any financial issues by paying cash for these houses this week, she does need to move quickly to sell one of them, so she has reserves in case something comes up. She has been so profitable lately, it might be time to take some profit from one of these properties and increase her cash reserve, so she doesn't miss out on new opportunities. It is something to think about in the morning, as she's getting tired, and ready for bed.

The next morning Emily was up at her usual time. This had been a week for her, and it was only Thursday, or Friday Eve, as she liked to call it. She was looking forward to the weekend, so she could have more time with Miriam. They had some shopping planned for their Colorado trip, and some retail therapy sounded exactly like what both of them needed. In just over two weeks, it would be just the two of them in Colorado for a whole week. She could hardly wait, and she suspected that Miriam felt the same way.

After her shower and getting ready, Emily headed to the kitchen to prepare breakfast for her and Miriam. Today was one of those days when she wished she had more time for breakfast. A big country breakfast with meat, biscuits, and potatoes sounded really good, but she didn't have the time. Looks like it was a breakfast sandwich kind of morning, which was OK. Miriam entered the kitchen, just as the sandwiches were finished cooking.

"Wish I had more time to make a big breakfast for you."

"It's OK. I love that you always have something good for me to eat."

"I'm glad. I hope you are feeling better about things today."

"Yeah. I have a lot of things that the other kids don't have, so I need to focus on that, and not on what I don't have."

"Glad you feel that way. It's almost time to head out."

"OK. Let me go grab my stuff, and I will be ready to go."

Emily drops Miriam off at school and heads to the office, for what should be a quieter day. She doesn't mind these days. She's had a busy week, with a lot of activity, which is good for her business, but a down day now and then is good also. It can give her a chance to catch up on where her various projects are in their stage of redevelopment. It is also a chance to research new projects, though today she thinks she will do some Colorado research, since Miriam is not here, and see what fun activities she can plan.

Before she has a chance to dig into the research, her phone rings, and it is Alexis, her residential real estate broker. Alexis is the one who markets and sells the properties when they are finished, and she sometimes assists in buying properties. When Alexis calls, it is usually a sign that a property is close to being sold, which is always a relief.

"Hey, Alexis. How are things."

"Things are good Emily. I was calling about one of your properties. It is the one in South Tulsa off of Yale."

"Oh, that thing. That was the closest I have come to just starting over from the foundation. They put a ton of work in it."

Yeah, that is the one. We have a potential buyer. I am familiar with him. He's likely buying to make it a rental. I spoke with his realtor and he has financing in place. He's just asking for $15k off the price of the property."

"Tell him he can take it at that price. I will be glad to be rid of that one. Schedule the closing ASAP. I would love to have the funds before I head out to Colorado in two weeks."

"Sounds good. I will let him know about the time issue. I am sure that it won't be an issue, as I am sure he wants to get a tenant in there ASAP anyway. Oh, I saw your information on your two new acquisitions. You need to quit dumpster diving to find stuff, but somehow you manage to clean them up. I don't know how you do it, but I enjoy working with you."

"Thanks. I am closing on the 2nd one tomorrow. Once I close, why don't you come by and get started on the pictures? I am not planning on doing anything serious to the outside. You could start to market it, and hopefully, the inside won't take long. It won't be a full restoration, just a quick clean-up, so I am hoping it will be done before I leave for Colorado as well."

"Sounds like a plan Emily. I will see you then."

"Have a good one Alexis."

Emily was glad to hear the news on that property. It was a major pain to work on and presented many challenges, but she will make a very nice profit off of it. Some of that profit will help prop her cash reserves so that she will be able to buy more properties with cash. She will of course take some of that money and pay herself, which couldn't come at a better time with their Colorado trip in two weeks.

Emily spent the rest of the day checking up on her other properties, but not much has changed since she just closed on two of them this week. She found a few ideas for their Colorado trip, including an afternoon horseback riding trip. She went ahead and booked it, and it would remain a surprise. She had a feeling that Miriam would love it, with the two of them riding horses through a mountain trail.

    Before she knew it, it was time to head to the school and pick-up Miriam. Miriam was in a much better mood today, which Emily was glad to see. They headed home for a relatively quiet evening together. After dinner, the two of them watched a movie together, and Miriam headed to bed to get a good night's sleep for her presentation in the morning. Emily stays up a little later to think through some stuff but heads to bed not long after Miriam.

The next morning Emily is glad she went to bed a little earlier than normal, as she woke up a little earlier as a result. After finishing her morning coffee, she rushed to get ready. She wanted to make Miriam an extra nice breakfast this morning, as she had her presentation. She headed to the kitchen and got some biscuits in the oven. She found some breakfast potatoes and fried them. To finish off the breakfast, she cooked some sausage patties along with some scrambled eggs. She hurried to put everything on the plate before Miriam came out.

Less than a minute later Miriam came out, and much to Emily's surprise was dressed in her business suit along with the heels.

"Well, don't you look just stunning!"

"Thanks. I wanted to look nice for my presentation, so I decided to dress like my mom, and show them how a professional lady dresses for a presentation."

"You're going to make me cry when you say stuff like that."

"I'm sorry. I don't want you to cry."

"It's OK. Breakfast is ready."

"I could tell. I was smelling it in my room when I was getting ready, and I could tell it was going to be extra nice today, and it looks it."

"Well, thanks. I wanted you to have a nice breakfast for your presentation later. While you eat, I have something that I think will complete your look." Emily heads out to her office and comes back later with a soft-sided briefcase with a strap. "I don't use this anymore, so I will give it to you. You can use it today for your stuff, and you will look so professional."

"Thanks, Mom! I love it, and I love that I will look so much like you!"

"You are too sweet. I would say hurry up and eat, but it looks like you are doing that on your own."

"Well, this breakfast is so wonderful! I love it, and it is one of the best breakfasts that I have had in a while. I appreciate the effort you took to make it for me."

"You are something else, Miriam, but I love you for it!"

"Oh, Mom. I love you too!"

After finishing their breakfast, the two of them head off to school. Emily wishes Miriam well on her presentation and lets her know how proud of her she is, with how she has been taking things since they talked. Miriam is something special, and Emily is so glad that she is a part of her life. With Miriam dropped off at school, Emily heads to the office to get her things for what will be the third closing this week.

Her closing is first thing in the morning, and it was relatively simple. Once it was done, she took Alexis through the house to get her opinion on it. Alexis agreed that while it looked bad, once it was cleaned up and the repairs made, it would be very desirable. She agrees to take pictures of the exterior of the house since little work will be needed there. She could then create the listing to bring attention to the property. By the time people were expressing interest in it, she would be able to update it with interior shots as rooms were done. After another walk-through, she did see a few rooms, or angles that were undamaged and she took some pics of those as well.

After her morning meetings, Emily decided to head out for some lunch. She knew Miriam would be giving her presentation soon, and she wished she could be there for it. In the past week, she has seen a lot of growth in Miriam. She is turning from a young lady with some potential to a really strong lady that is ready to take on the world. It's almost like she's turning into her mother! Emily is so proud of her. Before she picks her up, she decides to get her a little surprise. She heads to the florist and picks up some pink roses and writes a note and attaches it to the flowers.

She can't wait any longer, so she heads to the school, and finds a great parking space close to the school. She sends Miriam a text letting her know that she's here and where she's parked at. After what seems like an eternity, she can hear the bell ring, and the kids begin to pour out. A minute later she spots Miriam, wasn't hard to do today. Miriam gets into the car and is surprised by a dozen pink roses.

"Oh, Mom! What are these for?"

"I know you did well, and I know you put so much effort into it. Don't forget to read the card."

Miriam reads the card, which says, "To the best daughter a Mom could ask for. Keep kicking butt and showing them you're the boss. Love Mom."

"Oh, Mom! I love it! How did you know that I did well on my presentation?"

"You're my daughter. My daughter is going to kick butt."

"I'm so glad that you have so much confidence in me. That is something that I have been missing for most of my life. I don't know what it was, but when I got up to speak, something in me changed, and I felt confident, and I spoke like I was in charge. I told them about my family and the many things that I had that they did not. The teacher and many of the students were impressed with me. It was awesome!"

"That's my girl! I knew you could do it! I think you get to pick dinner tonight."

"Since I look so nice, just like my mom, we need somewhere special."

"Well, I think you deserve it, and you do look fantastic."

They head off to their favorite steakhouse and enjoy a great evening together. Miriam received so many compliments and many thought she worked for Emily, and that this was a work dinner. Miriam loved it, and Emily could tell that she was enjoying the attention. After a great evening out with dinner and some light shopping fun, they head home to relax a little before bed. Emily helped get Miriam's flowers into a vase.

They get changed into something a little more comfortable for relaxing on the couch. Miriam asks if they can watch a scary movie, which is becoming pretty common. She has discovered so many classic ones from way back. Emily has always enjoyed the classics and she loves that she gets to watch many of them with her daughter. It's after nine before the movie ends, and they are both ready for bed, especially with lots of Colorado shopping planned for tomorrow.

The next morning Emily doesn't get up till shortly after six. She gets her coffee and heads to the living room. There is no rush to shower, get dressed, and make breakfast today, so she'll enjoy some extra quiet time in the living room until Miriam wakes up. Once she wakes up, then they can plan out their day, which in addition to shopping, will likely include breakfast and lunch out. That was fine with Emily, as she enjoyed the break from cooking. While the food out would not be as healthy, Miriam eats well during the week, so a day or two of eating out will be just fine.

It was not until 7:30 that Miriam came out from her room, still dressed in her pajamas. She comes over to the couch and lays down on it, using her mom's leg as a pillow.

"Well, good morning sleepyhead. Hope you slept well!"

"I did. Kicking but and giving presentations is very tiring work."

"Tell me about it. That's why I drink coffee."

"So, what's the plan for today?"

"I was going to leave that up to you. I am sure you want breakfast soon, but you'll need to get dressed first, which means you need to get off the couch first."

"OK, but five more minutes. You make a great pillow."

"I'll give you two before I head to breakfast by myself."

"Oh, OK."

Miriam finally gets up and heads to her room to get dressed, with Emily soon behind her. Emily decides to keep it casual, so she finds a longer casual dress and pairs it with some wedge sandals. She heads to the living room to wait for Miriam, who just came out of her bedroom wearing a similar long dress but paired with her flats. They glance at each other and just smile, before heading to the car and finding breakfast. They head to a diner near where they will be shopping later. The diner is known for their country breakfasts and has chicken fried steak on their breakfast menu, which attracts Miriam's attention. Emily decides on breakfast with just about one of everything.

Miriam enjoys the chicken fried steak and devours it. She also samples many of the items that her mom ordered. Many were things that she had not had before. Emily was glad that she was willing to try new things, she was also glad that Miriam left her something to eat. Miriam ate like crazy but was small enough that Emily thought she would blow away in a windstorm. After breakfast, they headed to one of the western stores in town to pick up some of their clothing for Colorado, and they were promptly greeted as they entered.

"Welcome! Is there anything that I can help you find today?"

"We are heading to Colorado in a few weeks and are looking for some clothing."

"Excellent. What in particular are you looking for?"

"Well, a few dresses, a pair of boots or two, and a hat."

"We are going to be cowgirls!"

"Yes, you will be when I am done with you. Let's start with the dresses, and then go from there. Let me take you over there. What did you have in mind, casual or dressy?"

"Likely a variety."

"OK. Here are some plain dresses with a denim jacket, they are a great all-around look. Over here are some denim skirts, which you could pair with some of these shirts. It is more of a casual look., and back over here are the dressier dresses. I will leave the two of you to look around and see what you like. Once you have picked out the clothes, we can go from there."

"Thanks. Well, Miriam, what do you think?"

"There are so many pretty dresses."

"I think so too. I like the lady's idea, and to pick out a few things. I think we should pick out some of these dresses with the denim jacket. They will go great for a variety of events. I'm taking these two. Go ahead and pick out two."

"Oh, these are adorable, and this one is pink."

"Go figure. Pick out two denim skirts, two different lengths would be fine."

Miriam grabs the shortest one she could find and holds it up so Emily could see how short it would look on her.

"Uh, not in a million years, Miriam."

"I know, Mom, but that look on your face was pretty funny. I like this knee-length one and this longer one."

"Well, both of those are cute. Go ahead and grab a few shirts to go with them."

Miriam once again grabs the most revealing top she can find, and she holds it up for her mom to see. This time Emily just gives her a look, and Miriam just laughs at her mom. She grabs a couple of tops, and each of them grabs one formal-looking dress, and head to the dressing rooms.

After a few minutes, both of them have tried on everything they had picked out and were comfortable with their selections. The sales lady joined them to see what they had picked out.

"Both of you have some great choices. For the young lady, I would recommend two different boots. The standard-length boot, and one that is a little shorter. The shorter one will look great with the longer denim skirt, along with some of the dresses. I would go with the pink floral boot here, and this pink and brown shorter one. Go ahead and try them on and let me know what you think."

"Those are so cute."

"And for you, I can tell that you like heels, so I would go with a pair of ankle boots over here along with the more traditional boot. Go ahead and try them out." She heads back over to Miriam. "What do you think?"

"I love them! They fit great and will look so cute with my dresses."

"I'm glad to hear that." She heads back over to Emily, who has finished trying on both pairs. "Well, was I right?"

"About the ankle boots, oh yeah. I love the heel on them. The others felt great too, but I felt so short in them. I'm so used to wearing heels. I think we will take all the clothes we have picked out along with both pairs of boots. Now, we just need a hat."

"Well come over here and I will get you set up. For the younger lady, I love this white hat with the pink trim, and for you, this black hat with pink trim will look great with your selections."

"I don't know how you do it, but the hats are perfect as well. Miriam looks so cute in hers, and I look sophisticated in mine."

"Well, thanks. That is what I had in mind when I picked them out. Let me gather all your stuff and I will meet you at the register." She rings up everything, and Emily almost faints when she sees the total, but she knows they will have fun. "Well, thank you two for coming in today. Hope you have fun in Colorado!"

"Thanks for all your help"

They head out to the SUV to load everything in the back.

"Thank you so much for everything, Mom! I just love it all, and I know we will have so much fun!"

"You're welcome! Now, where should we head next?"

"Well, I know you spent so much on the clothes and stuff."

"Miriam, it is OK. I have done well over the years. Don't worry, we are not going without food, because we bought some clothes."

"Well, I could use some luggage."

"Now that I think about it, you didn't have much, so that sounds good to me. I have some nice business ones, but I might look for something fun, as well."

After some searching, Miriam finds a great 4-piece set, which of course is pink. Emily finds that same set, but in a burgundy color. Miriam jokes that she picked that color since it looks like red wine. Emily tells her that is exactly why she picked it out. Miriam asks where they are going next, and Emily informs her that unless they are buying a trailer to haul more stuff, they better head home to drop some of the stuff off, so they pick up lunch on the way home. After the large breakfast, they order some turkey wraps.

"That was a lot of fun, Mom. I can't wait to see Colorado."

"In two weeks, we will be there. I know you will have so much fun. I have some surprises planned, which will stay a surprise."

"Really?"

"Yes. I planned a few activities when you were not around. The hotel in Denver is a surprise, as are some of the activities we will be doing."

"What about the activities that we talked about?"

"Everything that we talked about is booked as well. This will be a trip that neither of us will ever forget!"

"Oh, Mom you're the best!"

"Well, for you I try. You do deserve the best. Well, what sounds good for the rest of today?"

"Can we go for a drive?"

"Anywhere in particular?"

"Some people in the class were mentioning a city north of Tulsa, called Bartlesville. They said it was an interesting town."

"That sounds wonderful. I know the route you are talking about. Well, let's go!"

They drove off to Bartlesville and enjoyed the scenery along the way. While in town, they checked out some of the local shops, along with some of the unique sights. Miriam thought the town was quite quaint. After a great afternoon checking out the sites, they headed back to

Tulsa, but not the way they came. After a few minutes, Miriam could see why. The scenery had become quite scenic. Instead of some hills, she could see valleys and some of the best scenery she had seen in Oklahoma.

"Oh Mom, I just love the scenery. It is so beautiful. I would love to live in some of the houses by the valleys."

"I did business up here a few times, and some people told me about it, and I love it. It is one of my favorite drives. We do have one more surprise to go."

"I love surprises!"

"I know you'll love this one!"

They began to slow down, and they made a right turn in an interesting place.

"Where are we?"

"This is your surprise. It is a nature preserve. Keep looking around and you might see something."

"After a moment or two, Miriam saw some large creatures near where the car was going."

"What are they, Mom?"

"Those are bison. They used to roam this part of the country in large herds."

"They look like big hairy cows."

"I guess they do."

After a moment Miriam spotted some other animals.

"Now that looks like a cow, with large horns."

"That is a Longhorn. Many people in Oklahoma don't like them."

"Really?"

"Yeah, but that's another day."

"Now those look like big deer."

"Those are elk. They are cousins of deer."

"I like them."

A few minutes they pulled by some buildings.

"What are these?"

"It is also a museum. This was the ranch of one of the main business people in Bartlesville. It is filled with lots of things that are part of Oklahoma's history, as well as the town. It closes shortly, so we don't have much time, but enough time to give you an idea."

Miriam seemed quite interested in the things that she saw. Emily was glad, as she always a daughter that was interested in history and learning outside of school. They both had a great time looking around in the time that they had. Emily let her know that they will have to come back when they have more time.

After driving for a few minutes, they pulled up to a stop sign.

"You had better hold on to something for the next few minutes."

After a few moments, Miriam could see why. This road had so many twists and turns in it. During one of the turns, Miriam said this was like a roller coaster. She was loving it. Her mom was doing this for two reasons. The first is it was fun. The second was to show Miriam that Oklahoma is not flat and boring like so many people think.

Since it was already getting late, they picked up dinner on the way home. It had been an incredible day of shopping and lots of fun together. They were both enjoying their new reality. Emily had a shopping companion and someone she could mentor and help grow. Miriam was finally able to receive the one-on-one attention that she had desperately needed. It was looking like they were what each other was looking for and needing.

    The next day was relatively quiet. They bought some groceries in the morning, while the afternoon was spent making sure Miriam was current on her schoolwork. Miriam was pretty good at keeping up with her work. Emily just liked looking over everything, as she liked knowing what Miriam was working on in school. Once the schoolwork was done, there was enough time for dinner and a movie before it was time to head to bed.

Monday morning Emily was up at her usual time. She got her coffee and headed back to her room. They had less than two weeks until their Colorado trip. She wanted to get some of these properties sold before they left. She wasn't facing a cash crunch, it would be easier to relax if she didn't have to worry about as many properties. A property that is vacant and being renovated seems to attract attention. People with bad intentions know no one is living there and likely has many new appliances being put in, along with lots of pricy tools. Once they were sold, she no longer had to worry about any of that.

It sounded like one should close in the next week or so, which had been finished for a few weeks now. It was a pricier home, so those tend to take longer to move. She is also hoping that one of her new acquisitions can be turned around quickly. Alexis had mentioned that she has the listing available online, along with the pictures that she has taken. She did have a few inquiries, but mostly to ask about the rest of the pictures. The other house would likely take a few weeks. The kitchen was going to be rebuilt, and that will take time.

Realizing that she can't spend all morning contemplating business, she heads to get ready for the day. Once she's done getting ready, it is off to the kitchen to figure out breakfast. Yesterday they had a big breakfast since they were home most of the day. Emily didn't mind those kinds of breakfasts, she just didn't want to do them every day, so it would be a breakfast sandwich kind of morning.

Miriam came out just as the sandwiches had finished cooking. She gave her mom a hug before sitting down to eat breakfast.

"Well, that was nice. Glad you are in a good mood this morning."

"It's your fault you know. We had so much fun on Saturday and just relaxing on Sunday. Also, there are less than two weeks till Colorado!"

"Well, I guess I'll take the blame then. I don't want you to lose focus these next two weeks and forget about your schoolwork. I know I need to do the same with my work. Got to push those houses."

"Don't worry Mom. I know you do a great job of checking up on me, so I know I won't be able to get behind."

"I like how you think. Finish getting ready, as it is almost time to leave."

Emily dropped Miriam off at school and headed to the office. When she got there, she saw she had a text message from Rachel asking if she was available today, as she had the paperwork for Colorado. Emily let her know that she'd be at the office all morning, and Rachel said she would stop by shortly.

Emily decided to give Alexis a call to see what the progress was on the houses. Alexis let her know that there was quite a bit of interest in the one property, mostly from investors who would rent it out. They wanted to see what the complete house looked like before they made a serious offer. The good news is there was interest, but it needed to be completed.

Once she was done talking to Alexis, she sent a text to the team leader handling the property, to let him know that this property was a priority, and she wanted it done ASAP, even if that meant more expenses. He let her know that he was there right now and that the property was not as bad as it looked. He would likely be done on Wednesday if there were no issues or unforeseen circumstances.

A few minutes later, Rachel arrived at the office.

"Hey, Emily. Is this still a good time?"

"Of course. I was just finishing up some emails."

"Great. Well first of all, how has Miriam been doing?"

"I have seen such an improvement in her over the past two weeks. She has really opened up and has been flourishing. Last Friday, she gave a presentation at school. She dressed up professionally for it and nailed it. She said many people were impressed. Here is a picture of her that morning."

"That is amazing! She looks so grown up. Doesn't even look like the little child that I dropped off just two weeks ago."

"I know. I can hardly believe the difference myself. I'm so proud of her."

"I am as well. I thought it would be a few months before we saw this kind of improvement. Well, here is a copy of the paperwork for you to take. Make sure you keep it with you. It authorizes medical care if needed and authorizes you to take her out of Oklahoma for the dates listed. I just need you to sign this one, which we will hold onto. If anything happens, you have my cell phone, but I'm sure there won't be any issues."

"I'm sure as well. She's so excited. I have a few surprises for her. One of the hotels we are staying at has a haunted themed floor, and we are staying there."

"She will love that!"

"Also, in Aspen, we have horse riding planned."

"That will be wonderful! I'm sure skiing planned as well."

"Of course."

"Well, it sounds like she will have so much fun, and I know you will as well. If anything comes up between now and when you leave, let me know. Don't forget to take lots of pictures!"

"Don't worry we will. Thanks for stopping by. Hope you have a great one!"

"You as well!"

Rachel headed out, and Emily glanced through the paperwork she had been given. She wasn't sure what half of it meant, as it was clearly written by an attorney. She was just glad that it let her take Miriam on a trip that they would love. Hopefully soon, she wouldn't need permission to take Miriam out of state, and they would be able to see the world together. Hopefully, this summer the hotel will be done and sold, and they would be able to get away for a few weeks somewhere.

While daydreaming about travel was nice, she needed to be able to pay for the travel, so she got back to work looking through some properties. Today was not an exciting day to look at properties online. It was a nice today, so she decided to check out some neighborhoods. There were quite a few nice neighborhoods, but many of the residents thought they were sophisticated enough to sell their houses on their own. These were known as For Sale by Owner, or FSBO. They were easy enough for her to buy, especially if they needed some repair work, which many were.

She stopped for some coffee before hitting the streets. She wasn't too concerned about looking suspicious driving through the neighborhoods. She was a woman driving a Volvo SUV. Most people would think she was looking for the house for book club. When she saw something of interest, she would take a pic of the sign with the information, along with a pic of the house. This would give her a reference point for when she called them later. She spent most of the rest of the workday driving around some neighborhoods, before ending up in the neighborhood near Miriam's school, which was also near the University of Tulsa. When she had finished the last neighborhood, she headed down the street to Miriam's school to wait for her. Shortly after arriving, the bell rings, and Miriam is on her way to the car.

"Hey Miriam, how was your day?"

"It was OK. I had Colorado on the brain today."

"I know the feeling. I couldn't concentrate in the office today, so I drove around checking out some neighborhoods."

"That sounds like fun. Likely more fun than school."

"I might take you out sometime."

"I'd like to spend time with you while you work."

"Why doesn't that surprise me. How about a rotisserie chicken for dinner, since we are both too distracted by Colorado to cook dinner?"

"That sounds great."

They pick up dinner and head home. After dinner, Emily helps Miriam with some of her work. She doesn't want it to pile up and make Miriam spend a lot of the weekend trying to get caught up. The work was pretty straightforward this time. She has no major stuff planned for the coming week, which is good, but on the last day of school, before Colorado, her math teacher has a major exam scheduled. After the work was done, there was enough time to watch a classic horror movie from the 1960s starring Vincent Price. He made quite a few based on Poe's works, so it was almost horror and education at the same time.

Once the movie was over, it was just about time for bed for Miriam.

"I hate that we don't have much time together during the week. We come home, eat, do a little schoolwork, and are left with an hour or two to spend time together before it is time for bed."

"I know Miriam. We have all weekend though, and in less than two weeks, we will have a full week together!"

"I know Mom. It's just hard sometimes."

"We just need to enjoy our time together for now. Now go get ready for bed."

"Alright, Mom."

Miriam headed off to her room to get ready for bed, and Emily headed off to get a glass of wine, and then to her room. She liked that Miriam was into horror movies and that they did not need to be modern slasher movies with lots of blood and stuff. She was glad that she enjoyed some of the classics as well. Miriam was definitely a unique young lady, and Emily just loved her. She couldn't believe that only a few weeks ago she didn't know that Miriam existed, but today she couldn't imagine her life without her. She finally feels like she has a purpose, beyond moving real estate.

She finished her glass and decided it was time to head to bed herself. While this week looked a little quieter than last week, she needed to be ready, which meant making sure she was well-rested.

The next morning Emily was up at 5. She got her coffee and headed back to her room. Something felt different today. It wasn't a physical thing, but somehow something seemed different. She wasn't sure what was causing this feeling, so she felt it better to go work on getting ready and making breakfast.

After getting ready for work, she headed to the kitchen to cook breakfast. She had extra time today, so pancakes sounded good, but not just any pancakes. She found some fresh cranberries and added them to the cooking batter. When Miriam came out for breakfast, the cranberries had begun to weep, which made it look like the pancakes were "bleeding".

"Mom, why are the pancakes bleeding?"

"It's because they are haunted pancakes."

"Oh, Mom! You're the best! Is the bacon haunted as well?"

"You better believe it is!"

"I love you, Mom!"

"Love you too, Miriam!"

They finished their breakfast and headed off. After Miriam was dropped off at school, Emily headed to the office to plan for the day. Shortly after she arrived, she received a call from Andy, the prospective hotel owner.

"Good morning, Andy. What can I help you with today?"

"Well, Emily. There has been a minor change, and I wanted to talk to you about it."

"I hope it is a good change."

"It is a very good change for both of us. We had some developments since we last spoke. Some new events were announced for this summer, and this hotel would be a prime location to host many of the participants. What we would like to do is close on the property before it is finished. This would give you your money earlier, but you would continue to work on the property. We would then be able to open earlier than planned, though with not a fully done hotel, but with the majority of it finished."

"That sounds like a very intriguing plan. So basically, the title would transfer earlier, but work would continue until finished?"

"Exactly. We would sign a contract for the work that was not done, so it would get done. All we ask is that the focus is on the meeting rooms, along with some of the top floors."

"Well, that will not be a problem. One crew is working on the lobby right now, while the other is on the 10th floor. One team will work down, while the other works up."

"I'm glad to hear that, as that was exactly what I was hoping we could get done."

"So, when were you planning on closing?"

"It would still be a few months, but we can begin to market the hotel in time to take advantage of these new events. We would likely close shortly before the new year if we can come to an agreement."

"Well, I am shocked, but it all sounds great. I will talk with some of my team and let them know what you are proposing, but I don't see an issue."

"Wonderful Emily! Hope you have a great day."

"You as well Andy."

Emily couldn't believe it. This was wonderful news. This would allow her to transfer the hotel earlier and make her profit much earlier. It would be easier to relax and do something with Miriam if she didn't have to worry about this hotel as much. While she would still be responsible for the work that still needed to be completed, she had teams that were working on it, so there was less for her to do. She would need to let Kelli and Brooke know about these developments and see what they thought.

Kelli seemed to like the idea. It showed a lot of faith in her and her work if they were willing to buy the property before it was finished. Brooke on the other hand had a few reservations. Normally the bank would receive the funds, pay off the loans, and the rest would go to Emily. In this case, the loan for renovating would still be being used. She would need to talk with some people to see how they would handle this if this would happen. So far, it looks like this would be a great opportunity for her, but there are a few bugs to work it before it can become a reality.

After checking on some arrangements for tomorrow's closing, Emily headed off to lunch. Today had seen some unexpected developments, was that the feeling she was having this morning? Maybe she had read something about that area being busy this coming summer and thinking that the hotel would be an ideal location for many of those events? It would bug her if she dwelt on it much, so she focused on checking out the weather for Colorado. At this point, many weather stations would have an idea for that distance out, so she checked and their first day looked like a great day for travel. Saturday night was showing snow, which was good if they wanted to go skiing.

Emily had called a few of the FSBO listings yesterday, and none of them seemed overly exciting. Most were good homes, they just wanted to not pay someone a commission for selling their house and were not ready for fixing up. It was a little disappointing, but not unexpected. She would take Miriam out this weekend and try some more. Maybe she will bring some better luck?

It was a quiet afternoon, after a pretty eventful morning. She picked up Miriam from school and they headed home. Miriam's day was pretty uneventful. It was just one of those in-between weeks at school, where nothing major was going on. Miriam quickly finished her homework before Emily had a chance to even think about dinner.

"I'm done with my homework, Mom. What's for dinner?"

"That's good. I hadn't thought about it yet. How about we head out for some dinner and maybe a little shopping?"

"That sounds great!"

"So where should we go?"

"You know I love Utica Square."

"Yeah, yeah, that's where we met, and stuff and we had our ladies' night there. Yeah, I love it there too, so let's go!"

They headed off and stopped for some Italian where they shared their first dinner. After dinner, they walked around some. There was something about that place that they enjoyed. They checked out a few shops, and Miriam found a beautiful teal dress, which she said she would wear on their next ladies' night. Emily told her she would look beautiful in it. After a few hours of walking around, Miriam was getting tired, so she headed home. She enjoyed the night out with her mom, and her mom enjoyed some time with Miriam. There was something different about being out with someone, and just sitting on a couch next to someone.

    Emily was not far behind Miriam for heading to bed. She had a lot to think about and wanted some time to process things.

On Wednesday, Emily was up at her usual time. She felt like she slept well last night. Maybe it was the evening out with Miriam that helped? All she knew is at least once a week during the week, they will need to do something similar. It will prevent them from getting in a rut of coming home, doing schoolwork, eating dinner, and ending the day with a movie or show every day. While a relaxing evening was good, it was not ideal for every day, at least for them.

After getting ready for the day, she headed into the kitchen to see what looked good for breakfast. After a few minutes, she determined it was a biscuit and gravy kind of morning, which she knew Miriam would not object to. Sure enough, just as soon as the biscuits were being pulled from the oven, Miriam was appearing ready to eat them. There was just something about that child, that while odd at times, Emily just couldn't resist. They greatly enjoyed their breakfast together, and before they knew it, it was time to head out the door. Emily dropped Miriam off at school, and instead of the office, headed to the closing for her one property.

She was glad to close on this property and be done with it. This was a very trying property, but she did learn a lot through it. It also represented a good amount of profit, which was a relief. She was going to take the majority of the profit and move it to her cash reserves for buying more properties with cash. She liked being able to buy properties with cash, as she could close quicker and many times at a discount. With their Colorado trip less than ten days away, this would be an excellent opportunity to bring a little profit home and use it for the trip. The remainder would stay with the business for taxes and other expenses. She figured the remainder would pay about two months of expenses for the business.

By the time the closing ended, and she was heading to the office, it was closing in on lunch, so she stopped for an early lunch before heading in for the day. Once she was at the office, she was looking through some of the listings, when she got a text from her project manager from one of the residential properties, she had bought recently. They had finished all the drywall yesterday and were busy painting today. They could stop by this afternoon to take the remainder of the pics. It was a relief for Emily. She let Alexis know to stop by the house this afternoon and finish all the pictures and get them updated ASAP. She would love to close on it before heading to Colorado.

The other house that she had looked at with Miriam was another story. It would be at least two months, just in the kitchen depending on what needed to be done. With a couple of holidays coming up, that would likely push the project to mid-January. That was typical for more involved projects, which most of hers seemed to be.

She got a call from one of the properties she drove by the other day. It was one of the houses near Miriam's school, which is in a pretty desirable neighborhood. The owner was a widow, who was not far from retirement. Her husband had passed not too long ago from a long illness. The house had been well maintained until he became sick. Now, she was looking to move into a senior community and wanted to sell the house. She was getting conflicting information from people on what to do. When she heard Emily's voicemail, she was relieved. She knew Emily's reputation and was hoping that she would at least look at it and give her an honest assessment. She agreed to come after she picked up Miriam, as she thought Miriam would enjoy looking at this house.

It was nice to know that Emily had a reputation of being fair, and her advice was sought after. She always treated others the way she would want to be treated. She knew many real estate investors that would take advantage of sellers and try to buy it cheaper than needed. She was all for making a profit, but she did not want to take advantage of people to increase her profit.

She didn't have much planned for the afternoon, so she researched the property that she was going to take a look at, along with the value of neighboring properties. She wanted to be prepared, so she could give the seller the best information that she could. Sellers appreciated when you could give them numbers, so they knew you weren't just making things up.

Before she knew it, it was time to go pick up Miriam from school, so she headed over there, and parked in her usual space. A few minutes later Miriam was heading out of the school and coming to the car.

"Hey, Miriam. How was your day?"

"It was good. Did you do anything fun today?"

"Closed on that one house finally, and we are heading to look at another house that is just down the street."

"I like looking at houses with you."

"I always suspected that you did."

"It is owned by a lady and she is looking to move, but the house hasn't been well maintained lately, so I don't know what to expect."

"Sounds like fun."

It was at that time, that they were pulling in front of the house. The owner was waiting for them on the porch.

"It looks nice on the outside."

"Yeah. It needs a little bit of work, but not bad."

"Well, you must be Emily, and who is this pretty young lady?"

"This is my daughter and assistant, Miriam."

"Well nice to meet you, Miriam. You can call me Mrs. Weber. Well, come on in and I will show you around."

As soon as they enter the living room, Emily can see what the seller meant. It was clear that the living room was in serious need of an update. It looked like it was out of the early '90s. Most of the rest of the house was in a similar condition. The bathroom and kitchen did need some work done as well. The one issue that she was seeing was there was a lot of clutter. She could see why the seller was getting lots of conflicting information. When they had finished the tour, she wanted to ask the seller some questions to see what was going on.

"It's a very nice house, Mrs. Weber. Like you said I can see some things that need to be worked on, which while not huge, do need to be done at some point. I wanted to see what your plans were."

"Well, as I had mentioned on the phone, I am wanting to move into something that would better accommodate my situation and age. The issue is my stuff. I need help sorting through it. My kids are far away and can't afford on their own to come here and help. I don't have the money until I sell the house. Most of the people who said they could buy it, want me out in a week or two. That just won't happen."

"I see your dilemma. What kind of prices were they giving you?"

The seller tells Emily some of the offers, and she is shocked.

"Yeah, they were taking advantage of you. Let me think for a minute. I will tell you what I can do for you. I will give you $15,000 more than their best offer. I will also give you 60 days to get things straightened out. That way if they can't come for Thanksgiving, they could still come for Christmas and help you. If you want, you can talk to your kids tonight and see what they think. If it sounds good to you at that point, we can either meet tomorrow or Friday and have you sign some papers, and I will give you a check for the house."

"Oh, Emily! You are the best! That solves so many of my problems. I will let my kids know tonight, and I will talk to you in the morning! Miriam, your mom is such a wonderful person. You are lucky to have her!"

"Thanks, Mrs. Weber. She's pretty special to me as well."

They headed out and got in the car to go home for the evening.

"Mom, what you did for Mrs. Weber was nice."

"Thanks. I do my best to help people out when I can. I could see she was in a predicament, and instead of trying to make things worse, I wanted to make things better for her. That's how I like to do business. I should do just fine with selling her house when I am done, and if not, oh well. We will be fine if one property doesn't bring in a ton of profit."

"I'm so glad that you're my Mom. You're pretty awesome."

"You're a pretty awesome daughter as well!"

"Thanks, Mom. What's for dinner?"

"How did I know this conversation was moving over to talk about food. How about we pick something up on the way home?"

"Sounds good to me."

They pick up a chicken meal on their way home. After dinner, Miriam works on her schoolwork. After all the work had been completed, they watched some shows together before heading to bed. Emily is pleased that she is putting so much effort into school. She's seen an improvement in her grades as well. Is it possible that the real Miriam is finally able to come out now? Hopefully, this isn't just temporary.

Emily woke up the next morning and saw it was shortly after five. She wanted it to be the weekend, so she could have lots of time with Miriam, but she had two more days. Instead of thinking of today as Thursday, it sounded better to call it Friday Eve. Friday Eve or not, she still needed to get motivated to get out of bed and start her day. She finally managed to get up and go get her coffee.

After she got her coffee, she headed to the couch. The next two days should be relatively quiet. She may meet with Mrs. Weber, but that is the only potential meeting, as of now. With so much effort going into renovating the hotel in addition to the one house, she didn't want to take on too many projects, especially with the Colorado trip coming up. Her usual team of people was getting stretched pretty thin, while there were others out there, she didn't like the thought of untested people working on her projects.

This morning, in addition to business, she had Miriam on her mind. She has seen such a huge improvement in her. She can't help but wonder if this is genuine, or an act? Everything seems to be perfect, but is it too perfect? She expected more resistance from a teenager, especially with the history that Miriam has. For now, all she can do is hope this is real, and continue to keep an eye on things to see if anything changes.

Realizing that she finished her coffee fifteen ago, Emily decided to go get ready for the day, as she wouldn't be very productive holding an empty coffee cup all day, staring blankly at the wall. When she comes out, she decides to try something different, so she prepares a frittata along with some breakfast potatoes. Once again, a moment after the food is put on her plate, Miriam comes walking out, ready to eat.

"Mom, this looks good. It almost looks like a different type of scrambled egg."

"It's an Italian omelet."

"Well, it is really good, and I love the potatoes are exceptional!"

"I'm glad you approve. I was just thinking how much you have improved since you have moved in. I'm so proud of the hard work you have been doing with your schoolwork. You're such an awesome young lady!"

"You're so sweet, Mom. I feel so different being here. I feel like I can finally be myself."

"Well, I must say that I am loving the person that I am seeing you become!"

"Oh, Mom! It's easy when I have you as a good influence on my life."

"Oh, Miriam! How did you get so sweet!"

On her way to drop off her plate in the sink, she walks by her mom and kisses her on the cheek. "I love you, Mom!"

"Love you too, Miriam. Now go finish getting ready for school."

A few minutes later they headed out and Miriam was dropped off at school. Emily reminded her that she had two more days till the weekend. She headed to the office to wait for what the day would bring. It would not take long, as her phone rang shortly after arriving, and no surprise, it was Mrs. Weber.

She talked with her kids about their deal, and they could not believe that someone would be so generous with their mom. It was exactly what their mom needed. She wanted to meet to sign everything. They set up a time for the afternoon, so Alexis had time to draft the paperwork, and also so Miriam could be there. Mrs. Weber liked Miriam and wanted to see her again.

Once she was done with scheduling with Mrs. Weber, she gave Alexis a call to let her know. She was pleased that something could be worked out that would benefit everyone. She was also curious to see the house Alexis also let Emily know that since she put the pictures online, there has been quite a bit of interest. She has three people looking at it today. Two are investors with cash. She is confident that one of the two will make an offer once they see it. Emily is glad to hear that and reminds her that they have a little flexibility in the price if needed to move it quickly. Alexis says she will keep Emily updated and will see her this afternoon.

It has already been quite a morning, now came the waiting game. Emily hated waiting for news. She needed something to occupy herself, while she waited for word from Alexis or this afternoon's meeting. She decided to head to the University of Tulsa and walk around for a bit, especially in the business building. It had been a few weeks since she had been there for business, so she thought it was time.

Emily loved walking around the university. She could just feel the creativity as she walked around. After a few minutes, she was walking past the finance department offices, when she decided to walk in. She was greeted by the receptionist, who quickly called the department chair out to say hi. As soon as he saw her, he had this relieved look on his face. He quickly called her back to his office to talk.

During the school year, they had a monthly luncheon called "Friends of Finance" where they would bring in different speakers, who would speak over lunch. Emily was a regular member, so she was very familiar with the organization. Their speaker for the luncheon next Thursday was suddenly unavailable due to a family emergency. He wanted to know if Emily would take his place. Emily was surprised but was honored to do so. She was used to speaking to student groups, but this would be a much larger group and include many in the business community. They talked for a few minutes more about what had been going on in her life and if she had been working on any new projects.

She headed out shortly after lunch. She had the feeling if she stuck around any longer, she might end up teaching a class or two. She was hoping to see a few old friends and feel refreshed, now she was speaking to several hundred people in a week. Hopefully, the next few days would be relatively quiet, to give her the ample prep time needed to prepare. Miriam will be so excited to hear about it, and of course, she will want to come. With not much else to do, she headed back to the office to look through some listings and wait till it was time to pick up Miriam.

She was excited to go get Miriam today. She had much to share with her and was also looking forward to hearing how her day was. It seemed like an eternity before Miriam was walking out of the building and heading to the car.

"Hey, Miriam! How was your day?"

"It was OK, I guess. Didn't do much today. Mostly review in my classes. I hope your day was better."

"Oh, just a tad. We are heading back to Mrs. Weber's house to have her sign the paperwork. I also got invited to be the speaker at a luncheon at the University next Thursday!"

"That's awesome, Mom! I hope I get to go."

"Of course, you do! Wouldn't have you miss this for anything."

"I'm so glad to hear that! I would love to hear my mom give a speech."

"Well good. I don't know what I am talking about, but we are already at Mrs. Weber's."

Alexis is already there and heads quickly over to Emily.

"Hey, Miriam. Nice to see you again." She turns her attention to Emily. "Well, both of the investors looked at the property and they both loved it. The first one put in a written offer before he left for a slight discount from our listed price. The second investor put in an offer for our listing price. A bidding war has broken out and it is up to $15k over our asking price!"

"That is incredible to hear! At this point, whoever can close quickly has the property."

"I will let them know. I did take a look around, and it does need some work but is not bad. Mrs. Weber seems nice, and she thinks you are wonderful!"

"Well, that is good. Let's go inside and take care of this."

They headed in and Mrs. Weber signs the paperwork selling Emily the house and an agreement that she can stay in the house till the start of the new year. When it was done, they gave her a cashier's check for the purchase price of the house. Mrs. Weber was so thankful and agreed to keep Alexis updated on what was going on. When it was done, Emily and Miriam headed home. They stopped along the way for a nice salmon fillet to cook for dinner along with some veggies.

After dinner, Miriam didn't have much schoolwork, which was a relief. Emily had done enough thinking and was looking forward to a quiet, relaxing evening. She wanted something different instead of watching something, so she poured a glass of wine and headed to the couch to talk with Miriam.

"Miriam, we have this Colorado trip planned well. I know we are both looking forward to it. I wanted to know some of the places that you would like to visit next."

"Well, there are so many places in this country I would love to visit. I would love to go to New York and Washington DC. There is so much history there and many things to do and see there. I would love to travel outside the country as well, at some point. I would love to go to many of the places in Europe or Asia. I love learning about those places, and I would love to be able to see them someday."

"I'm glad to hear that. I am originally from NJ. I was thinking about visiting there for Christmas. It would allow you to meet many members of my family and learn more about me. It is also really close to many of the cities in the Northeast. We could do a long trip and see so many sites while we were there. I was going to mention it after Colorado but wanted to get your input tonight."

"That sounds wonderful, Mom!"

"OK then. I don't know when we can travel internationally, but I think we found our next trip. I will work out some of the dates and get approval for them. I enjoy talking about things like this with you. It is so much fun, almost as fun as spending time with you!"

"Oh, Mom! I love our time together. OK if we watch something before it is time for bed?"

"That would be great. I will let you pick."

They enjoyed some time together watching some things that Miriam picked. Emily was beginning to think that she would enjoy almost any activity with Miriam, as long as she got to spend time with Miriam. She kind of suspected that Miriam felt the same way that she did. She held Miriam a little closer until it was time to head to bed. It wasn't long after that Emily felt the need to head to bed, to think about the day and what on earth she should talk about next week.

Friday morning and found herself waking up at 5:15. Just one more day and she had the entire weekend with Miriam. It was their last weekend before their Colorado trip, so they likely weren't doing a lot, other than spending quality time together. She was OK with that and she was sure that Miriam was OK with that as well. She enjoyed their talk yesterday about traveling and now has some great ideas for potential things to do over Christmas. Before she did any more planning, she wanted to see how this trip went and see what went well and what did not. It would help to make the next one better.

After finishing her coffee, she headed to get ready for the day, then to the kitchen to cook breakfast. She decided on pancakes with some bacon. She added some blueberries to them, so she felt like it was somewhat healthy. She found some food coloring and once Miriam's pancakes were done, she drew a ghost on them for her. Sure enough, just as she was finishing, Miriam walks in.

"Breakfast smells good. What are we having?"

"Haunted blueberry pancakes!"

"That's awesome Mom! You're the best!"

"Now you can be haunted by the pancakes all day when you are at school."

"Oh, Mom! You're so funny."

"Well hurry up and eat before they haunt the house."

Miriam finished up her pancakes and bacon and got ready for school. She loved when her mom did something special for her. She was not used to the extra attention, and it was something that she loved. It gave her a sense of security, which she had been missing since she lost her parents.

After Miriam was dropped off at school, Emily headed to the office to see what may happen today. Once again, it didn't take long for things to start to unfold. Alexis was calling, hopefully with updates about the house.

"Good morning Alexis. I'm hoping you have some good news for me."

"Don't I always Emily. Consider the house sold!"

"Well, that is wonderful news!"

"The final offer is $20k over asking!"

"That is stunning!"

"I know. It was one of the investors and he would like to close ASAP. Would tomorrow afternoon work for you?"

"I guess. I normally like to spend that time with Miriam, but this won't take long. I will talk to her about it when I pick her up. Let's go ahead and schedule it and let him know that everything sounds good on our end. Great job Alexis!"

"Thanks Emily. I guess I will see you tomorrow."

Well, that is a nice way to start a day. That property was one of the easiest jobs she had, with only a few days of work, but it was one of her most profitable ones. She was excited and it is a major relief to be done with this one. She wanted to have this one done before Colorado, but she didn't think it would be possible. Now she can relax some more and have a nicely funded cash reserve to buy some more properties.

Emily decides to go for a coffee run and come back and get some ideas for her speech next week. She needed a topic, and she was not sure what it should be. She didn't want it to simply be a business lesson on real estate investing, though she could incorporate some of it in there. She wanted something more, though. She spent the rest of the day working on some ideas, only stopping for lunch. Before she knew it, it was time to go get Miriam and begin their weekend.

Once Miriam got in the car, Emily decided to ask her about tomorrow.

"Hey, Miriam. How was your day?"

"It was good. I'm glad it is the weekend, as I am looking forward to spending time with you."

"I'm looking forward to spending time with you as well. I sold one of the houses today, and they would like to meet tomorrow to sign the papers and give me the money. It won't take long, but I wanted to see if that was OK with you first."

"Can I dress up like you and can we have a ladies' night out after?"

"Absolutely. You like dressing up like me, don't you?"

"You always look so pretty, and I love how you look."

"You are too sweet. Ladies' night it is tomorrow night!"

They headed home, stopping to pick up dinner. Emily let Alexis know that Saturday would work for them. After dinner, they changed into something more comfortable and enjoyed some classic movies for the rest of the evening. Not the most exciting evening by many standards, but it was a wonderful start to their weekend.

Miriam loved to cuddle up next to her mom on the couch and Emily loved it. She knew it made Miriam feel safe and secure as well as loved, and it was a feeling that she was glad she could share with her. After two classics, they decided to head to bed and get some rest for another ladies' night tomorrow. They were becoming a highlight in their lives.

Saturday, Emily woke up a little after six. She got her coffee and headed to the living room for a bit. She had some time to relax and take things in before Miriam woke up and they planned out their day. It was nice to have some quiet time without feeling rushed as she did on most weekdays. In a week from now, they will be boarding a plane for Colorado. While most of the work had been done, there were always last-minute things that needed to be purchased or planned. The weather was continuing to look promising, with ideal conditions for skiing.

It was close to seven before Miriam got up and came out to the couch to lay next to her mom while using her leg as a pillow.

"Well, good morning!"

"Good morning, Mom! What's for breakfast?"

"I see what the priority is here. What are you wanting?"

"I'd like to stay here for breakfast."

"Well, then I need my leg back so I can go to the kitchen to cook breakfast."

"I suppose you can have it back, but it's very comfortable. I'll need it back later."

"Well, OK then."

Emily headed to the kitchen to work on breakfast. She put some biscuits in the oven and started some breakfast potatoes along with sausage and scrambled eggs. She felt like she needed a big breakfast, even if they were not eating out. She knew Miriam would appreciate a big breakfast, as she loved breakfast, and would routinely eat her mom's as well, especially when they went out.

They sat down to eat breakfast, and Miriam thought everything tasted great. She would eat like this every morning if she could, though Emily couldn't imagine having the motivation to cook breakfast like this every morning, though a generation or two ago, this was normal. They discussed their day and Miriam wanted to stay home for a bit before they headed out later. Emily suggested that they work on their stuff for Colorado. This would give them an idea of what they might need more of, and they could pick it up later when they were out.

Miriam wasn't used to planning for a trip like this, so her mom helped her plan out the days and what she might need. Emily was glad that they had purchased the western boots, as they would work in a variety of situations and would eliminate the need for many other pairs of shoes, which would take up space. After about an hour, Emily felt good about what she and Miriam had for the trip. She made a note of a few items to pick up.

With some time to go before their meeting, Miriam suggested a movie. Emily suspected she just wanted her pillow back, and sure enough, by the time the movie had started, she had it back. Emily didn't mind, she loved that someone could feel so at peace being with her. She knew Miriam felt safe when she was with her. Emily was going to do what she could to keep her safe as long as possible. She had already been through too much for a young lady.

After the movie, Emily made a quick lunch for the two of them. While they were eating, Emily asked if they could drive around for a bit and look at some properties before heading to their closing and then to their night out. Emily loved the idea and asked if they were getting dressed now, and Miriam suggested they look their best, so they headed off to get ready for the day.

When Emily was done, she headed to the living room to wait for Miriam, who a few minutes later came out wearing her new teal dress, black tights, and ankle boots.

"Miriam, you look so beautiful!"

"Thanks, Mom! You look wonderful too!"

"I know you're just saying that cause you're so sweet, but I appreciate it. I'd ask if you are ready to head out, but you look like you are ready to take on the world!"

"Just trying to be like my mom!"

The two of them headed out and Miriam drove around some of her usual neighborhoods, along with a few new ones. She drove Miriam around some of the best neighborhoods and some of the less than best neighborhoods. It gave them a chance to talk about some of the differences. Miriam got to be her mom's assistant by taking the pictures and writing down the information for later.

After a few hours of driving around, they headed to the closing. Alexis was impressed with how Miriam looked and thought she looked like she was ready to take on the world as well. She thought it was sweet that she wanted to look and act like her mom. The closing did not take long, and Emily and Miriam were soon on their way to their night out.

"Well Miriam, what should we do first?"

"Well, it is a little early for dinner. Can we walk around a little bit?"

"That is always a good idea."

The first store they went in had some scarves that they thought looked cute, and they could use in Colorado. They walked around a few stores and didn't see anything they had to have, so they headed off to dinner. Tonight's dinner was at their favorite steakhouse. Not only was the food wonderful, but the atmosphere was perfect for a night out, and they attracted lots of attention, which they both loved.

After dinner, they walked around some more and headed to some of the larger stores to look around. Miriam found a few dresses that she loved, while Emily found a dress with a matching jacket that would look nice for work. They were almost done when they passed the shoe department and they had to stop. Emily got Miriam some more dress shoes, as that is what she wore a lot of. She wanted her to have a variety of colors and styles. Miriam was thrilled with the new shoes. After a great evening of food and shopping, they decided it was time to head home.

"Mom, I had such a great time with you tonight, and it just wasn't the food and shopping. I loved driving around looking at the houses and talking about the neighborhoods. I enjoyed the meeting, even if I didn't understand all of it. I love being a part of your life and not just at home."

"Miriam, you don't know how happy that makes me. I love having you come with me. I love that we can spend time together and it is just not at home but also when I am working as well. I love you so much!"

"Love you too, Mom! Now I think I will head to bed, as I am tired."

Miriam gives her mom a big hug and a kiss on the cheek before heading off to bed. Emily grabs a glass of wine and takes off her heels before sitting on the couch for a few. She loves her time with Miriam and having her around makes work much more enjoyable. She made two-plus hours of driving around looking at houses enjoyable. Miriam just made every part of her life more enjoyable. She finished her glass of wine and headed off to bed.

Sunday was a relatively quiet day for them. They went to the grocery store to pick up a few things to get them through to Friday. When they got back, they cooked a pizza and spent the afternoon relaxing on the couch watching classic horror movies. It was a perfect day for Miriam as she had lots of time to spend with her mom, and they were watching lots of new movies that she had not seen before.

The next few days were also relatively uneventful. Emily spent most of the next three days working on her speech for Thursday. She did take some time to peruse some of the real estate listings, but nothing popped out at her. She was not worried, as it was almost Thanksgiving and it was a quiet time. Also, she made enough profit last week on that property to last for many months, and that was after she paid herself a nice bonus.

Miriam was continuing to do well in school. She was preparing for her math exam, which was coming on Friday. She had begun to settle into a routine, which was good as it kept her on track. She would need to stay on track this week, as she had her exam and didn't want to spend time on her trip trying to get caught up.

Thursday morning, Emily was up at five. She made sure she made extra coffee this morning as she would need it. She was going to give the biggest speech of her career today. She was used to more intimate settings, but this was several hundred people. Her topic was a little different, so she was not sure how it would be received by the group. She finally finished her coffee and headed to get ready for the day.

Once she was dressed and ready for the day, she headed to the kitchen to prepare breakfast. She was so nervous that she wasn't that hungry, but she knew if she didn't eat, that she would regret it, so she cooked some eggs and biscuits. Miriam headed to the kitchen, dressed in one of her professional-looking dresses and heels that Emily had gotten her. She was excited to see her mom speak. She was also glad that she was going to miss most of her school day. She had math early in the day, so she would attend to review for the exam, but still be able to attend the luncheon and hear her mom.

"Good morning, Mom. You look fabulous!"

"Thanks, Miriam. I don't feel fabulous right now."

"I know you'll do great! I believe in you!"

"You're too sweet. You look wonderful as well. Are you sure you're not supposed to speak instead?"

"Oh, Mom! You're funny."

"Thanks. Now finish up breakfast, so I can get you off to school for a bit."

Miriam finished her breakfast and went to finish getting ready for her abbreviated school day. Emily dropped her off at school, then she headed to the office to grab what she would need for the speech. She had already emailed a copy of the presentation, but she had some notes that she wanted to get. She decided to stay at the office and review things before it was time to head back to the school to pick up Miriam and head to the University.

After she picked up Miriam, they headed to the University of Tulsa for the luncheon. It was held in one of the larger meeting rooms. She got checked in and received her name badge, along with one for Miriam. They headed in to grab their food and find their seats. The food looked wonderful, which it usually did. Today, it was beef with mashed potatoes, gravy, steamed veggies, and a roll. Miriam wished her school food looked like this every day.

Since she was the speaker, they were seated up front along with a few other VIPs, mostly from the University. They were interested in Miriam and were asking her lots of questions. They couldn't believe she was only in 8th grade. They thought for sure she was ready for college. Miriam was enjoying the food and especially the attention.

Before Emily knew it, the Finance chair was at the podium welcoming people and would be introducing her momentarily. She couldn't believe that she had volunteered for this, especially this close to a vacation. She would need a vacation after today. The finance chair had finished the announcements and was introducing her. She grabbed her glass of iced tea and finished it. In her mind it was wine, and it would help her relax. She was heading to the podium as people were clapping for her.

"Thank you for the kind welcome. It is so nice to be speaking at my favorite University. Today my presentation is entitled "My Greatest Achievements". Since I am known as a real estate developer, by most, and I was introduced as such, I will start by showing a few of my recent projects."

She shows them a few before and after pictures of some of her recent residential properties. She then moves on to her hotel project. She can tell by their reaction that they are impressed.

"While these projects that I have shown you have been wonderful works, and I am indeed proud of them. They are not my greatest achievements. Let me tell you about my real greatest achievements."

She talks about the many young ladies that she mentored or gave internships to while they were students here. She also talks about what mentoring has meant to them and how it impacted their lives.

"Now I will finish with what has been my greatest achievement so far. A few weeks ago, I was talking with a former classmate and she mentioned to me that I could take the mentoring to the next level. I was intrigued. A few weeks later I met a sweet girl named Miriam, and it was love at first sight. A week later she moved into my home and my heart. In that time, she has learned a lot about my business world and accompanied me to many meetings and events.

It would be an understatement to say that I have taught her many things and her life has been forever impacted. She has also taught me so much, and she has forever impacted my life as well. In a few months, she will formally be adopted and legally become my daughter, but to me, that has already happened. She is here today to hear me speak, and she had no idea she was the topic. So,

Miriam please stand, so others can see my greatest achievement."

Miriam stands and receives applause and has a tear or two visible. She is very touched, to say the least.

"In closing, you don't need to be a successful businessperson to do great things and have great achievements. All you need is a willingness to do great things and change the world for a handful of people, then you will truly be a great person with memorable achievements. Thank you!"

The majority of the crowd stood to cheer and clap. The finance chair came back up to close and brought Miriam onto the stage as well. She ran to her mom and gave her a big bug and they held each other for a moment before heading back to their seats. Once the luncheon was over, Emily stayed around for a few to answer questions from people. There were quite a few that had kids that were grown and on their own. She had inspired them to look into adopting older kids like Miriam. Miriam was glad to hear that, as she knew quite a few older kids who would love a home.

It was close to 2 till they were finally done. As they were heading out, Emily joked that it would be time to pick up Miriam from school soon. Miriam just laughed. They decided that they had done enough for today and would head home. Once they got home, they both changed into something more comfortable. Miriam came out and laid next to her mom on the couch.

"Am I really your greatest achievement?"

"Of course. Just look at how much you have improved in the past month. Imagine how much change there will be in the next couple of years? That is the kind of achievement that excites me."

"I'm so glad you feel that way, Mom. I had a great time today."

"That's good. Was it just my speech?"

"That was my favorite part, but I loved dressing up, the food, and talking with the people."

"Why doesn't that surprise me? So, what should we do for the rest of the evening?"

"Well, I should probably review my math for tomorrow. I don't have much else to do for school."

"That sounds like a plan. Should we pack everything tonight or wait till tomorrow?"

"Let's do it tonight since we have more time and then we can relax tomorrow evening."

"I like your plan."

Emily helps Miriam review her math for tomorrow's exam. They spend about an hour reviewing everything. Emily feels confident in what Miriam knows, so she works on dinner, while Miriam finishes up an assignment for another class. Once they are done with dinner, they go ahead and pack everything that they set out the other day. It takes two large suitcases each to fit their stuff plus a smaller carry-on-sized suitcase. They would be gone for a week, and winter clothes, especially for skiing are quite bulky. Emily had the feeling that transporting all of these suitcases was going to be fun.

With everything ready and packed, they decide to relax and watch some TV before heading off to bed. It had been an incredible day for both of them. Emily took a risk with her speech and it really paid off. She didn't know what it might mean for her career, but she was relieved. She was looking forward to taking a few days off and spending some much-needed time with Miriam.

After a few shows, it was time for Miriam to head to bed. Emily would be following her soon, but tonight was one of those nights that she could use that glass of wine. While she drank, she thought of all that she had worked so hard for the past few years. She had worked hard and enjoyed a lot of success, but somehow it couldn't compare to being with Miriam. She finished her glass and was off to bed.

The next morning, Emily was up at her usual time. She wasn't feeling the motivation to get up this morning, and if she didn't have to get Miriam ready for school, she would likely stay in bed. She had given the speech of a lifetime yesterday and tomorrow she will be on vacation, but what about today? She didn't have much to get done today. She finally got up and got her coffee while she contemplated the day.

Once she was done with her coffee, she headed off to get ready for the day. She decided that she didn't need to head to the office today, so instead of her usual office attire, she found a wrap dress with wedge heels. This was as casual as she liked to be on non-holiday. Once she dropped off Miriam, she would head back home and take care of things at the house. She headed off to the kitchen to work on breakfast. Today was a variety of things that she was wanting to finish off. Miriam headed to the kitchen just as things were being finished.

"Wow, Mom. That is a cute dress."

"Thanks. I will be working at the home office today, so I didn't feel like wearing my normal work attire."

"Wish I could stay home with you as well."

"Me too, but you missed most of yesterday and I don't want you to get behind. It's just one day and tomorrow we will be on vacation!"

"I am very much looking forward to it."

"I know, Miriam. I am as well."

Miriam finished her breakfast and headed off to finish getting ready for school. Emily dropped her off at school and headed back to the house. She checked through a couple of listings to see if anything was exciting, but there wasn't much. She received some updates on a few of her projects and things were where they should be. With not much else to do, she looked through some of the activities that they had planned for the next few days. She thought they had a good mix of planned activities and free time to find something to do or to simply relax. She checked some of their travel arrangements to see if there had been any changes, but everything was looking good. It was only lunchtime and everything she felt she wanted to do today had already been accomplished.

    She decided to head to the store to look around. She wanted to see if there were any travel items that she might need or want. She saw some cute neck pillows, so she picked up two. They could come in handy for the flight or the drive to and from Aspen. She also saw some snacks that would be good to take along. She walked around some and was checking out some things for Miriam. She saw a few things that she might have to come back for another day. Though it seemed like an eternity, it was finally time to go pick up Miriam.

    When Miriam got into the car, Emily asked her, "Who is ready for a vacation?"

    "After today I am for sure!"

    "That bad?"

    "No. I did OK on the exam, but it was a long and slow day."

    "I had one of those as well. Oh, I picked you up something." She reached into the bag and pulled out one of the neck pillows and placed it around her neck. This one was purple and glittery.

"I love it! Not as comfortable as you, but still comfortable."

"Thought you might need one on the plane or the longer drives."

"Thanks, Mom. It's really cute."

"Well let's pick up dinner and head home."

They picked up some tacos and headed home to begin their vacation. Once dinner was done, Miriam made sure all her work was done, so she wouldn't need to worry about it till she went back to school. Luckily, everything was done already so she put her schoolwork away and went to sit next to her mom on the couch.

"Well Miriam, what should we do now?"

"Watch a movie?"

"That sounds good."

They find a good movie and spend a relaxing evening, with just the two of them. They enjoy the quiet, as they know the next few days will be fun, but busy at times. After the movie, Miriam heads to her room. She wanted to look through some last-minute stuff to make sure she was ready in the morning. They would be getting up like it was a school day. With Miriam in her room, Emily got a glass of wine and headed to her room to check through everything as well. She was a little nervous traveling with somebody, as she hadn't traveled with anyone in a while. She finished her glass and headed to bed.

The next morning, Emily was awake at 5. She headed to the kitchen to get her coffee and headed back to the room. Though it was a Saturday, she didn't have much time to relax. She finished her coffee and headed to get ready. She heard Miriam's alarm go off when she was getting her coffee, so she was sure she was up and getting ready as well.

She headed to the kitchen. Instead of her usual business attire, today was definitely more western looking. They were saving their new clothes while they were there but found some stuff that would work. Emily was wearing a knee-length dress that had some sparkle to it. She opted for the ankle boots, as she knew she would manage fine in them for travel and didn't want to risk the other boots when she wasn't used to them. Miriam had a long denim skirt with her shorter boots and a sparkly top. Of course, both ladies had their hats with them. Breakfast today would be a breakfast sandwich, which would get them on the road quickly.

They finished breakfast and loaded all the suitcases into the car and were off to the airport. Emily had opted to use the valet service, as she could pull up to the terminal and unload all the suitcases, with most of them being checked and she wouldn't need to worry about them until they arrived in Denver. That left them with a bag each that they could carry.

Miriam was looking around quite a bit. This was her first time at an airport, and she was very curious about things. Emily was a seasoned traveler, so she was the perfect person to answer questions and knew what to do to ensure a smooth trip. They headed off to security. Luckily, they were flying first class and Emily had a status that got them to an easier line. It was not much of a hassle to get through. Once they were though, it was much easier to relax. They stopped at the large glass window and watched the planes for a moment.

"I love the planes, Mom. I didn't think there would be this many."

"Well, many people like us are heading out for Thanksgiving. See that large white plane over there?"

"Yeah. Is that our plane?"

"You bet. We have a few minutes till we start to board, so we can walk around some. If you see something to eat or drink, let me know. I know we were rushed a little bit this morning."

"OK. I could use a drink."

"There is a store here. We can stop in and get some drinks, as I could use some extra coffee."

After getting their drinks, they walk over to their gate and prepare to board. It doesn't take long, especially since they are in first-class to board the plane. Miriam is so excited as she walks down the jetway and up to the plane. They walk in and take their seats in the second row. Emily let Miriam take the window, as it was her first flight and she wanted her to be able to enjoy the view. They get their bags under the seat and wait for everyone else to board. Miriam is busy watching all the activity including them loading the bags, she can see all of hers get loaded.

Once everyone is on board, they begin their departure procedures. Miriam is fascinated by the safety briefing and is following along. She is started when they begin to push the plane back from the gate. Luckily, her mom is there to reassure her that everything is normal. They start the engines and make a short trip to the runway. They pause for a moment before lining up on the runway. Emily tells Miriam to hold on. At that moment, the plane begins to accelerate down the runway and is soon airborne. Miriam has a look that is partial excitement and partial not sure what to expect. Once they begin their climb, Miriam is looking out the window watching the city get smaller and farther away.

 It wasn't long before the flight attendants were bringing the cart through the aisle to hand out drinks and snacks. Emily let Miriam have her choice of soda, while she had one as well. The wine was tempting, but with several hours of driving ahead of them, she wanted to be a good example to Miriam. Miriam spent most of the remainder of the flight alternating between looking out the window and reading the inflight magazine. The flight was relatively smooth until they got closer to the mountains, then the turbulence picked up some. Emily could tell that Miriam was unsure what to think.

 Miriam enjoyed the landing but was surprised at how far away the airport was from the city. She didn't see many buildings at all during decent. She was also surprised by how large the airport was. When they exited the plane, it took several minutes of walking just to get down the terminal. Emily was quick to point out some of the various cities that were listed at the various gates, including some international ones.

 When Miriam thought they were at the end, they arrived at a station and waited a few minutes for a train to come by, which they took past another concourse before finally arriving at the main terminal, where they picked up their checked bags, which was followed by more walking before they exited, only to wait for a bus to take them to the rental car facility down the street. After a few minutes, they were finally dropped off, along with their bags. Luckily for them, they were able to bypass the long line of car renters and head straight to their vehicle, where they were directed to a line of trucks to choose from.

"Well Miriam, that is a lot of trucks to choose from. What do you think?"

"I don't know. I do like this pretty red one."

"Me too. We will take it. Let's grab our bags and put them in the back row."

Once they loaded their bags, they headed to the gate to check out the truck and were soon on their way. After a few minutes of driving, they were on the interstate and began to see the town. Miriam was excited to see the Rocky Mountains in the distance, and Emily let her know that they would be heading there soon enough. When they passed the downtown area, Miriam was excited with what she saw. Her mom let her know that they would spend the 2nd half of their vacation at a hotel in the downtown area and would have lots of opportunities to see the sights.

Shortly after passing downtown the mountains were getting closer and closer, and they were soon beginning their climb into the mountains, and about 90 minutes after leaving the airport, they were coming up to the Eisenhower Tunnel. Emily let Miriam know the story about this tunnel, and what the route would have looked like before the tunnel. It was about two hours after passing through the tunnel that they arrived in Aspen and found the resort. It was just as beautiful as the pictures showed it would be.

They gathered their bags and headed into the hotel. The inside of the hotel was beautiful and looked like what a ski lodge in Colorado should look like. There were quite a few fireplaces around the lobby, where people could gather. Emily headed to the desk to check-in, while Miriam stayed and looked around in amazement. Emily got checked in, and they were soon heading to the elevators to go to their room.

When they got to the room, Miriam was surprised at the size of it. This was no ordinary hotel room. There were a living room and kitchen. When her mom showed her around, she saw that it had two bedrooms as well. It would be just like being at home. They got their bags settled and sat down for the first time since they left Tulsa in the morning.

"Well, Miriam, what do you think?"

"I love it, Mom! It is so beautiful out here. I loved the drive here, as there was so much to see. I love the mountains."

"Well, there is one more surprise." She walked over to the back of the living room and opened the curtain, revealing a balcony that overlooked the mountains.

"Oh, Mom! I want to go out now!" Miriam unlocked the door and went out on the balcony. She noticed two chairs and a small table out there as well. "We could eat out here."

"We could, though it might be a little cold."

"It's just so beautiful out here."

"Yes, it is. I'll let you stay out here for a few, while I unpack a few things."

"OK, Mom."

Emily went in and sorted through some of their things. She had unpacked what they would need for the next few days. Tomorrow would be horse riding in the morning. Miriam still had no idea, but she would be so excited. It was supposed to start snowing tonight, and by the afternoon, there should be sufficient snow to at least do some skiing lessons. Once she was done, she went to check on Miriam.

"Hey Miriam, are you getting hungry?"

"Yeah, we haven't had much today."

"I know. That happens many times when you travel. Let's head to the restaurant to see what looks good."

"Sounds great, Mom."

They headed to the restaurant to see what they had. The hotel had quite a few food options. In addition to the sit-down restaurant, there was a place to get food to go. After a busy day of travel, the thought of taking something to go back to the room sounded appealing, so they found some food and headed back to the room. It was nice to be able to finally relax and enjoy time with each other. When they had finished, they decided what to do next.

"Well Miriam, we can relax here for the rest of the evening or there is a pool we can head to and a hot tub as well."

"That sounds great. I haven't been swimming in a while."

They headed to the pool for a bit. After all the travel, they were both a little stiff and it felt great to move around. After some time in the pool, they headed to the hot tub and relaxed for a bit before heading back to the room. By the time they got back, it was getting late, so they just watched TV together for a bit before heading to bed and getting ready for their first full day in Aspen.

The next morning, Emily woke up earlier than she expected she would, but then realized she was an hour behind her normal time zone. She headed to the kitchen to make some coffee and wait in the living room till Miriam woke up and headed out of her room. She hadn't discussed any time to wake up, so she was not sure when to expect her. It was nice to be away for a bit. The past few weeks had been extremely busy in more than one way. Between adding Miriam and a lot of real estate activity, the past month seems like it has been non-stop with little time to breathe. She had begun to realize that she needs some time to get away and recharge. This week would go a long way to doing so.

It was about 30 minutes later that Miriam came out and sat next to her mom and gave her a big hug.

"Well, good morning to you as well! Hope you slept well."

"The bed is not as comfortable as my bed, but I loved the view."

"I'm sure you did. We have some activities this morning, so we should likely get dressed soon so we can have breakfast."

"OK, Mom."

They get dressed for the day and head to the restaurant for breakfast, where Miriam is excited to see that breakfast is a buffet, where she can get what looks good, which is just about everything there. She even tried a few new things and liked quite a few of them. When they had finished, Emily led them out back and they began to walk around. After a moment, Miriam saw two horses and asked if they could go take a look at them. Her mom obliged, for obvious reasons.

"These are such pretty horses. Can I go pet the horses?"

"Of course, Miriam." She begins to pet them.

"How would you like to ride on one of them?"

"Really? I'd love to." The person helps Miriam up into the saddle. "Oh Mom, this is fun!"

"Well, your fun is just beginning, because this is the surprise for the day. We have a short lesson on riding then we get to go on a ride through the trail."

"Oh Mom, you're the best!"

Emily climbed onto her horse and the two of them learned some of the basics of riding before they went on their ride through the trail. It was a great time for the two as the trail was quite scenic and they enjoyed the quiet time together, away from the rest of the busy world around them. It was just the two of them and their horses, and nothing else at the moment mattered to either of them. It was about two hours that they were gone. When they got back, Miriam wanted to ride some more. It was clear that she was hooked, as was Emily.

They headed to the restaurant and grabbed some to-go lunch, which they took up to the room. They had a little time before their skiing lessons, and they were very much looking forward to it. Neither had any experience with skiing, so it would be something that they could experience together. After finishing their lunch, they headed out to where the lessons would be. The instructor had them try on the skis and started with some basic maneuvers. After a few minutes, they were able to move around on the skis, and he felt that they were ready to try some of the basic slopes.

They headed off to enjoy the rest of the afternoon on the slopes. After a few minutes, they were able to get a hold of it. Though they were on the beginner slopes, they were enjoying themselves. It wasn't long before the sun was beginning to set, and it was time to head back to the lodge for the night. Once they got back, they decided to head to the restaurant for dinner and they changed into one of their cowgirl dresses and boots that they had picked up. The restaurant had great food, and they felt great to be in their dresses again, after a day of riding and skiing. After dinner, they headed to the room to see what they should do next.

"Well Miriam, what should we do now?"

"I have had one of the best days ever with you, Mom. I'm not ready to get ready for bed, especially now that I am dressed up."

"Well, you are an adorable cowgirl. We could drive around some and see what we can find to do."

"That sounds wonderful."

They head to the truck and drive around town, where they find a couple of clothing stores that they loved. They found some clothes that were Western-themed, so they had to add to their cowgirl collection. After a few hours of seeing the town and shopping, they decided to head back to the lodge. They decided to sit on the couch for a few, before heading to bed. Naturally, Miriam was laying against her mom. It was a day that she would never forget. She was so thankful and appreciated all the effort that her mom put into planning this day.

"Well, before you fall asleep on me Miriam, you might want to go get changed and head to bed."

"I suppose, Mom. This was one of the best days ever. I love you so much!"

"Love you too, Miriam. Now go get some sleep, so we can have more fun tomorrow!"

They headed off to their rooms and were both asleep quickly. It was an incredible day for both of them, and one for the ages. Tomorrow would bring another set of adventures for them to enjoy.

Monday morning, Emily was up at 6:30, which was late for her, especially considering the time change. She headed out to get her coffee. When she got out to the living room, she was surprised to see Miriam already out on the couch.

"Well, good morning, Miriam! I'm surprised to see you up already."

"I was too excited to sleep."

"It was my morning to sleep in. Let me get my coffee and we can talk."

After a minute, Emily had her coffee and sat on the couch next to Miriam, and tried laying on Miriam, like Miriam usually does to her.

"You're right. This is quite comfy."

"Oh, Mom!"

"OK. I guess we can switch."

"That is much better!"

"So, what should we do today?"

"Can we ski some more?"

"Well since it is our last full day here, I suppose we should. Should we go to the same slope or try something new?"

"Can we try skiing on the trails?"

"That will be a lot of work, but it could be fun. We can head out after breakfast."

They got dressed and headed down for another breakfast buffet. Miriam loved the variety of food that was available, and she could get used to eating breakfast like this every morning. Once they had finished breakfast, they headed out to the slopes and decided to try the trail, instead of downhill skiing. They quickly realized that it was more of a workout than they had planned. When they wanted to rest, they would find a large rock or tree and sit for a few, before continuing along the trail. It took them over three hours to complete the trail. They headed back to the lodge and got changed for lunch. They went back to the restaurant for lunch and discussed what to do for the rest of the day.

They quickly realized that they were too tired to ski anymore, and they wanted to shop some more, so they decided to do a ladies' night in Aspen. After an afternoon of shopping, they headed to a nice restaurant and enjoyed some of the best of what Aspen has to offer. They loved driving around in their red truck, looking like cowgirls. They got a few looks from people, mostly from those who thought they were from Texas. It was another wonderful evening, and they had so much fun together. It was hard to believe that it was their last night in Aspen, so they stayed out and enjoyed the city as much as they could.

It was after nine before they got back to their room. Miriam hugged her mom and let her know how much fun that she has had the past few days and how much she appreciates everything. She heads off to bed, and Emily does the same. The past two days have been incredibly busy, and she had a drive back to Denver in the morning. She made a note to find some quiet time while they were in Denver, as she was going to need a vacation from her vacation.

The next morning, Emily was up at six. She headed out to get her coffee and contemplate the day. She had about a three-hour drive to get back to Denver. She wasn't looking forward to it, but Denver should be a little more relaxing. They will be there for a few days more, and they don't have nearly as many activities planned. It should be a chance to relax a little more. She was enjoying the time with Miriam, she wasn't expecting it to be non-stop all day long.

It was about thirty minutes later that Miriam got up and came into the living room. She laid next to her mom and asked what the plan was for the day.

"Well, we should probably get breakfast. At some point, we will need to pack everything and take it out to the truck and then head to Denver."

"I like breakfast."

"I've noticed. Well, let's go get dressed and go get breakfast. Today would be a good day for one of our cowgirl outfits."

"Sounds great, Mom."

They headed off to their rooms to get dressed for the day. They each picked out one of their more casual dresses, along with the standard cowgirl boots. Once they were ready, they headed to the restaurant for the breakfast buffet. Miriam once again had her fill of just about one of everything in the buffet. Once they were done with breakfast, they went back to the room to get everything packed. They had done a bit of shopping while there, and it was going to be a tough fit to get everything in their bags. Looks like they might need to purchase another suitcase to fly back to Tulsa, but that was a few days away, so they could worry about it later.

Once everything was packed, they decided to load up the truck and head out. Emily would need to stop for gas. If they got to the hotel a little early, they could park the truck in the garage and walk around downtown. It was an uneventful drive into Denver, though the roads were not as clear as they had been when they arrived. It ended up being close to check-in time when they finally arrived at the hotel.

Miriam was impressed with downtown. They had seen the Colorado Capitol when they entered downtown. There were also quite a few sports stadiums/ arenas that were quite impressive as well. There was much to see downtown, and they had quite a few days to take in the sights. They unloaded their luggage in the lobby and a bellman took their luggage to deliver to their room, while they parked and officially checked in.

While the hotel looked nice, Miriam knew her mom had mentioned something special, but she wasn't seeing it. When they got into the elevator, and Miriam asked what floor. Emily smiled and said, "the 13th floor." Miriam got really excited until they got to the floor and the elevator opened. She heard a family voice say "Here's Johnny! Welcome to the 13th floor!"

"Oh, Mom this is awesome!" She walked out and saw large pictures from some of her favorite horror movies. She had to take pictures with many of them.

Emily could tell that she was loving this, "I don't know about you, but I think this floor is haunted!"

"You're the best!" She gave her a big and kiss on the cheek.

At this hotel, they had their own room, but they were adjoining, so they could move back and forth without entering the hallway. Emily wanted her to have some space for herself. This would allow them time to be together, but still give the time she might need, such as in the evening or the morning, considering her mom is usually up a little earlier than she is. They got Miriam's luggage moved to her room and they unpacked a little before deciding what to do with the rest of the evening.

"Well, Miriam. What should we do now?"

"We could walk around for a bit and maybe find something for dinner."

"I think I know the perfect place to head."

It was a nice cool evening when they walked out of the hotel and traveled a few blocks. Miriam saw what looked like red busses heading back and forth up ahead.

"What is that up ahead?"

"That is the 16th street mall. Those busses travel up and down the street. When we see something, we can hop off and get back on when we are done."

"That sounds like fun." They wait for the next bus and travel for a bit before they see some places that they want to shop at, so they get off. After a little bit of browsing, they found a place that looked good for dinner, so they ate dinner there, before continuing to browse the stores. When they felt that they had seen everything, they headed back to the hotel. Miriam was wanting to hear Johnny again.

When they got back to the room, Miriam wasn't ready for bed yet, especially when she could lay on her mom. She laid on her mom for a bit, just enjoying everything. She felt so at peace being with her mom. After all she had been through, it was like being protected from the storm that was surrounding her. After a few minutes of peace, she began to doze off, and that is when her mom helped her into her bed and kissed her goodnight, before heading to her room.

Emily could see the look on Miriam's face when she was laying with her, and she could tell that she was at peace. That feeling meant so much to her, especially knowing how much Miriam had been through. She couldn't wait till Miriam was officially hers, though it would only be in legal terms, as Miriam was already officially hers, and no one could change that feeling.

Wednesday morning Emily awoke at six. She got her coffee and sat on the couch and waited for Miriam to wake up. She had planned some activities today and was a great opportunity to show Miriam some of the Denver suburbs. She had enjoyed the sights and the uniqueness of the area and she wanted to share that with Miriam. It was about an hour later that Miriam joined her mom on the couch.

"Good morning, Miriam. Did you sleep OK in the haunted room?"

"Oh, Mom! It was wonderful!"

"That's good. Before we get started on our day, I wanted to talk to you about something."

"Like what?"

"Well, I feel so bad. We've been so busy planning this trip that I haven't done anything to plan for your birthday next week."

"This trip has been the best birthday present ever, especially since I have been spending it with you."

"Well, I'm glad to hear that. Did you want to do anything for your birthday on Sunday, when we are back in town?"

"I just want to spend the day with you, maybe do something for dinner?"

"Sounds great. Ready to go eat breakfast?"

"Do you really need to ask?"

"I guess not. Well, let's go get ready and get some breakfast."

They got dressed in their cowgirl outfits and headed to breakfast, before heading out for the day. They started the day in the suburb of Centennial and enjoyed many of the shopping centers in the area, many had stores that were not available to them in Tulsa, including a large furniture store. Afterward, they headed out to Lone Tree, where in addition to checking out more stores, they picked up lunch. Miriam was enjoying the scenery, with the Rockies a constant in the background. It was a beautiful sight and one that they both wished they could see more often.

After lunch, they headed west and drove through some of the western suburbs. They stopped at a bakery to pick up some snacks and checked out some more shopping areas. They started to head downtown, but Emily had one more surprise. They stopped at Casa Bonita for dinner, and Miriam enjoyed the food and the show. The experience there reminded her of her home. After dinner, they headed back to the hotel to relax for the rest of the evening.

After a busy day of seeing the town, they got changed and decided to catch a movie and enjoy their bakery treats. After a busy day of running around, it felt great just to be together. They enjoyed two movies before Miriam was ready to head to bed. She was looking forward to tomorrow, which would be Thanksgiving. She had so much to be thankful for this year, and she was looking forward to spending it with her new mom.

For Emily, she also had much to be thankful for. It had been another great year for her, but nothing could compare to having Miriam in her life. She was also looking forward to spending Thanksgiving with Miriam. Having Miriam in her life gave her a greater purpose beyond buying and selling real estate. She felt that she was creating a legacy, that could be passed on.

Thanksgiving morning and Emily was up at 6:30. She got her coffee and headed to the couch for a few. Sleeping in the next room was something that she was incredibly thankful for. For some time, she had wanted kids but had relationship issues that had prevented her from having a child. At the time, it was disappointing, but looking back, it meant that she could make a clean break and not have the other person hanging around for the rest of the child's life.

She is so glad that Miriam is in her life. What amazes her about Miriam, is how much they share in common. She expected to have some things in common with a child, especially a daughter, but how much they share in common would be amazing if they were genetically related, but the odds that two strangers would have this much in common is phenomenal. That is one of the reasons why they are celebrating today.

It was shortly after seven when Miriam entered the room and laid on the couch next to her mom.

"Well good morning, Miriam, and Happy Thanksgiving!"

"Happy Thanksgiving to you too, Mom! So, what's the plan for today?"

"Well, we can go get some breakfast, which I know you are ready for. The hotel is doing their Thanksgiving dinner this afternoon. Other than that, I don't have anything else planned. We can either stay at the hotel today, walk around downtown some more, or drive around some more, but most things will be closed today."

"I think I'd like to stay here and spend the day with just you."

"I'd like that as well. Well, let's go get dressed and get some breakfast, then we can come back and find something to watch."

"Sounds great, Mom."

They headed off to get dressed and went on to eat breakfast. When they were done with breakfast, they came back to the room and changed into something more comfortable. Emily was able to connect her laptop to the TV and they spent the next few hours watching horror movies together, many of which were depicted out in the hallway. When it was close to dinner time, they got dressed in their nicest cowgirl dresses that they had bought and headed to the restaurant for their first Thanksgiving dinner together.

The dinner was set up in a buffet-style, to allow each person to take what items that they wanted. Miriam had taken a lot of everything, so she could try out a variety of items and see what she liked. Emily, however, stuck with the classics. It was a very enjoyable dinner for the both of them. The more formal atmosphere reminded them of the many evenings out that they had enjoyed together. For some reason, the two of them enjoyed getting dressed up and eating out. It was one of many reasons that they were thankful for each other today.

After dinner, they headed back to the room and got changed for bed. They watched two more movies till it was time to head to bed. It had been a wonderful day together. While they didn't do a lot of activities, it was nice to just spend some quiet time together. Tomorrow would likely be a busy day, and Saturday would be a busy travel day, so it was nice to just relax and forget about the world for a day and just enjoy what matters.

On Friday morning, Emily was up at six. She got her coffee and was reflecting on how wonderful yesterday had been for the two of them. Today was going to be a busy day, and they would get started once Miriam woke up. Today they would head to Colorado Springs, which is about an hour south of Denver. Emily had been to Denver many times but has never made the trip south. She was looking forward to some of the sights, and she heard that the Rockies were even closer to the interstate there.

It was about seven that Miriam came out and once again laid on the couch next to her mom. She looked up at her mom with this adorable smile.

"Well good morning to you! I'm guessing you had a great day yesterday as well?"

"It was a wonderful day, Mom. I could get used to days like that."

"I know, Miriam. I could as well. Let's go get ready and get some breakfast so we can get started on our day."

They headed off and within an hour, they were on the road to Colorado Springs. They enjoyed the closeness of the mountains as they approached the city. They passed the USAF Academy and Miriam enjoyed seeing some of the jets flying around. After a few minutes, it felt like they were leaving town. Straight ahead was a rather large mountain and Miriam was intrigued.

"What mountain is that?"

"That is Pike's Peak, and that is where we are heading this morning."

"Really?"

"Yeah. We are going to drive straight up it to the top."

"Awesome!"

It took another hour for them to make it up to the top. Once they were there, they enjoyed the view for a few minutes until it was too cold, and they headed to the visitor center at the summit for lunch and some shopping. Emily was glad that they had spent the past week at a mile elevation or higher, as it made it easier to deal with the higher altitude they were at. Miriam had mentioned that there were mountains back where she was from, but one could not simply drive up to the top. She had always wanted to climb a mountain, now she can say that she has.

When they had finished their time at Pike's Peak, they headed back to the city to see some of the other sites and check out some of the shopping areas. They ended their time in Colorado Springs with dinner, before heading back to Denver and the hotel. Since they had an earlier flight the next morning, they decided to pack most of their stuff tonight. This would save on time in the morning, and it also made sure they had adequate space in their suitcases, which they surprisingly did.

Once the packing was done, they decided to sit on the couch and chill for a bit. Miriam let her mom know that this trip has been the best vacation that she has had. She also really loved Colorado and hopes to come back again. Her mom let her know that this was also one of her favorite vacation spots as well and that they would be back soon. Colorado, especially Denver, was close enough that a long weekend was sufficient time. Miriam was tired and headed to bed. Emily wanted to have a glass of wine before heading to bed. It also gave her a chance to plan out the next morning. They would be able to be up at their usual times but would need to be on the road pretty quickly.

Saturday morning, Emily was up at six. She got her coffee and headed to the couch. This past week has been incredible for the two of them. She can't remember having this much fun on a vacation before. She is sure that Miriam feels the same way. This was a much-needed break for the two of them. They needed to make sure that they took regular trips whenever possible. They have many years' worth of trips to make up.

Miriam was up about thirty minutes later. She laid by her mom and had this look on her face.

"Not ready to go home?"

"This place is too nice, and we don't have mountains back home."

"I know, but we will be back soon, I am sure of that. Well, we better get some breakfast, so we can get to the airport."

They get dressed and head to the restaurant for their last meal in Colorado. Once they are finished with breakfast, they load the bags in the truck and head to the airport, first dropping off the truck, then heading to check most of their bags. The Denver airport is much larger than Tulsa. In Tulsa, the walk from checking luggage to security to gates is not long. In Denver, that is not the case, as there are longer walks and multiple security areas to choose from. Luckily, they found one that was not busy and with Emily's status, they were quickly through security and heading to the train to get to their concourse.

Once they were at their concourse, it was another long walk to get to the gate. By the time they were at the gate, they were ready to sit for a few. They had another 30 minutes until boarding began. Miriam was having fun looking at the other planes in the area and seeing where they were going to be heading. Many were going to wonderful places that she would love to go to, while others were heading to places that she was not familiar with.

Before they knew it, it was time to board. This plane was smaller than the first one, but they were still upfront in first class. The flight to Tulsa was relatively uneventful. It was too short for much food service, though they were given a snack and a drink. It took about five minutes to walk from the gate to pick up the checked bags. Once they had their bags, they went outside to the valet, who went and picked up their car and brought it to them, along with helping them load their stuff in the back. They were soon on their way home, stopping to pick up lunch.

It did feel good to be back home, though Emily was not looking forward to the piles of laundry that awaited her. She was happy enough to move all the luggage to the laundry room and work on it tomorrow. She just wanted to relax with Miriam, after a busy day of travel. They decided to watch a bunch of movies and order some pizza at dinner time. After a week of running around, it was nice to just relax and enjoy each other's company.

Tomorrow would be another relatively relaxing day, other than needing to do laundry and get groceries. It was also Miriam's birthday, and they would celebrate it with dinner out, which was becoming one of their favorite things to do together, especially if it involved dressing up. Miriam was heading to bed a little early for her, but with a busy day of travel, she was ready for some sleep. Emily stayed up for a bit with a glass of wine, to contemplate this trip and where they should go for Christmas, which was now only a few weeks away.

Sunday morning and it felt good for Emily to be back in her own bed. While the hotels had been nice, it felt great to be back home. She headed to the kitchen to grab her coffee and wait on the couch for Miriam to wake up. She was feeling like she needed a vacation to recover from her vacation. Luckily, there was not much planned for today, which would allow them to relax and get some things done. She was looking forward to celebrating Miriam's birthday today. The past few weeks had been incredible, and she knew that there was much more to come.

It was about thirty minutes later that Miriam awoke and entered the living room and laid on the couch next to her mom.

"Well, good morning birthday girl! How does it feel to be fourteen?"

"It feels good that I am here with you! Between finding you and the trip to Colorado, this will be the best birthday ever!"

"I am so glad to hear that! You are way too sweet though. So, what does the birthday girl feel like doing today?"

"We can start with breakfast and just watch some movies for a bit, before heading out for dinner."

"How did I know that breakfast would be a priority for you? Should we go out or stay here."

"I'm not leaving this couch."

"OK. I will go make breakfast then."

Emily headed to the kitchen to see what she had. Luckily, she could make pancakes along with biscuits and some bacon. It would be a filling breakfast for both of them, and something Miriam would love. They enjoyed breakfast together then headed back to the couch to enjoy a few movies before the birthday festivities began. After the second movie, they took a quick lunch break and made a sandwich. They took their lunches and headed back to the couch for a few more movies.

It was about four when the last movie ended. They headed off to get ready for their dinner out. While they enjoyed their cowgirl outfits and boots, it was nice to wear their typical dresses and heels. They headed off to their favorite shopping center, for dinner and some shopping. Dinner was at their favorite steakhouse. Miriam had never been a big steak fan until she started eating there a few weeks ago. Not only was the food wonderful, but the atmosphere was excellent, and many people there would smile at the two of them.

After dinner, they enjoyed walking around and looking at the various shops. Since it was her birthday, Miriam was able to pick out a few things that she liked, which were mostly more dresses and dress shoes. She was quickly becoming more and more like her mom, which thrilled Emily. After a great evening out, they headed back home, but not before stopping for a few snacks.

When they got home, Miriam wanted to cuddle up next to her mom and enjoy her snack. She had an incredible day and wanted nothing more than a few more minutes with her mom. While Emily wished this could continue all night, she knew Miriam had school in the morning and wanted to make sure she had a good night's rest. When she had finished her snack, Emily gave her a hug and kiss on the cheek and told her she hoped she had a great birthday, and to have a good night's rest. Emily stayed up for a little bit more, before heading to bed herself. It was back to the office tomorrow.

Monday morning and Emily was up at 5:30. She got up and got her coffee before heading back to the bedroom for a few. After almost a week and a half off, it was back to the office for her and school for Miriam. The past few days with Miriam had been wonderful and she enjoyed every minute that the two of them got to spend together. She would almost seem alone today at the office. She was not looking forward to being away from Miriam and she was sure that Miriam was not looking forward to being away from her mom.

After she finished her coffee, she headed off to get ready for the day, before heading to the kitchen to prepare breakfast. It had been a while since she had made breakfast, which was a nice break, so she decided it was time for biscuits and gravy. It was always a favorite of Miriam's. Sure enough, just as she was finishing, Miriam was walking into the kitchen saying something was smelling pretty good.

"Well, good morning to you as well! You're looking very nice today, Miriam."

"Thanks, Mom. I don't want to be at school today, but I thought if I looked good, I might at least feel good about going back."

"I like your attitude. I made one of your favorites. I was hoping it would help a little bit this morning."

"Oh, Mom."

"You do realize that one of these days, your face will get stuck like that."

"You mean like this?" Miriam crosses her eyes and sticks out her tongue.

"Yup. Just like that. I'll still love you even then though."

"Oh, Mom. I'll still love you even if you're making fun of me."

"I'm glad to hear it. Now finish eating and getting ready for school."

Miriam finished her breakfast and headed off to finish getting ready for school.

A few minutes later, they were headed out the door. After Miriam was dropped off at school, Miriam headed to the office. It seems like it had been forever since she had been here. She went through her emails and there wasn't anything important. Many people had taken off the majority, if not the full week, so she was not expecting much.

She decided to take a look through the listings, as it had been a while since she had looked. She found a few that were of interest to her and decided to call and get more information and possibly schedule a showing. There was one in particular that looked appealing, so she called that realtor first. Her instincts were correct on this one. It had fallen into disrepair through years of not being properly maintained. She saw it was between Miriam's school and their house, so she scheduled a time to look at it this afternoon after Miriam got off school. She would enjoy looking at this one.

After she was done looking through the listings, she decided to update Rachel on their trip and let her know what she was thinking about for Christmas. Rachel was thrilled to hear how well things had gone in Colorado. She had received some of the pics of Miriam and Emily and passed them on to her supervisors. Everyone was so amazed at how well things were going with Miriam. They knew that Emily was the right person for Miriam. Rachel thought the Christmas plans were exciting as well, and they would give Miriam a chance to learn a lot about the history of the country as well as do some sightseeing. She was OK with the trip and would give final authorization once the dates and locations were finalized.

Emily spent the rest of the day planning out their Christmas trip. Unlike the Colorado trip, this would cover a lot more cities, but would also be almost two weeks long. She had to balance the desire to see many of the sights with the desire of her family to not only see her but to also meet Miriam. She let them know that she would be in the area for almost two weeks, and they would have their time with her in the middle, which would happen to be Christmas. Before she knew it, it was finally time to go get Miriam and check out the listing.

Miriam was excited to see her mom and was practically running to the car.

"Hey, Mom!" Miriam reached over and gave her mom a big hug.

"Well, I missed you too! I have a few surprises for you. The first one is we are checking out a house on the way home."

"I hope it's haunted."

"After seeing the pictures, I wouldn't be surprised if it was."

"Awesome."

After a few minutes, they arrived at the house, and Emily could instantly see that this house needed work. The realtor greeted them at the porch and welcomed them in. The house had potential, but it looked like it had been neglected for a while. It turns out that it had been owned by an investor, who was new to the business. He rented it out but never kept up with the upkeep. As the house fell into disrepair, it became harder and harder to attract quality tenants. He finally decided to get out of it and do something else. Emily was very interested and called her inspector friend to see when he could look it over and make sure there was nothing major hiding. He said he was already in the area and could head over. Emily let the realtor know that her inspector was heading over and if everything were OK, she would make a written cash offer. The realtor seemed excited by the news.

Emily and Miriam stopped to pick up dinner on their way home. When they were done with dinner, Miriam worked on the little schoolwork that she had to work on. When she was done, she headed to the couch to sit next to her mom.

"Earlier you said you had a few surprises, and seeing the house was one of them. Are there others?"

"Oh yeah, I did say that. Well, I was waiting till we could sit down and talk, like right now. Well, the second surprise is we will be traveling for Christmas!"

"Awesome!"

"I thought you would like that."

"So, where are we going?"

"Glad you asked. On the first day of the break, we will fly to Washington DC. We will spend a few days there. On Tuesday, we will head to NJ and you will get a chance to meet my parents and family. We will spend Christmas with them. On the following Tuesday, we will head to New York City for a few days, and fly back to Tulsa on Saturday."

"It sounds so wonderful! I've always wanted to see those cities!"

"We will have a chance to see a few others as well, while we are there."

"It sounds wonderful! I just hope your family will like me."

"Oh, Miriam. You have nothing to worry about. I've talked to my parents quite a bit about you, and they can't wait to meet you. I know my two sisters will love to meet you as well."

"It would be nice to have some family again, besides the best mom around."

"Nice try. Well, let's watch some TV till it is time for bed."

"Sounds great, Mom."

They watch a few shows before heading to bed for the night. It had been a busy day for them both, and they were looking forward to getting some rest. They were two and a half weeks from another travel opportunity and more quality time together. The next few weeks would likely drag on.

The next morning, Emily was up at her usual time at 5:30. She got up and got her coffee, before returning to the room to contemplate the day. She was expecting a report on the house this morning, which would let her know whether or not to purchase the house. It had potential, so she was hopeful. She was also glad that she and Miriam would be spending their Christmas together. This time it would be a tour of the northeast portion of the country, along with visiting her family.

After finishing her coffee, she headed off to get ready for the day and make breakfast. Today she felt like a breakfast sandwich was what she wanted to make. As she was finishing them, Miriam was heading out to the kitchen.

"Good morning, Miriam. You always look so nice for school."

"Thanks, Mom. Some of the kids think I'm different since I don't wear a t-shirt and ripped jeans every day like they do."

"Well, don't worry about them. You look beautiful! I never understood why teens think everyone needs to conform and dress like they do. I think it says a lot about your maturity when you dress how you want to."

"I'm glad you're my Mom. You know what to say to make me feel better!"

"Well, I'm glad that I could help. Now finish breakfast and make sure you're ready for school!"

Miriam finished breakfast and went off to finish getting ready for school. While she was waiting, Emily went ahead and made another cup of coffee for her travel mug. It was soon ready to head out and take Miriam to school and head for the office.

Shortly after she got to the office, her phone rang, and it was her contractor that had looked at the property when she left. The good news is that the damages were mostly cosmetic. The foundation and structure were sound, so it would be another project to clean up the property and sell it. She just needed to decide how deep she wanted the work to go. She could fix it up and have it look how it did a few years ago, or she could renovate a room or two, which would add to the time to fox the property but could increase the profit potential.

First, she needed to purchase the property, so she sent the realtor a written cash offer for the property, and her offer was $10k below the asking price. While she was waiting to hear back, she decided to see if any of the other listings from yesterday were worth scheduling an in-person look at. After a few minutes, her phone rang and this time it was the realtor for the property she had just sent the offer to. The realtor saw that it was a cash offer and wanted to know how quickly she could close. When the realtor heard that she only needed 24 hours, she said they would accept the offer and decided to meet the next day at noon.

When she got off the phone, she gave Alexis a call to let her know about the closing. Emily wanted her to take a look at the house and see what she thought as far as how much renovation should be put into the house. Emily already had an idea, but it doesn't hurt to get a second opinion, especially from the person whose job it would be to sell the finished product.

With not much to do at the office, Emily decided to head to the future hotel and see how it has progressed since she last saw it, which has been a few weeks. The first floor was looking great and was finished. The lobby was very welcoming, and the meeting rooms were ready to be furnished for whatever even they were holding. Work was progressing on what would be the guest rooms, and quite a few were already done. She took quite a few pics and sent them to Andy, who was very pleased with the results so far. He was looking forward to being able to move in and start serving their guests.

After a few hours of checking out the hotel, it was time to pick up Miriam from school. Emily let her know that they were going to purchase the house that they had looked at yesterday. She also let her know how the hotel was looking. Miriam said it sounded like her mom had a more exciting day than she did at school.

When they got home, Emily started on dinner while Miriam worked on her schoolwork. Miriam did a great job of keeping up with during the school day so that she didn't usually have much to work on when she got home. She liked being able to spend as much time as possible with her mom.

After enjoying a great chicken and steamed veggies dinner, they decided to head to the living room and watch a few shows. After a week of travel, it was nice to spend some time just relaxing on the couch, enjoying each other's company. After a few shows, it was time for Miriam to head to bed. Once she was off to bed, Emily poured a glass of wine and sat on the couch for a few.

Emily was feeling pretty good about how things have been progressing, both with Miriam and professionally. She couldn't wait till Miriam was finally her legal daughter, though she has long been her daughter in her heart. She knew it would be a few more months till she could finally adopt Miriam. She was also pleased with how the hotel was turning out. She had dreamed of doing a project like it, and it was turning out wonderfully. With her glass empty, she decided it was time to head to bed herself.

The next morning, Emily was up at her usual time. She headed off to get her coffee and contemplate the day. She was closing on another property today, though she was unsure how involved she should be in it. She knew it needed lots of paint and some maintenance, but should she just clean up the bathroom and kitchen or completely renovate them? Completely renovating a room can add weeks at a minimum to the project. It will also increase the cost, but it will bring a higher price. The question is, does the increase in price she gets compensate for the increased cost? She decided to think it over later after Alexis had a chance to look it over and give her opinion.

After she was done getting ready, she headed to the kitchen to make breakfast. She was in the mood for biscuits and gravy, which was always a favorite of Miriam. On biscuits and gravy morning, Miriam seemed to get to the kitchen a little faster. Today was no different.

"Something smells good, Mom. Smells like biscuits and gravy!"

"How did I know you would smell it from your room and come running?"

"You know how much I love biscuits and gravy!"

"That's why I make it often."

"You're the best. So, anything fun planned today without me?"

"Buying that house this afternoon that we looked at on Monday."

"I would much rather be buying houses than going to school."

"I'm sure you would. Just remember that I went to school for a long time before I could run my own business and be successful."

"I know, Mom. It's just frustrating at times."

I know, Miriam. You're doing great though. Now go finish getting ready for school."

Miriam headed off to finish getting ready for school. Emily couldn't help but love Miriam. She had a wonderful attitude about her. She understood why she needed to do things like go to school, though she wasn't always fond of going. Her facial expressions when she is complaining about the school are priceless and adorable. Emily tried hard not to laugh, though it wasn't always easy with Miriam's facial expressions.

It was soon time to drop Miriam off at school and head to the office. She had some time before her closing at lunchtime. She was preparing some things for the closing when Andy called.

Andy had shown some of the pictures of the hotel to some of his business partners and they were greatly impressed. They were so impressed that they wanted to move their offices to the new building soon, which means they would like to acquire the building before it is finished but they would pay the price for the finished product, and Emily would continue to renovate it. They would like to close before Christmas so they could be moved in by the start of the new year. Emily loved the idea and let them know to contact Kelli, so she could make preparations.

Once she was off the phone with Andy, she called Brooke to let her know the news. Brooke was thrilled with the news and said she would talk with her supervisor to see how they would handle the finances since the renovations would be continuing even after the building was officially sold.

A few minutes later, Kelli called to congratulate her. They had worked out an agreement and the building would officially transfer ownership in two weeks. The best news is that once all the costs were accounted for, Emily would take home over a million dollars! Emily couldn't believe it. She was shocked to hear the news. She knew she would do well, she had no idea it would be this well. She got off the phone and cried for a moment. Years of hard work had paid off and she was now having incredible success. There was a lot of struggle in her early days, but now that hard work had come to fruition.

She decided to take an early lunch to celebrate, though the real celebration would wait till Miriam could join her. When she was done with lunch, she headed off to her closing for the house. It was pretty straightforward and no surprises. When it was done, she walked through it with Alexis to get her opinion. Alexis could see that it needed a lot of paint and cleaning up. She didn't think the kitchen needed a full renovation, just replace the "cheap landlord" appliances. The bathroom would also benefit from some new fixtures, which wouldn't add much to the costs, but would make the place look much better and less like a cheap rental house. Emily thanked Alexis for her help and would let her know when she could begin listing the property.

It was close to time to get Miriam from school, so Emily decided to drive around for a bit and make her way to the school. She didn't see anything overly interesting and was at the school a few minutes before Miriam was dismissed. It wasn't long till she saw Miriam heading to the car.

"Hey Mom, how was your day?"

"It was wonderful! The guy decided to buy the hotel earlier than planned, so in two weeks it will be his, though we will continue to work on it."

"That's awesome!"

"I know. I think we need to celebrate!"

"Ladies' night out!"

"That's what I was thinking."

They headed home to get changed and head out to celebrate. Miriam loved getting dressed up, especially when she gets to go out with her mom. Emily was already dressed up for work, so she swapped her heels for heeled ankle boots. When Miriam saw how her mom was dressed, she wanted to have a similar look, which was fine for Emily. She loved that Miriam wanted to dress like her.

There was no discussion on where they were heading. They were heading to the same place they always go to on ladies' night. It was where they first met, and where they had many evenings out. Since it was a little early for dinner, they decided to do some shopping first. They enjoyed looking at things and trying clothes on, even if they didn't buy something every time they went shopping. Today, Miriam got a warmer pair of boots for the coming colder months. She loved that they were dressy enough that she could still wear her dresses with them. Emily told her she would look adorable in them.

After a bit of shopping, it was time for dinner, so they headed to their favorite steakhouse. Once they had placed their orders, Emily decided that she needed to talk to Miriam about something.

"Miriam, I wanted to talk to you about something."

"Sure, Mom. What is it?"

"Well, when the hotel sells, there will be a lot of money coming in. A lot of it will stay in the business to be used for other projects, but a substantial amount will be coming in the coming months. There will be enough coming in that I can take off most of the summer and the two of us can travel!"

"OH, Mom! That is so exciting! Where would we go?"

"I don't know yet. It depends on a few things, but we can worry about them later."

"This sounds so wonderful! I can't wait to travel with my mom and see so many different places."

"Well, I knew you would be excited, which is one of the reasons that I wanted to head out tonight. I wanted to celebrate a wonderful day with my daughter and tell her the good news."

"I'm glad that you feel that way about me, as I feel the same way about you. I love our nights out and I love dressing up, especially when I can dress up to look like you!"

"You're the best Miriam! You know I love you so much!"

"Love you too, Mom."

The two of them enjoyed their dinner followed by a little bit more shopping and some walking around. It was a nice night, and they loved walking side by side holding hands. When they were together, nothing else seemed to matter. Soon, it was time to head home. There were still two more days in the school/ workweek. Miriam thanked her mom for another wonderful evening and headed to bed.

      Emily stayed up a little longer and enjoyed a glass of wine. It had been quite a day. Her dream project was becoming so successful, that it would allow her to take most of the summer off to travel with Miriam. She was hoping to travel overseas with Miriam, but the timing may not work. She can't get her a passport until the adoption is final, which may not leave enough time. At least they could travel all over the US, which neither of them had done before. When her glass was empty, she decided it was time to head to bed herself.

The next two days were relatively uneventful. With Christmas vacation a little over two weeks away, Emily wasn't needing to do a lot of purchasing right now, especially with the sale of the hotel coming. She did get word from Alexis that Mrs. Weber had moved out over Thanksgiving, and that her family had finished getting the last of her stuff out of the house, so they were free to start working on it. That house along with the one she purchased earlier in the week gave her two new projects. They were still working on the one house that had needed a new kitchen. She was getting stretched thin for workers. The house she just purchased could be done quickly, so she will prioritize it.

Their first week back from Colorado had been a busy one, at least for Emily. She was looking forward to relaxing some this weekend with Miriam, though they hadn't planned anything yet. That didn't matter. All that mattered was that they could spend two whole days together, doing whatever they pleased, which was what they loved to do.

Saturday morning Emily awoke at six. She headed off to the kitchen to get her coffee and head to the couch to wait for Miriam to wake up. It had been quite a week for her, and she was glad to have a day off. She had several projects going on right now and some of them would take some time. She didn't need to do much these next two weeks, except keep an eye on her projects. She wasn't sure what to do with her time.

It was close to seven before Miriam came out and laid on her favorite spot on the couch.

"Well good morning to you Miriam! What would you like for breakfast today?"

"Can we eat out today?"

"You mean I don't have to cook? Sounds good to me. Let's go get dressed and head out."

Miriam decided she was in the mood for one of her cowgirl outfits, so she picked the one with the denim skirt and the shorter boots, along with the hat. When she came out, she was surprised to see that her mom was also wearing a long denim skirt along with ankle boots. They both laughed and Emily said she would need to grab her hat, and they were off to breakfast.

They were in the mood for pancakes today, so they headed to a place that was known for their pancakes. They each ordered a short stack along with a few sides. Emily was glad that she didn't have to cook, and she knew that Miriam loved a variety of sides, which was harder to do when it was just the two of them. Over breakfast, they decided to spend the day traveling around to some of the best shopping places in and around Tulsa. They weren't looking for anything in particular, perhaps some clothing for their trip.

One of their first stops was a store that specializes in western clothing and items for a ranch in the largest Tulsa suburb. A friend had recommended that they check it out since they had so much fun in Colorado playing cowgirls. There was quite a bit of clothing that they liked along with items to decorate the house. They were also surprised at the selection of items for a ranch. It felt like everything they could use, including lots of stuff for horses. Miriam was so excited. After their riding adventure in Colorado, she wanted a horse of her own. Emily didn't say no, but she needed to look into some things first.

After their first stop, they went to a neighboring shopping center to see what they had that looked interesting. They checked out a few of the stores, before getting lunch at a burger place. After lunch, they headed to a shopping center in the Tulsa Hills area to see what was there. They found a bookstore along with a department store that had some really cute dresses that were perfect for Christmas, so they purchased them. This was turning into a great day of shopping and spending time together.

It was about mid-afternoon when they had finished the second shopping center, so they decided to check out one more in the northern Tulsa suburb. They were starting to see many of the same stores, so it didn't take long till they had seen what they wanted to see. Before heading home, they saw a restaurant that was a Mexican grill. They thought they were dressed appropriately, so they enjoyed a great dinner together, before heading home.

Once they got home, they changed into something more comfortable for relaxing. They had enough time to watch a movie before it was time for Miriam to head to bed. Emily stayed up for a bit with a glass of wine to think about some things. She really liked the store that sold the ranch items. The thought of her owning a ranch was intriguing to her. The only issue was she considered herself to be a city girl, who enjoyed wearing dresses and heels. That is not exactly ranch attire. It was something to consider another day, though if Miriam knew she was even considering it, she would be beyond thrilled. Best not to say anything until it can become a reality.

Sunday morning and Emily slept in till 6:30. That was unusual for her, but it was Sunday and it felt great to get a little bit more sleep. She headed off to the kitchen to get her coffee and wait for Miriam on the couch. She had a weird dream about horses, and she didn't know what to make of it. Was she simply thinking back to her horse-riding experience back in Colorado, or was this her subconscious telling she needed to do something? She needed way more coffee than she had in her cup to figure this one out.

It wasn't long after she started contemplating her dream that Miriam came into the living room, to cuddle with her mom on the couch. It was always a highlight for her. She loved that Miriam was able to show affection to her, and she loved to return the affection as well.

"Mom, can we go out to eat for breakfast then do our grocery shopping?"

"That sounds like a good idea. What should we do after that?"

"Can we stay home the rest of the day and watch movies?"

"That sounds like a wonderful plan to me. Let's go eat."

They headed off to a diner for a country breakfast, filled with a variety of meat, biscuits and gravy, grits, and of course pancakes. Afterward, they headed to the store to buy groceries, including snacks for the movies and a pizza for dinner. Today would be a ladies' night in, which was almost as good as a ladies' night out, except they didn't have to get dressed up. When they got back, they enjoyed a great day filled with movies, laughter, some crying, and lots of great time together. After a busy day of shopping yesterday, today was exactly what they needed. Tomorrow would be the start of a new week work and school week, and the closer it got to Christmas, the longer the week would seem to be.

Monday morning and Emily was back to her usual time of 5:30. She headed to get her coffee and decide what she was going to do today. She had a lot of projects going on, so she wasn't in a hurry to add more to her list. She had one that could possibly be ready to sell before she leaves for Christmas vacation. Other than the closing for the hotel, which was next week, she didn't have much planned for the next two weeks.

When she was done with her coffee, she headed off to get ready for the day, then to make breakfast for the two of them. After eating out for the last two breakfasts, she thought they could use a breakfast sandwich today. Miriam would just be happy to have something to eat. It didn't take her long to come out, ready to eat breakfast.

"Good morning, Mom!"

"Well, good morning, Miriam! You look so nice today."

"Thanks, but you say that every day."

"Not my fault if you look nice every day."

"Oh, Mom!"

"You know I still love you, even when you make that face. It's so cute."

Miriam just sticks her tongue out, then they both laugh. Miriam heads off to get ready for school, but not before giving her mom a hug. Emily loved that Miriam was so sweet and had a sense of humor. She was just hoping that it would not change much as she entered high school next year. It was soon time to drop Miriam off at school and head to the office, though today she headed home to work from her home office. It felt weird being dressed up and at the house, but she wanted to be ready in case she needed to meet with someone.

It wasn't long into the morning when the phone rang, and it was Brooke. She had talked with her supervisors about the closing. They would take the check, hold onto the amount of the loan plus a little bit for reserves. The rest would be released to Emily. This would allow payments to continue from the same account, and the bank would also have the money to pay back the loan. Once the project was finished, anything left in reserves or if it comes in under budget, that money would be released to Emily at that time. Emily was thrilled to hear that the details had been worked out, though when she heard the amount of the check that would be written to her company as profits, she almost passed out.

After that conversation, she was trying to get her mind back on work, when Rachel called. She wanted to see if Emily was available Wednesday morning for a phone call with her and her supervisors. They just wanted to talk about Miriam's progress, and this would be a routine meeting, so she had nothing to worry about. Emily let her know that Wednesday morning would be fine, and she looked forward to talking with them at that time.

The workday had barely started, and she already had two phone calls with really great news and hopefully good news. While Rachel had said it was routine, the fact that her supervisors wanted to be in on the call made her feel like something was going on. Their meeting was in forty-eight hours, so she didn't want to spend all that time worrying, especially when there may not be anything to worry about. She decided to go for a drive to clear her mind. Since she had a few hours until it was time to pick up Miriam, she decided to head out of town.

After about 30 minutes of driving, she came across a nice-looking property that had a for-sale sign on it. When she slowed down to take a look at it, she saw it was a ranch. She saw there were some cars parked at the main house, so she decided to stop and see if someone was available to talk to her. By the time she had parked her car, a couple was walking out to see who she was.

"Is there something we can help you with?" the man asked her.

"My name is Emily, and I was driving by and I saw this property was for sale, and I wanted to see if I could talk to you about it."

"Sure. Well, this ranch has been ours for many years. It has been a great place, but we are nearing retirement in a few years and all of our money is tied up in the ranch. We'd love to stay here for a few more years, but we could use some cash today."

"Well, I may be able to help. I happen to be a real estate investor."

"Well, that would certainly explain your dress. Most people out here don't usually dress like you unless someone has died."

"I understand. What if I were to purchase a portion of the ranch? It would give you some cash soon. You would still be able to work and live here. In a few years when you are ready to retire, we can decide what to do at that point."

"That sounds like a nice plan. I will talk it over with my wife and see what we want to do. Let us get your contact information."

"Here is my business card. It has my cell phone number on it."

"Well, thank you for stopping by Emily. It was nice meeting you and we appreciate the offer. It sounds more appealing than selling the ranch and moving elsewhere."

"Well, thank you for talking with me. I look forward to talking to you soon."

Emily headed back to Tulsa to get some lunch then headed back to the house to finish a few things before it was time to pick up Miriam. She was able to finish her list of things just in time before she needed to go pick up Miriam.

When she picked up Miriam, she asked what her mom had been working on today. Emily let her know that she was checking out a new property, and would show Miriam soon if they were able to come to an agreement. Miriam always liked checking out properties, and Emily let her know that she would have liked this one. They headed home and picked up dinner. After dinner, Miriam worked on a few assignments, before joining her mom on the couch to watch a few shows before it was time for bed.

After Miriam headed off to bed, Emily got a glass of wine to think about the developments of the day. She was excited that she got to check out that ranch. It seemed like the perfect opportunity for her and Miriam to learn the business before fully diving into it. It would also allow them to purchase horses for them to ride and they would have a place to keep them. She needed to do some more research on the property and running a ranch. Tomorrow would be an excellent opportunity to do that research. With her glass empty, it was time to head to bed.

The next morning Emily was up at her usual time. She headed off to get her coffee and come back to the room. She had a lot on her mind. She had a potential new business venture to think about. Yesterday they briefly discussed some terms but didn't get into details. She was unsure how much money they were thinking about. She had quite a bit coming from the sale of the hotel, but she was unsure what the ranch was worth. Hopefully, she will get some clarity from the owners in the coming days if they are interested in her ideas. With her coffee finished, she headed off to get ready for the day and make breakfast.

For breakfast, she decided to try a version of a country breakfast, with hash browns, biscuits, sausage, and pancakes. She knew Miriam would approve, and sure enough, Miriam was in the kitchen just as breakfast was done.

"Something smells good today!"

"Thanks, Miriam. Thought I would cook a few things today."

"It all looks so good."

"Well, I hope you will enjoy it."

"It is so good, Mom!"

"Well, I'm glad you enjoy it."

They finished their breakfast, and Miriam headed off to get ready for school. Emily decided she would head to the office today to do some research. She only liked to work from home when it was beneficial to getting things done around the house. When she didn't have things to do at the house, she could become distracted and less likely to work. Soon, it was time to drop Miriam off at school and head to the office.

When Emily got to the office, she decided to give Kelli a call and see if she knew anything about ranches.

"Hey, Emily. What's going on?"

"Hey, Kelli. What do you know about ranches?"

"Not a ton. I usually stick with Tulsa, which doesn't have a lot of them. What's going on?"

"Well, I was driving around yesterday and saw one for sale just across the Mayes County line. I talked with the owners and they love the property and don't want to leave, but they need some cash as they are getting close to retirement. I had mentioned investing in their ranch and getting some ownership, which would give them the cash they need and let them continue to stay and run it."

"Wow, Emily. I know you and Miriam had fun riding horses. I didn't know you had THAT much fun."

"I know. Am I crazy for thinking about this?"

"You've always been crazy, which is why I enjoy working with you, but this makes sense. You could take the majority of the profits from the sale of the hotel and buy into the ranch. It would save a lot of taxes and give you a stream of income."

"I hadn't thought about that."

"Have you looked at the property yet?"

"Not yet. We just talked for a few minutes by their house. It did look nice though."

"Well, if they do invite you, I'd like to go."

"Sounds great Kelli. You've been such a help."

"Glad I could help Emily."

Emily spent the rest of the day reading about ranches and everything she could find out about them. If she was thinking about doing this, she wanted to have a good understanding before she met with the owners again. There was so much info and she was learning quite a bit, which was helping her realize that this could be a possibility.

It was soon time to get Miriam and head home. When they got home, Miriam finished up her schoolwork, while Emily was cooking dinner. Tonight, she was preparing some salmon fillets along with some veggies. They were a great combination and they both loved it. After dinner, Emily sat on the couch and Miriam leaned up against, while her mom put her arm around her for a few minutes. After a busy day of research, it felt great to be home and have Miriam by her side.

They decided to watch a movie tonight and just enjoy being with each other. Emily had thought that she didn't have to have someone in her life, but she realized that she needed Miriam. Miriam was just as good as an influence that Emily was on her. They were both better off when they were together. Emily was OK knowing that she needed someone in her life, and she was more than OK knowing someone needed her in their life.

Wednesday morning and Emily was up at 5. She headed off to get her coffee and think about the day to come. She had her phone meeting with Rachel and her supervisors later in the morning. Even though Rachel said it was a routine meeting, she still felt nervous. She didn't want anything to happen to her relationship with Miriam. It was the best thing that has ever happened to her. She still had a few hours till the meeting, so she needed to focus on something else, or she could spend that time worrying when everything is fine. She headed off to take a longer shower to get her mind off of things, before getting ready for the day and making breakfast.

After she was done getting ready, Emily headed to the kitchen to prepare breakfast. There was only one thing on her mind, and it was biscuits and gravy. As they were finishing, Miriam walked into the kitchen.

"It smells like biscuits and gravy!"

"Can't hide anything from you, can I?"

"Not if it's biscuits and gravy."

"I'll remember that for next time."

During breakfast, Emily kept looking over at Miriam.

"Why do you keep looking at me, Mom. Do I look bad?"

"You look beautiful as ever, Miriam. I was just thinking how much better my life has been since I have you in it!"

"My life is so much better with you in it too! If you keep looking at me though, I'll make that face."

"Oh, you know how much I love that."

Miriam crossed her eyes and stuck her tongue out, with some food on it.

"Oh, that is so adorable! I just love it."

"Oh, Mom!"

Miriam finished her breakfast and before heading off to get ready, she gave her mom a hug and kiss on the cheek and told her that she loved her very much. Emily told her that she loved her very much as well, along with her goofy faces, and gave her a kiss on the cheek.

It was soon ready to drop off Miriam and head to the office to await her phone meeting. This meeting couldn't come soon enough. She just wanted to know what was going on, so she could relax and enjoy the day.

When it was time, she called Rachel, who let her know that they were ready.

"Hello, Emily. This is Lauren, and I am Rachel's supervisor. How are you doing today?"

"I'm a little nervous at the moment."

"Well, don't be. This call will be nothing but good news for you and Miriam. I have been so pleased with the progress that we have seen since she has moved into your house. We expected some improvement, but what we have seen has been incredible. We were all so worried about her. Every aspect of her life has vastly improved since she has moved in with you, and we simply don't know what to say."

"Well, thank you so much. I have loved every minute that we have spent together and am looking forward to many more great memories with her. She is such a sweet young lady, and I am in love with her. I would do anything for her. We have a relationship that I never thought was possible."

"That is so wonderful to hear and what we love to hear from the parents that want to adopt. We do have a surprise for you though. The children routinely appear before a judge to get a status update on where they are in the process of finding a family and getting adopted. I was at one the last week for another child and the judge asked how Miriam was doing, as he heard that she had been placed, but had not seen her since she had been placed. Well, I will let him tell you himself. Judge Wilber, the floor is yours."

"Thank you, Lauren. It is a pleasure to meet you, Ms. Gardner."

"Thank you, you Honor."

"Well, I could not believe the updates that I was hearing. For years, it was nothing but sad story after sad story with Miriam. We were almost to the point of losing hope with her, but then she met you. I asked Lauren about who she had been placed with and when she mentioned your name, I was not surprised. You see I have a daughter, Kristen, who was struggling at the University of Tulsa a few years ago until she met this wonderful mentor, who put things in perspective for her and she changed her life around. She is now a very successful young lady."

"I remember Kristen, she was such a sweet young lady. I am so glad that I was able to help her out. I knew she had been struggling but did not know that she had turned things around that much."

"Well, she did and was thanks to you and now we add Miriam to that list. To thank you, we have talked it over and instead of waiting the full six months to finalize the adoption, we have decided that it is in the best interest of everyone if the adoption is finalized soon. On the first Monday in January, you two will appear before me, and the adoption will be finalized. Merry Christmas, Ms. Gardner, you've earned it."

"Oh, my! I don't know what to say but thank you so much!"

"You are very welcome. I will leave you now, and you can discuss the details about the time and other details."

"Well, Emily, we told you not to worry."

"I just can't believe it."

"You better believe it, because, in less than a month, Miriam will legally be yours!"

"I know we can't wait."

"I will send you the details for the hearing. Hope you have a good one Emily."

"Thanks, Rachel and Lauren. Same to you."

That was a completely unexpected phone call for Emily. She was hoping they would have some good things to say, but the rest was not even something she had considered, but she was thrilled to hear it. Miriam will be beyond excited to hear the news. She will want to celebrate, which would be fine with Emily, as she will want to celebrate as well.

Emily decided to try and focus on her research for a bit. After a while, her phone rang and she didn't recognize the number, but it was local, so she answered it.

"Hello, this is Emily."

"Hello, Emily. This is Al. You stopped to look at our ranch the other day."

"Yes. How can I help you?"

"Well, we liked the idea of your offer. We realized that we hadn't discussed any financial terms. How much were you looking to put in?"

"I have a project that is selling next week, so I'd like to roll over the majority of the profits, so it would be about a million dollars."

"Well, that would buy up half of the ranch. If you are serious, we'd like to have you come by and we can show you around and give you a better idea of what the ranch has before you commit to it. When would be a good time?"

"I'd love to come by for a visit. I do have a 14-year-old daughter, who would love to come also and see the place, so would Saturday work?"

"That would be great. We will be here all morning, so once you are up and have had breakfast feel free to head over."

"That sounds great, Al. I will see you then."

Once she was off the phone, she let Kelli know that they were going to look at the ranch on Saturday. Kelli said she would be ready, just to text when she was heading out and they would ride up together.

Emily decided to spend the rest of the day researching some more about ranches and give her some more ideas for Saturday.

When she picked up Miriam, she said she had some good news to share, but wanted to wait till they got home to share it. Miriam begged the entire way home to hear the news. When they finally got home, they went into the living room.

"Well, I had a phone meeting with Rachel and her supervisor this morning. They were very pleased to hear how well you have been doing. Well, the judge who was overseeing your case had heard how well you were doing as well. Long story short is they decided I don't have to wait the full six months till I can adopt you. So, when we come back from Christmas, I get to adopt you!"

"Awesome! I am so excited! We need to celebrate! Ladies' night out!"

"How did I know that would be your reaction?"

"You just know me too well."

"You better believe it!"

They embrace and hold each other for a few minutes.

"Well, if we are going to celebrate, we better get changed so we can head out!"

Miriam decided it was a special occasion, so she wore her new teal Christmas dress, along with black tights and ankle boots. Her mom was already similarly dressed, so she swapped her heels for her heeled ankle boots. This time Miriam said her mom wanted to look like her. They both just laughed and hugged before heading out to their favorite place to celebrate.

They were both too excited to eat right away, so they enjoyed walking around and looking at the various stores together. After walking around and looking at a few stores, they decided to head to the restaurant to eat. This was their place and they loved being there. They had wonderful food and the atmosphere was perfect for two ladies celebrating. While at dinner Emily told Miriam that they would be looking at a place on Saturday. She was intrigued that it was not after school, and Miriam wanted to know more, but her mom insisted that it was a surprise.

After dinner, they walked around some more. Though they didn't buy anything this time out, they had a wonderful time being with each other, celebrating the fact that they would soon legally be mother and daughter, though, to them, that had happened months ago. In their mind, a piece of paper wouldn't change how they felt about each other, though it declared to the world that they were in fact, mother and daughter.

The next two days were relatively uneventful. Miriam was busy was school, while Emily was busy reading everything, she could find about ranches for their Saturday meeting. She was anxious to see the place and learn more about it. It looked like a great opportunity for her and would give her and Miriam something to do on weekends. They would also be able to purchase horses and ride them regularly. Miriam would love that idea and would likely insist that they ride the horses every day. It would teach her responsibilities, which was a good thing for a teen to learn.

    She did get word from her workers that the house that she recently purchased was nearing completion, so she let Alexis know to take pictures and get the listing ready. On Monday, they would start on Mrs. Weber's old house. It would take some time. That other house that needed a new kitchen was also nearing completion, so Emily had Alexis take pictures and get the listing ready. She was hoping at least one of them would sell before they left for Christmas vacation, but it would likely be the beginning of January before either would close. That was OK, as she was not hurting for money.

Saturday morning found Emily waking up at six. She got up and got her coffee, before heading to the couch to wait for Miriam to wake up. She was feeling a little nervous. She had looked at countless properties before, but this was different. This would not be a flip. This is something that Miriam could potentially run and manage as an adult. She had read a lot this past week and had some ideas, but this would still be a new opportunity for both of them. It was the new opportunity that was making her feel a little nervous.

It was close to seven when Miriam woke up and came out and sat on the couch in her favorite spot.

"You know I never get tired of looking down and seeing that sweet face staring back at me."

"Well, how about this face?" She crossed her eyes and stuck her tongue out.

"Same thing with that sweet face." She leaned down and kissed Miriam.

"Oh, Mom."

"Well, we have a property to look at after breakfast. Since I know you'll wear a skirt, wear a longer denim one with one of the cowgirl boots. I'll wear something similar, and yes you can wear your hat since I will too."

"Two Saturdays in a row dressed as cowgirls. This will be fun."

They headed off to get dressed and then headed out to a diner for a big country breakfast. Miriam loved the variety of food that was included and would likely eat breakfast like that every day if her mom would let her or, she wanted to cook that much food. For the time being, it would remain a special treat when they went out. When they were about finished, she texted Kelli to let her know that they were about to leave the diner.

When they were done, they headed out to the car. Emily let Miriam know that Kelli would be joining them, and she was going to follow them up to the property. After a moment, Kelli pulled in and they headed out to the property.

During the ride, Miriam was becoming intrigued. Usually, it was Alexis who would be joining them to look at a house. She liked Kelli, but she usually only handled larger properties, like the hotel. They were also heading out of town, which was odd for her mom to buy something that was not in town. Something was definitely up.

After about thirty minutes they pulled into the ranch. As soon as they pulled in, Miriam's started to get excited.

"Is this the property that we are looking at, Mom?"

"Yes, it is, Miriam."

"Awesome!"

They parked by the house and Al and Carol came out to greet them.

"Well, I can see you have dressed a little more appropriately for out here," Al commented before he laughed along with Emily. "Well, who is this pretty lady with you?"

"This is my daughter, Miriam. Miriam this is Al and Carol. I also brought a friend with me, who helps me with my properties. Al and Carol this is Kelli."

Everyone shakes hands and says their greetings. Al started by showing them the main house. It was your typical three-bedroom farmhouse. There was also a smaller one-bedroom guest house near it. It wasn't being used at the moment. By the two houses was a garage that houses some of their equipment like tractors. It had enough room that it could also be used to work on equipment.

They were now off to look at the heart of the ranch, the place where the animals were kept. The first barn was where the cattle were kept overnight. They were usually out by now, but they wanted them to see everything first. Miriam was loving the barns and wanted to see all the cattle. The next barn had what excited Emily and Miriam the most, the horses. For a large barn, there weren't many horses. There was a third barn, but it was empty for the time being. Al had told them, that for years, they did great with cattle and the few horses they had. Lately, it had become apparent that they needed to branch out more, which was one of the reasons that the property was for sale.

When they were done with the tour, they asked Emily and Miriam what they thought of the place. Before Emily had a chance to speak, Miriam gave her opinion.

"I absolutely love it! Mom, we so need to buy this place. It would be so fun to have horses. We could also have other animals like sheep and goats as well."

"I think Miriam speaks for both of us on this one. We are definitely interested. We just need to come to an agreement on how things will work."

"Sounds great. The four of us can head in and talk while Miriam can go back to the barns and play with the animals."

Before he finished speaking, Miriam was off to the barns and the other four headed into work on the details. After some, they came to an agreement. Emily would purchase half of the ranch. Since Al and Carol were living and working there, they would receive a salary. Any profit above that would be split equally. In a few years when they were ready to retire, they could revisit and see what Emily wanted to do then. They would meet next Friday afternoon to sign the paperwork and Emily would bring a check for the purchase.

Emily got Miriam from the horse barn and they headed back to town, but not before stopping at the ranch store to look around again. They had fun looking at everything. Emily wanted to check out some of the food prices for other animals that she was considering purchasing. After some time in the store, they headed out for lunch then headed home to relax for the rest of the day. Miriam was so excited that she spent the next hour talking about the horses and everything she wanted to do at the ranch. Emily just couldn't believe it.

After getting Miriam to calm down, they changed into something more comfortable. After a busy morning, they wanted to relax and just spend time together. Next weekend they would be traveling, so it felt good to relax while they could. Miriam picked out a few movies and they spent some quality time together, only taking a break long enough to cook a pizza for dinner.

After a busy day and a couple of movies, Miriam was ready to head to bed. Emily stayed up for a bit and poured a glass of wine to think things through. She could not believe that she would be purchasing half of a ranch in a matter of days. Two months ago, she never would have considered such a purchase, but two months ago she was living alone with no concept of adopting a child. The funny thing is she didn't miss the old life. While it may have been more predictable, she wouldn't trade it for the many adventures that Miriam had brought with her. She didn't know where all these changes were leading her, but she didn't mind as long as Miriam was along for the ride as well.

Sunday morning and Emily was up at six. She got her coffee and waited on the couch for Miriam to wake up. It had been quite a week for Emily. Next week was looking like quite a week as well. There were so many highlights this past week, but there was only truly one best, and that was when she found out that she could adopt Miriam earlier than they had thought possible. That feeling beats out any business deal that she has done or likely will do in her life.

It was about 6:30 when Miriam came out and set next to her mom on the couch.

"Did you dream about horses all night?"

"Of course not. There were also sheep, goats, and other animals in there as well."

"Why doesn't that surprise me."

"So, what's the plan for today?"

"Well, next week is going to be crazy, and we leave Saturday morning. Today would be a good day to get organized for the trip and start packing many of the clothes we won't need till then. It would also give us a good idea on what we need to pick up, which today would be a good day for that."

"Can we have breakfast first?"

"Like I could say no to that face. Go get dressed and we will go get breakfast and a few groceries, then we can come back and get started."

"Good, cause I'm starving."

"Oh, Miriam!" Emily made that face that Miriam usually makes and the two of them just laughed.

They headed out to a diner for breakfast and the grocery store to get a few things, since it would be a shorter week for them. When they got back, Emily started the laundry. Miriam was not used to packing for two weeks and didn't think she had enough. Emily let her know that her mother said not to pack too much as they could do laundry when they were visiting. Emily said it would likely be colder than it was here, so Miriam decided to pack lots of long skirts. Emily just laughed, as she was doing the same thing. She also reminded Miriam that they would likely be doing a lot of walking, so Miriam packed lots of flats and slip-on shoes. Emily couldn't complain because she had lots of wedge heels and stacked heeled shoes. They made a list of what they needed from the store.

 With most of the work done for the day, they headed off to the store to get the things that they needed. They loved looking around at other stuff when they shopped. It didn't matter that they weren't going to buy it, it was just fun to look at stuff and spend time together. Once they were done with their shopping, they headed out and drove around for a bit, and found some other places to check out.

 It was about dinner time when they got home, and Emily worked on diner while Miriam got changed. It was another great day for them, though a little different, but any time they could spend together was a good day. This next week would be busy, especially for Emily with selling a hotel and buying a ranch within days of each other. Saturday they would head to the Northeast for two full weeks of adventure. If their Colorado trip were an indicator, this trip would be full of lasting memories and lots of great times together. Neither one of them could wait to see what the trip would bring.

Monday morning and it was back to the usual 5:30 wake-up time. She headed off to get her coffee and come back and think through the day. She didn't have much planned for the day. There were two closings this week, so far, but they were later in the week. These two weeks off couldn't come at a better time. She felt like she needed to take some time to reevaluate things. She enjoyed buying and selling properties, she just seemed to have a lot more downtime since she knew what she was doing. She could think about this later as it was time to get ready for the day.

After she was ready, she headed to the kitchen to cook breakfast. Today seemed like a good day for a nice breakfast, so she prepared some pancakes, hash browns, biscuits, and bacon. She knew Miriam would appreciate it, which is what mattered to her. She had barely finished putting everything on her plate when she walked in.

"Mom, this all looks so good!"

"Well, thanks, Miriam. I thought you would enjoy it."

"Oh yeah, very much."

"Well, I am glad. Hopefully, this next week of school doesn't drag on for you."

"It will. It always does."

"Well, in five days we will be at the airport heading to DC to start our two-week Christmas vacation."

"I can't wait. It'll be so much fun."

"I feel the same way."

Miriam finished her breakfast and headed off to finish getting ready for school. Emily decided that she could use another cup of coffee for this Monday morning, so she prepared another and had it in her travel mug. It was soon time to drop Miriam off at school and decide what she was going to do with her day.

After she dropped Emily off at school, she decided to drive around some of the neighborhoods and see what might be available. On days like today, it was nice to be out of the office and not sitting at a desk all day. She also enjoyed listening to music as she drove around. She saw a few new ones including an FSBO that looked intriguing.

She opted to call about the FSBO right away to get more information. A lady answered and said it was recently listed. It had belonged to a relative that had recently passed. The house needed work, which the family didn't feel like doing or putting in the money to have it done. They just wanted it sold. Emily let the lady know that she was very interested in looking at it, and if she wanted to purchase, she would pay cash. They set up a time in the afternoon to come to look at it. Emily had the feeling that Miriam would love to see it.

With not much else to do, she decided to drive to her various properties and walk around to see how things were going. Two of the houses were indeed just about done and the workers should finish by the end of the day. She thanked the workers for their hard work and ordered lunch for their teams. She also let the one team know about the project that they could start tomorrow. She headed to the hotel to see what had changed since her last visit. She spent some time looking around, very pleased with what she saw. It was no wonder that the new owners paid what they did for the property. By the time she finished with the hotel, it was time to get Miriam and check out the new property.

Miriam was excited to check out another property, especially when she heard the story behind why it was for sale. She was hoping that it would be haunted. When they started looking around the house, they could see why the family was wanting to just sell it. It needed a lot of work, from painting and general upkeep to replacing things that had been neglected. Emily could see the potential, which was why she was in this business. When she was done looking at it, she asked the family member what they were asking, reminding them that she would be paying cash and could close in 24 hours. They gave a reasonable offer considering the circumstances. She said she would go ahead and purchase it at that price and would send written confirmation as well. They decided to meet the next afternoon.

Emily and Miriam headed home for the day. Emily started on dinner, while Miriam finished up her schoolwork. They both enjoyed the end of the day when they could be together and enjoy their time together again. Dinner was a time to catch up on the little events of the day, before heading to watch TV or a movie. Today, there were a few shows to watch before heading to bed. It felt great to enjoy a quiet evening before the hustle and bustle of their vacation began. After a few shows, it was time for bed for Miriam, with her mom following not far behind.

Tuesday was a relatively quiet day for Emily and Miriam. She spent most of the day preparing for her hotel closing the next day. She wanted to make sure there were no surprises, so she talked with Kelli and Brooke during the day to ensure everything was good to go for the next day. This was a big project and she wanted things to go as smoothly as possible.

Emily had her closing in the afternoon. She had Alexis meet her there and she took a look at the house. She said it was going to be another decent clean-up project with likely needing the kitchen redone, as it was looking dated. That is what Emily had figured, she just always liked a second opinion, especially from Alexis, who would be responsible for selling the house when it was finished. Alexis knew what people in the area were looking for and what they were willing to pay for.

Once they were done looking at the house, Emily let her team know that they could get to work on the house, and she gave them the details on what they would need to work on. She now had two projects that just started this week and both of them would take several weeks if not a month or longer. This was fine with Emily, as she would be gone for two weeks. It made her feel like she was working even while she was on vacation. She also wouldn't need to have to worry about finding replacement projects till after she got back.

With only a few days till a long vacation, Emily and Miriam wanted to enjoy the quiet while they could. They spent some time packing a little more, as they didn't want to wait till the last minute, especially when they were heading to the ranch on Friday afternoon. They also talked about some of the cities that they would be able to see and what sights they would like to see.

Wednesday morning and Emily was up a little earlier than normal. She got her coffee and came back to think about the day ahead. Today was a big day for her. Even though it was not finished, possession of the hotel would transfer to the new owner today. In exchange, she would receive a large sum of money that would allow her to purchase half ownership in a ranch. She had spent years of her career to get to this point, and she couldn't believe that she had finally achieved this level of success. After finishing her coffee, she headed off to get ready for the day.

After she was done, she went to the kitchen to cook breakfast. She would need a good breakfast to get through today, so she cooked pancakes, biscuits, bacon, and sausage. She knew Miriam would love it. Sure enough, just as she was finishing up, Miriam walked into the kitchen.

"I love the smell of breakfast in the morning."

"Of course, you would. You also love the taste of breakfast in the morning."

"Oh yeah, especially when it looks this good!"

"I would say I hope you enjoy, but I can see that you already are!"

They finished off their breakfast and Miriam went to finish getting ready for school. Emily decided to prepare another cup of coffee to take with her. She had a feeling that she would need it this morning. The closing wasn't scheduled till almost noon, so she had a feeling that the morning would drag on, so she wanted that extra cup of coffee to help get through the morning.

It was soon time to drop off Miriam and head to the office to wait. She needed something to do, so she decided to look through the online listings to see what properties were available, even though she wasn't looking to add another property right now. She did see a few that looked interesting, so she spent some time looking into them a little more. She enjoyed this part of the business.

Later in the morning, she did get a call from Alexis. One of her finished properties had someone interested in purchasing it. It was the house that she had recently purchased that needed some minor work done on it. Another investor had just sold his property and was looking into something a little nicer. Since he already had the funds, they could close soon. His offer was a little below her asking price, but she would still make a good profit, so she let Alexis know to go ahead and schedule a time to close before Saturday.

It was soon time to head to the hotel for the big closing. It went according to plan, but it took a lot longer than her normal residential closings. A lot of that was because the hotel was still being worked on. A lot of agreements needed to be signed. The check was given to Brooke, and Emily let Brooke know to place her proceeds in her account for purchasing properties since the majority would be used to buy the ranch. By the time it was done, it was time to pick up Miriam from school.

Emily was so excited by the time she picked up Miriam that Miriam suggested they go out that night to celebrate. Emily thought it was a wonderful idea. She loved celebrating with Miriam. When they got home, Miriam changed into something a little dressier to match what her mom had worn that day. Emily just swapped her business heels for her ankle boots that she loved for evenings out.

They headed out to their usual location, which was their favorite. They walked around for a bit checking out some of their favorite stores. When they got hungry, they headed to their favorite steakhouse for dinner. After dinner, it was walking around some more and looking at a few more places. They loved that the shopping center was decorated for Christmas. It was one of the best places in Tulsa for lights. Everything looked so pretty, and they loved seeing all the lights and other decorations.

After a great evening out, they headed home. They both got changed into something more comfortable for relaxing in and sat on the couch. There wasn't a lot of time to watch something, so they decided to talk for a few. Miriam sat next to her mom and leaned against her. Emily asked Miriam if there were anything that she would change. Miriam said she was thrilled with everything. She loved her mom and she loved spending time with her. She just wished she had more time to spend with her, but she was glad when they had their nights out. She was also glad that they took vacations, where they could spend more time together.

After talking for a few, Miriam decided to head to bed, but not before giving her mom a hug and kiss goodnight. Emily decided to stay up for a few and enjoy a glass of wine. It was a nice way to finish an incredible day. She had worked for years to get to this point, but she couldn't help but wonder what was next? Where would she go from here? After such a large project, would she be fine with continuing with residential properties? The good news is she didn't need to answer these questions today. In just a few days, she would have two weeks off to think about stuff and more importantly, to spend lots of precious time with Miriam.

    She finished her glass of wine and headed to bed. She was looking forward to some much-needed downtime, which was soon coming. She had just two more days at the office, and she knew she would be busy on Friday. She was hoping that tomorrow would be a quieter more relaxing day, especially after the business of today.

Thursday was a relatively uneventful day for both Miriam and Emily. Alexis did call and let her know that a family and looked at the other property, which had the new kitchen, and made an offer. They would require financing but had been preapproved, so it would be after she got back from her Christmas vacation before they could close.

Later in the day, Brooke called to let her know that the bank had deposited her proceeds in the account that she specified. Brooke had her check the balance, and Emily couldn't believe it. She had never imagined that the account would have so many zeros in it. She let Brooke know the exact amount that she would need to have in a check to purchase her share of the ranch tomorrow. Brooke let Emily know that it would be ready for her to pick up in the morning.

After a great night out yesterday, Emily and Miriam wanted to relax at home for the evening. Friday they were going back to the ranch to purchase their share and the following day they were off on their vacation, so it was nice to relax for the evening and just be with each other. The coming days would bring a lot of wonderful memories but be chaotic at times.

Friday morning Emily awoke at her usual time of 5:30. As she was getting her coffee, she couldn't help but smile at the fact that it was her last day of work for another two weeks. Today would be a busy day with an investor purchasing one of her properties this morning and she and Miriam heading to the ranch this afternoon to purchase their share. It looked like it would be a good day, though a busy one. She headed off to get ready for the day.

Once she was done getting ready, she headed to the kitchen to work on breakfast. Since tomorrow would be a rush, today would be the last full breakfast at the house, so biscuits and gravy it would be. She also wanted to have them, as she wasn't sure if people in the Northeast knew what biscuits and gravy were. As soon as Miriam walked into the kitchen, she knew what was for breakfast, and she was excited. Since they were going to the ranch today, Miriam was also dressed in full cowgirl attire, including the hat. Since her mom had some meetings, she was dressed in her regular business attire but would change before picking up Miriam.

"I smell biscuits and gravy!"

"We may not have them again while we are gone, so I wanted to make sure we had them today, especially since I know they are your favorite."

"You're the best, Mom!"

"I do try. Hopefully, no one gives you a hard time about how you are dressed today."

"Well, if they do, I will just tell them that my mom and I are purchasing a ranch after school, and we wanted to dress appropriately."

"That's my girl!"

They enjoyed their biscuits and gravy before Miriam headed off to finish getting ready. She wanted her hair to look perfect with her hat, though her mom told her that she already looked perfect.

It was soon time to drop off Miriam and head to the office for a bit before her first closing of the day. She didn't have much to do at the office, so she organized it for a bit before it was time to head out.

The closing was very quick and straightforward. That tends to happen when both parties are experienced investors. Afterward, she met with Alexis for a few to talk about some of the properties. When she was done, she took the check to the bank to deposit it, while picking up the check she would need for this afternoon. With her morning meetings done, she headed home for lunch and to get changed for this afternoon. She would also take some time to continue with the packing for tonight, so it would be ready sooner. She wanted to relax as much as possible and not spend the evening running around.

After a few hours at the house, it was time to pick up Miriam from school and head to the ranch. Kelli was going to meet them there to help make sure everything ran smoothly. Miriam was excited when she got picked up. Not only was she heading back to the ranch, but she received many compliments for how she looked today. When she had mentioned to a few people that they were purchasing a ranch, many people suddenly started to show an interest in her. Her mom just laughed and said that was typical.

When they got to the ranch, after greetings were exchanged, everyone but Miriam headed in to go through the paperwork. Miriam, of course, headed off to check out the horses. She was hoping to have a horse of her own soon. She loved the thought of her and her mom coming out here on the weekends and riding horses around the ranch. It seemed like so much fun.

The meeting itself was pretty straightforward. For the time being, things would continue the way they had been, with Al and Carol running the day-to-day of the ranch. They would receive a salary for their work, and everyone would split the profits above that. Emily would be free to add new features to the ranch, after checking with Al and Carol first. She could also purchase horses for herself and Miriam and they would stay free, they would just need to pay for the food and other costs. After a few years, when Al and Carol decided to retire, they would revisit and decide what Emily wanted to do, and she would be given the first choice of what she felt like doing. She could purchase the other half, or find another partner, or sell her part along with Al and Carol.

Once it was done, everyone shook hands and walked out to talk for a bit. It was a nice day for mid-December, and they wanted to enjoy it while they could. Everyone decided to head to the horse barn to see what Miriam was up to. It was little surprise that she was grooming the horses and giving them treats. She looked like a natural and Emily knew she had made the right decision in buying the ranch, as it looked like it would be a positive influence on Miriam. It was soon time to head back to town, as it was getting dark and there was still much work to be done.

Emily and Miriam headed home, stopping to pick up dinner. After dinner, Miriam had no schoolwork to work on, so they finished their packing. Since they had been working on it for the past week, it didn't take long to finish, which left them plenty of time to relax and catch a few shows before it was time to head to bed.

Emily stayed up for a few to drink a glass of wine. She couldn't believe that she was now a half-owner in a ranch. She had never pictured herself as a country girl, but it was starting to grow on her. She would always be a city girl that loved to dress up and look her best, but now she could also be a country girl as well. It was a pretty good feeling. It was soon time to head to bed herself, as tomorrow would be a busy travel day, and it would start early.

Saturday morning and Emily was up at five. She wanted a chance to enjoy her coffee before the busy day of travel began. Unlike their last trip, this would be a much longer travel day with two flights. They would also lose an hour instead of gaining an hour by flying. She was curious how well Miriam would handle such a busy day. It would be close to dinner time before they arrived at the hotel for the night. Once she had finished her coffee, she headed off to finish getting ready for the day and make sure all the suitcases were ready to go, and moved to the living room.

By the time she was moving the suitcases to the living room, Miriam was up and ready to go as well. She grabbed her suitcases and moved them with her mom's, to help in loading the car. She asked Miriam if she would rather have her heat up a breakfast sandwich, or would she rather just grab something on the way to the airport. Miriam said to just grab something, so they loaded up the car with the suitcases and headed out, stopping to pick up a quick breakfast on the way to the airport.

They arrived at the airport shortly after six, and their flight was scheduled to leave at 7:30. Emily opted for valet once again. She liked being able to park close, especially when they had so many bags. It didn't take long for them to unload the car and drop off the majority of their bags, which would be checked to DC. They had cleared security by 6:30 and could take their time heading to the gate. Miriam saw some food that looked good, so they stopped and purchased a little more to eat.

Once again, Emily had purchased first class, and these planes were a little smaller with only eight first-class seats, which would make it a little quieter for the flight.

They were among the first to board and were relaxing in their seats when the main rush to board started. It would be an almost six-hundred-mile flight, taking close to two hours, by the time they landed in Chicago.

The flight would be relatively uneventful. Miriam was getting used to air travel, and she was beginning to love it. It was almost two hours later, about 9:30, by the time they got to their gate and had left the plane. They had 90 minutes until their next flight left, and the gate was not far away, so it was a great opportunity to relax.

They had just gotten to their gate when Emily saw something and told Miriam she would be right back. A few minutes later she came back with a small box. She said Miriam had to try something new. She opened the box and Miriam could tell it was pizza, but it looked a little different. Her mom told her that it was Chicago deep-dish pizza and she needed to try some. Miriam took a bite, and she loved it. The two of them easily split the small pizza that Emily had picked up. Though it was a little early for lunch, it would be a while before they had an opportunity to eat.

Boarding began about 10:30, and once again they were one of the first on the plane, which they were beginning to enjoy. They also enjoyed the special treatment while the other passengers were boarding. This flight would be a little shorter on time, taking about 90 minutes, but with the time change, it would be like 2 ½ hours.

This flight would also be uneventful, except for the scenery. Shortly after takeoff, they passed over Lake Michigan, and Miriam couldn't believe that such a large body of water was simply a lake. Her mom told her there was a reason why it was one of the Great Lakes. They also passed close enough to Lake Erie, that Miriam was able to see it as well. Miriam also saw some mountains, though they looked quite different than what she had seen in Colorado. Her mom explained that they were part of the Appalachians, another major mountain chain in the US, though vastly different from the Rockies.

It was about 1:45 when they arrived at the gate at the Reagan National Airport. It was a smaller airport than the others, so it didn't take long to get to where their bags were. Once they collected them, they were off on a shuttle to pick up the rental car. This time they hadn't picked anything specific, but Emily was able to choose from a selection of cars, and they had an SUV, which reminded them of what they had, so they picked it. After loaded their bags, they were off to the hotel.

Their hotel was in one of the Maryland suburbs of DC. Emily thought it was an ideal location for not only seeing the city but also the surrounding area, without always dealing with the DC traffic. By the time they got to the hotel and checked into their room, they were pretty tired for the night and opted to stay at the hotel. They headed down to a neighboring restaurant for dinner and headed back to the room to relax. At this hotel, they had their own bedroom and bathroom but shared a living room and kitchen. It made them feel like they were at home.

They talked about their plans for the coming days and flipped through the TV, before finding a good movie to watch for the rest of the evening. They had gotten some snacks at check-in, and they were perfect for spending time together, watching a movie. When the movie was over, they both felt it was time for bed. It had been a busy travel day, and tomorrow would be a busy day of seeing the sights in the nation's capital.

Sunday morning, Emily was surprised to wake up and the clock said it was almost seven, then she remembered that she was an hour ahead, so this was a normal time for her to wake up. She headed to the kitchen to get her coffee and wait for Miriam to wake up. Today would be her first visit to DC in a few years, especially to drive in the heart of the city. Luckily, today was a Sunday, so traffic should be a lot lighter and easier to navigate. She wanted Miriam to experience some of the historic sites in town and learn some more of her country's history.

It was about 30 minutes later that Miriam came out and sat next to her mom on the couch. Instead of laying on her mom, like she usually does at home, she gave her mom a hug and kiss on the cheek and thanked her for taking this trip. Miriam said she was ready to get going, so they got dressed and headed down for breakfast, which was a buffet filled with lots of great food. Emily told Miriam to eat all she wanted, so she had lots of energy for the day.

After breakfast, they headed out and got on the road to DC. They headed south from the city. After a few minutes, Miriam was commenting that DC didn't look all that different from many other cities, as she saw the same shopping stores and restaurants that they had back home. Her mom explained that much of the city was a standard city that people lived in, so much of it looked like a typical city. They were heading to a part that was not typical.

A few minutes later, and Miriam understood what her mom was talking about. She could see a large white building with a dome in the center of it. She recognized it from TV and some of her classes. It was the US Capitol. Her mom drove her around the National Mall, showing her some of the major sites. At one traffic light, they could spot the White House. After a lap around the mall, they parked, so they could see some of the museums.

They started with the Museum of Natural History since it was filled with animals. When they were done, they crossed the mall to head to another. Halfway across, Emily stopped them and had Miriam look down the Mall to the Lincoln Memorial. She explained that this area was filled with history and speakers. MLK gave his famous "I Have a Dream" speech there and people were lined up to where they were standing. When they looked the other way at the Capitol, she explained that the new presidents are inaugurated there, and people are lined up to where they are standing to hear the new president. Miriam couldn't imagine that many people gathered.

They explored a few of the other museums along the mall, taking a break for lunch. Emily asked Miriam if she had seen everything there that she wanted to see, and she replied that she had seen what she wanted to see. Emily let her know that they had two more places to see, but they would need to drive there.

They got into their car and headed across the river to Arlington, Virginia to the National Cemetery. When they walked in, Miriam was shocked to see all the gravestones. Her mom explained that this is where many people who served in the military are buried, many of them died in service. They spent quite a bit of the afternoon walking around and see much of what was to see. Miriam loved learning the history today, but Emily could see that she was getting tired, and it had been emotional for her.

After a few minutes of driving, they stopped and began to walk around. Emily explained that this part of the cities was filled with the embassies of other countries. Most countries would send an ambassador to the US, and this was where they lived and worked. Each embassy, though in the US, was considered a part of the country that had its ambassador there. They walked past a few that Miriam recognized their name and knew where they were. She then saw a flag that looked familiar. She walked up to the building and the sign said "Embajada de la República de Guatemala en EE. UU.". Emily could see a few tears as Miriam stood there. Emily explained that even though she was going to be adopted soon, and would become a US citizen, this would always be a part of her history and who she was. She didn't want her to ever forget her past, even though it could be painful at times. Miriam walked over to her mom and gave her a long hug for a few minutes until she could stop crying. Once Miriam had stopped crying, she wiped her face and had her picture taken, so she could show others some of her history.

  They decided that they had seen enough for the day, so along the way home, they picked up dinner. When they got back to the hotel, they enjoyed their dinner. The hotel had an indoor pool and hot tub, so they decided to head there for a bit to relax after a busy and emotional day of seeing the sights. After some time enjoying the water, they headed back to the room to watch some TV and enjoy being with each other. Miriam thanked her mom for showing her everything that she had today. She loved learning about history and seeing where so much history happened. Even though she cried a lot, she enjoyed seeing the Guatemalan Embassy. It was nice seeing a part of her home again. They hugged again, and Miriam headed off to bed.

Emily poured a glass of wine and thought about the day. She was glad that Miriam had enjoyed seeing a part of her history. She wasn't sure how Miriam was going to react, but she was glad that it worked out. Emily wanted Miriam to remember her past and where she came from. It was something that Emily had to learn more about, which Miriam could teach her a lot about. Emily also wanted her to learn more about US history, which is one of the reasons why they were here and spending so much time in this part of the country. Tomorrow would be another busy day, but hopefully not as emotional. Emily didn't like seeing Miriam cry like that, though she understood it and was glad that she did show emotions for something so emotional.

Monday morning and Emily was up at six. She headed off to get her coffee and wait for Miriam to wake up. She didn't have as much planned for today. She did have one thing planned for today, and she knew that Miriam would love it. Afterward, she just might see what Miriam felt like doing. Tomorrow they would make their way to NJ and had a few stops along the way, so if Miriam wanted to do less today, that would be just fine.

It was about 45 minutes later that Miriam woke up and headed to the living room. Once again, she hugged her mom and leaned against her for a few minutes.

"Well, good morning to you as well. I love these hugs in the morning."

"Thanks, Mom. I've had a great time so far, and I am so glad that we got to come here. I'm sorry I cried yesterday. It's not that I don't love you, I do. I just miss my family sometimes."

"That's OK, Miriam. I understand. They are an important part of your life, and I don't ever want you to forget about them. I don't want you to think of me as a replacement for them. I am just continuing where they left off. Now come here because I want a hug and kiss from you."

She gave Miriam a big hug and kiss on the cheek, just like Miriam loves to give her. Miriam just laughed and hugged her back.

"How about we go get dressed and go find some breakfast?"

"You don't have to ask that. I'm always ready for breakfast."

"I should have known that."

They got dressed and headed off to breakfast. Miriam got another plate with just about everything the hotel had for breakfast. Afterward, they headed off to their first destination, the National Zoo. Miriam was so excited to see all the animals, many like pandas, she had never seen before in person. They spent a few hours there walking around, taking a break for lunch. When they were done, Emily asked if she wanted to see anything else. She said she did but was a little tired. Emily then said they could drive around for a while, and they could stop if Miriam saw something that looked interesting. Miriam liked that idea.

They headed south towards the city, but then headed west to avoid the traffic. They entered Virginia and saw the Pentagon and passed by the airport that they flew into. After a few minutes, they were in Alexandria. Miriam loved the look of some of the older buildings and got excited when she saw some of the shopping opportunities, so they stopped for a bit to do some shopping. Apparently, Miriam was never too tired to do some shopping. They spent the afternoon looking around and stopped at a restaurant for dinner, before heading back to the hotel for the night.

It was their last night in DC and they both had a great time there. They got to see many of the major sites around town, learned some history, and of course, did some shopping. Though there was still much to see, they could come back another day to see them. Emily wanted Miriam to get an overview of some of the major places in DC, and not necessarily see everything there was to see.

Tomorrow, Miriam would get to meet some of her new family, and she was feeling a little anxious about how her mom's family would feel about her. She had not told her mom how she felt, as she didn't want to upset her or make her worry as well. She loved her mom so much, and her mom loved her so much. She just hoped that the rest of her new family felt the same way about her.

Tuesday morning and Emily was up at six. She headed off to get her coffee and wait on the couch. She hated to admit it, but she was nervous this morning. Later today, her parents and her sisters would meet Miriam, and she would meet her new extended family. While she had talked with them over the phone, meeting someone in person can be a very different matter. She knew Miriam had to be very nervous as well. They were scheduled to spend a full week with her family. If things weren't going well, it could be a very long week.

It was closer to seven when Miriam finally woke up and joined her on the couch. They were not in a hurry today. Her parents had said to be there by 4, so they had time to explore some on the way to NJ. She had a few activities planned for the day, that she was hoping that Miriam would enjoy.

"Good morning, Miriam."

"Good morning, Mom."

"Are you a little nervous about today?"

"More than a little nervous about today."

"I know how you feel. I am nervous too. I know they all love me, I am just hoping that they love you as much as I do. You mean the world to me and I want them to feel the same way that I do. I want you to try and relax some and try not to think about it too much, and I'll try and do the same thing. OK?"

"I'll try, Mom, if you try too."

"Sounds like a plan. Let's go get dressed, get some breakfast, and hit the road."

"I like the breakfast part of that."

"Oh, Miriam."

After getting ready for the day, they headed off to breakfast. Miriam was going to miss the selection of breakfast foods that were available each day. She loved having a variety of items to eat. Once they were done with breakfast, they headed back to the room to pack everything up and head out. After some driving, they were on the interstate heading north.

After a while on the interstate, Miriam saw a city up ahead that looked like they were going to pass. She asked what city that was, and Emily replied that it was Baltimore, and that is where they were heading this morning. They exited the interstate and headed to town. After passing the football and baseball stadium, they approached downtown. Emily let Miriam know that Baltimore had the National Aquarium, and that was their first destination of the morning. After seeing the aquarium, they walked around the inner harbor and saw many of the historic ships that were docked there.

After spending the morning at the harbor, they found some lunch. Before leaving town, they had one more place to visit. They headed east and a few minutes later they approached what looked like it was a military base or something. They got out and walked around. Emily explained that it was Fort McHenry. Emily explained the significance of what happened there in 1814, and what Francis Scott Key had seen that night as well as the following morning. Miriam said she finally understood what the song meant, and it was no longer just words to sing at the start of a sports game.

They headed back to the interstate and a few minutes later, they were passing through the Fort McHenry tunnel. Miriam said that the name sounded familiar and they both laughed. It was about an hour later that they saw two large bridges and Emily said they were approaching New Jersey. Miriam couldn't believe how big the bridge was. Emily explained that the Delaware River was below them. Up the river was Philadelphia, and at one time they had lots of shipbuilding and some of the largest ships around had to pass under this bridge.

Miriam was surprised at how open everything was and how many farms she was seeing. Emily let her know that yes, New Jersey was a very densely populated state, but that was mostly the Philly and especially New York City suburbs. This part of New Jersey had lots of farms and cows and in fact, had a rodeo that they were about to pass. They actually wouldn't see much till they got to her parent's house, which was about 30 minutes away.

After passing many farms, a few townships, and even a borough, they arrived at a nice-looking house, with a couple sitting on the porch.

"Well Miriam, this is my parent's house. This is where I grew up. Those are my parents waiting on the porch. Try and relax. I'll be with you the whole time!"

They got out of the car and walked up to the porch. Emily's mom got up and ran towards the ladies. Emily was expecting her to run towards her, but she instead ran straight to Miriam and gave her a big hug.

"I've been looking forward to meeting you for a while now! I'm so glad I finally get to meet you, Miriam! You are way prettier than your pictures that your mom sent me."

"Thanks. It's nice to meet you too. What should I call you?"

"You can call me whatever you'd like, but Grandma is just fine with me."

"Does Grandma remember that she still has a daughter over here?"

"Of course, but she's busy with her precious granddaughter." She glances over at Emily and smiles at her. "Of course, I have time for my daughter. Come back later tonight."

"You're hilarious, Mom."

"Well, I guess I can squeeze you in for a minute." She gives Emily a big hug. "It is always nice to see you, especially when you bring new grandkids for us to spoil with you."

"Maybe my dad misses me."

"Nope, still waiting to meet that new granddaughter."

Emily's mom walks Miriam over to her husband and they hug.

"It's so nice to finally meet you, Miriam. We've heard so much good about you. You're all your mom talks about. We can finally see why that is. You can call me Grandpa by the way."

"Thanks, Grandpa. My mom means so much to me."

"We are so glad to hear it. Why don't you two come inside? Dinner will be ready shortly. I'm sure you two have been busy traveling."

Everyone goes inside, and while Emily's mom finishes the last few things, Emily tells her dad about what they had seen since they left Tulsa. He loves to hear about how the traffic was and what the different sites looked like.

It wasn't long until dinner was ready and the four of them sat down to a nice dinner of roast chicken, mashed potatoes, some mixed veggies, and fresh-baked rolls. Miriam was loving it, and Emily's parents were pleased to see her enjoy the food. They remember Emily when she was that age, and she was more particular with her food. After dinner, they headed to the living room to talk some more for the evening.

They shared some stories about how Emily was growing up and what she liked to do. Miriam loved learning all about her mom. When it was time for bed, they let Emily know that she was in her old room, which was the usual guest room. Miriam was in the room just past it. They were both glad to get some rest after a busy day. Tomorrow would be another busy day of spending time with family and learning more about each other.

Wednesday morning Emily awoke at six. As she woke up in her old room, her first thought was she didn't want to go to school today. She then realized that she was an adult and didn't have school anymore. She decided to go get some coffee and wait for the others to wake up. They had not discussed any plans, but today would be a good day to go do something, as tomorrow was Christmas Eve. She was not fond of being out and dealing with the last-minute shoppers.

It was about thirty minutes later that her mom joined her on the couch.

"Good morning, Emily. Nice to see that you are still getting up early in the morning."

"Good morning, Mom. Yeah, I still love to get up, grab my coffee, and think things through."

"Your dad and I just love Miriam. She is an absolutely wonderful young lady. You were so lucky to get her."

"Thanks, Mom. I feel the same way about her. She was so nervous about meeting everybody. I'm glad to see she did well yesterday, though she does have a few more people to meet."

"I'm sure she'll do fine."

"I'm glad you feel that way, Mom. I'm sure she will too."

Miriam came into the living room and laid between her mom and grandma.

"Well, good morning, Miriam. Did you sleep OK?"

"Good morning, Grandma. Yeah, I slept OK."

"Glad to hear it. I was just telling your mom how glad we are to finally meet you. We think you are such a sweet young lady. We are glad you're here and that you're our granddaughter."

"Thanks, Grandma. It feels nice to have a family again. I love my mom, but it is nice to have others in the family as well."

"Are you two hungry? I can go cook breakfast."

"I'd love breakfast, Grandma."

"OK, then I'll go cook breakfast." She heads off to the kitchen, leaving Miriam and her mom.

"Miriam, what do you think of your grandparents?"

"I like them. Grandma can be silly at times and Grandpa is pretty nice."

"Yeah, Grandma has always been like that."

"So, this is where you lived when you were a child?"

"Yeah, we lived in this house most of my life. Later today, I can show you where I went to school."

"That would be fun. What else were we doing today?"

"I'm not sure. We'll have to talk to Grandma and Grandpa."

A few minutes later Grandma came out and let them know that breakfast was ready. The four of them headed into the kitchen to eat. It was a nice breakfast with a variety of items to eat, so Miriam was excited. Over breakfast, they discussed their plans for the day. The ladies wanted to head to Philly to show Miriam around, and to head to the outlet mall just north of the city. It was always one of Emily's favorite places to shop, and she went there every time she visited her family. Grandpa was going to stay home and work on a surprise for the ladies for dinner.

Once they had finished breakfast and got ready, the ladies headed out. On the way, they passed Emily's high school. Miriam couldn't believe that it was in the middle of a cornfield. Emily just laughed and said she would have loved to go where Miriam was going. She had it so much better than many others, so she should be glad. It was about 45 minutes later that they were crossing the Delaware River and headed into Philly. Off to the left, Miriam could see the airport and all the sports stadiums and arenas for the city. Off to the right was downtown Philly, which is where they were heading.

They found parking and walked around the historic part of Philly and showed Miriam some of the sites including Independence Hall and the Liberty Bell. They showed Miriam where the US Mint was, which was where so much of the country's coins were made.

After a bit of walking around downtown, they headed to the outlet mall for an enjoyable day of shopping. Miriam couldn't believe how big the mall was, as it took quite a while. Emily showed her some of her favorite stores to buy clothes for the office. Emily picked up a few new pieces for work, and they found Miriam a matching suit in her size. She could now really look like her mom when they went to look at houses together. Grandma loved it that Miriam wanted to be like her mom so much. It made her proud of her daughter.

After a busy day of shopping, they headed back for dinner. Grandpa had bought a smoker a few months ago and had smoked some ribs and pork shoulder for dinner. He had also invited Emily's two sisters over for dinner, along with their family. Emily was surprised to see everyone there when they got back, but she was glad to see her sisters, Lauren and Kristen. They loved meeting Miriam and thought the world of her. Lauren was the oldest and had two daughters, Finley and Josie, that were a little younger than Miriam. Miriam was thrilled to have people close to her age to spend time with, not that she didn't like spending time with the adults.

Dinner was ready when the ladies got back from shopping, so the entire family ate together. After dinner, the kids ran off to play and talk, while the adults sat around and got caught up with the changes in everyone's lives. Everyone wanted to hear details about Miriam and what they had been up to for the past two months. They were all thrilled to hear how well she had been doing. The family was kind of surprised to hear about the ranch, though. Part of why Emily left the area was that it was too country for her and now she was part owner of a ranch. Her sister said her country roots were finally coming out and Emily just rolled her eyes and laughed.

They discussed some of their plans for the coming days, as they wanted to spend as much time together as they could. They decided to spend most of Christmas together, including dinner. Lauren wanted to take Miriam for a night, so the girls could do a sleepover. Emily thought it was a good idea, and she figured Miriam would love some extra time with her new cousins. Saturday, they thought it would be fun to take Miriam to Lancaster, PA, and show her some of the Amish communities and enjoy some great food and shopping. Emily said that sounded great and she would be joining them.

After a couple of hours of catching up, Lauren and Kristen decided it was time to call it a night, but they would be back at some point either tomorrow or the next day. Miriam had enjoyed her time with her cousins and was looking forward to spending more time with them in the coming days. She was tired but wanted to relax with her mom for a few, before heading to bed. She was loving being around all these people, and it felt so good to have an actual family again.

Christmas Eve Emily was up at six. She headed to the kitchen to find some coffee and wait for others to wake up. Yesterday was a very busy day, but it was a good busy. Shopping with Miriam is one of her favorite activities, and she loved having her mom with her. She was so surprised to see her sisters and their families. It had been too long since she spent time with them and it felt good to finally be in the same room as them, and not communicating through a phone. A few minutes later, Miriam joined her on the couch and cuddled up next to her.

"I always love those morning cuddles. So, what did you think of your cousins?"

"I like Josie and Finley, but they are a little crazy."

"They get that from their mom, but you didn't hear that from me."

They both laugh at the statement.

"So, what are the plans for today?"

"I don't know. We never really did much on Christmas Eve. We would usually just watch some Christmas movies and snack on foods. I know it is not the most exciting thing in the world. We can always create new traditions for us."

"That sounds good. I like the thought of new traditions with my mom."

Grandma entered the living room and sat down next to the girls.

"Mom, do we have any plans for today? Miriam was curious."

"Not really. Lauren and Kristen are at the in-laws today, so they will be here tomorrow."

"How about the four of us go get breakfast and we can show Miriam around?"

"That sounds good to me. I'll go find your dad and get ready, and we will be down in a few."

Everyone got ready and they headed out. They went to a local diner for breakfast, as it was the best place around. After dinner, they headed to some of the Philly suburbs in NJ that were known for their shopping and had other interesting things to do. Miriam loved seeing everything, and she was surprised at the size of some of the shopping areas. She could spend days exploring some of the shopping areas. Her favorite was in the Chery Hill area. Her mom told her it was one of her favorites as well.

After a busy day of driving around, they headed home for dinner. Emily didn't want her parents to have to cook, so they stopped, and she picked up dinner for the family. When they got home, they enjoyed dinner while watching some Christmas movies together as a family. It was the perfect ending for a great day of spending together time together as a family. While they didn't purchase a lot, they enjoyed being together, and the memories that they created were priceless.

Tomorrow would-be Christmas, and it promised to be busy again. Lauren and Kristen would be coming over in the morning, along with their families, and would likely be there till the sun went down. It promised to be another busy day, but one filled with more priceless memories of great family times, good food, and time well spent.

Christmas morning Emily was up at six. After getting her coffee she sat on the couch to wait for the others. It had been an amazing year. She thought she might sell some properties and maybe be in a relationship. She never would have guessed the success she had professionally this year. While she didn't have the relationship, she thought she might have had, the best relationship she ever had was down the hall and would soon legally be her daughter. It was something she couldn't have imagined at the start of the year, but she wouldn't trade it for anything.

A few minutes later, Miriam came out and laid next to her mom.

"Merry Christmas, Miriam!"

"Merry Christmas, Mom!"

"Just so you know, all your presents from me are back home, and you can open them when we get back. Didn't want you to think that I forgot about you."

"I know, Mom. I didn't expect you to bring everything, just so I could open it and fly it all back. Don't worry, I already have the best Christmas present ever, and it's right next to me."

"You're so sweet, Miriam. I feel the same way about you. Having you has made this the best Christmas ever. I'm just so excited that I have someone special in my life to celebrate with."

As they were finishing their hug, Grandma walked in.

"Merry Christmas ladies. Might if I join in the hug?"

"There's always room for Grandma."

Grandma joins in and they hug some more.

"Well, should we open presents first or have breakfast?"

"East breakfast!"

"That's my Miriam!"

"Sounds good to me. I don't think Grandpa is up yet anyway, so I'll go cook breakfast and we can open presents afterward."

Grandma heads to the kitchen to cook breakfast, while Emily and Miriam stay on the couch and just cuddle up next to each other. They just enjoyed being a part of a family on such a special day. A few minutes later, breakfast is ready, and they head to the kitchen to enjoy breakfast together. Grandma cooked a couple of the girl's breakfast favorites, so it was a very enjoyable start to the day. Grandpa finally woke up and joined them for breakfast. He was glad to have Emily back for a few days, as well as having Miriam in his life. The two of them meant a lot to him. When breakfast was over, everyone headed to the living room to open presents.

There was not much organization to the presents. Everyone pretty much handed out their presents and people opened them. Emily had picked up a few things during their shopping trips, and she gave them to her parents. Her parents didn't want to overwhelm Miriam with a lot of things to bring back, so they kept it simple with a few books, so she had something to open, along with some gift cards, so she could buy the clothes that she wanted when they were back home. When Emily's sisters arrived shortly, the scene would be repeated.

After the presents had been opened, Emily's parents headed to the kitchen to start the large dinner for later. They had a turkey and a ham as the main courses, along with many sides. It would be close to mid-afternoon before the meal would be done, which gave the family lots of time to spend together. It was about an hour after they had finished opening the presents, that Emily's sisters, along with their families came over. Finley and Josie had brought a few of their presents over, and Miriam headed off to spend time with them. With her parents working on the meal, it gave Emily a chance to talk to her sisters.

They wanted to hear about some of her projects that she had been working on. They were also curious about what had led her to buy a ranch. She explained what had led her to purchase it, and they thought it was nice that it was something that she and Miriam were both interested in. She let them know that she didn't know what her plans were for the long term, but it was something to try for a few years, and she was able to get out of it if it was not what she wanted to be doing. She told Lauren that she should bring Josie and Finley out to the ranch sometime in the summer. They would love it, and they would get to spend some time with their cousin.

The ladies also spent some time talking about Miriam's background and some of what she had been through. While it was such a sad story, they were glad to see how great things were turning out for Miriam. They thought she was the best, and her cousins just loved spending time with her the other day. They asked if she planned on adopting any more kids after Miriam. Emily let them know that she hadn't thought about it much, as she was so focused on Miriam right now. She figured at some point she might, it would just depend on how things turned out. She also didn't know how Miriam would react, so she would worry about it at some other point.

After much talking, dinner was finally ready, and everyone headed to the kitchen for the family Christmas dinner. Emily's parents were so excited to have all three of their daughters here, along with the spouses of the two and three grandkids. The only thing that could have made this dinner any better would be more grandkids. Miriam loved the dinner. There were many new things that she had never had before, and she loved trying new things. There were many things that she was going to have to ask her mom to learn how to make.

When the family could eat no more, they headed off to the living room to watch a movie together. It was one of those things that they liked to do after Christmas dinner, and Emily had done many times as a child, and while visiting as an adult. It didn't matter if not everyone liked the movie, it was just something that everyone could participate in. After the dinner, they went around the room and everyone shared something that they were excited about this past year. Everyone knew what Emily and Miriam would discuss. Even though they all knew, they loved hearing it anyway, especially the way that Miriam told it. Her story was so sweet, and they could tell how much it meant to her to be a part of their family and to have Emily as her mom.

When everyone had shared their stories, it was back into the kitchen for dessert. It was either red velvet cake or pumpkin pie unless you were Miriam, then it was both. She just couldn't decide, so Grandma told her it was OK to take both and try them out. It was no surprise that she loved both of them. Once everyone had their desserts, the adults headed back to the living room to discuss the plans for the coming days. Tomorrow the ladies were heading to Lancaster to do some shopping and show Miriam some of the Amish communities, along with trying some of the food.

    Sunday, Emily was going to the girls on a shopping trip and some historical adventure. There were some things that she wanted Miriam to see, and she thought it would be fun to bring the cousins along, so they could spend more time with Miriam, and their parents could get a break. Emily was also curious about what it would be like to have multiple kids. They didn't have much planned for Monday, maybe come over for dinner. Tuesday, Emily and Miriam were heading to New York City to finish off the week.

    It had been an incredible Christmas celebration with the family. Emily and Miriam were both glad when the others left and they could spend a little bit with just the two of them, though they didn't stay up late as they were tired from the day, and there were more busy family days to come in the coming days. It would be tiring, yet emotionally filling at the same time.

Saturday morning and Emily was up at six. After getting her coffee, she headed to the living room to wait on the others. She was already dressed and ready to go, though her family hadn't discussed what time they were leaving, which was typical of them. They apparently thought that everyone communicated telepathically. It was one of those things about her family that had always bugged her, though if that were one of their biggest faults, things could always be a lot worse, so she tried not to let her bother her as much.

It was about thirty minutes later that Miriam joined her on the couch. She was also dressed in her typical long denim skirt, long sleeve shirt, and casual shoes, and ready to go.

"Good morning, Miriam. You're looking nice today."

"Thanks, Mom. That was actually what I wanted to talk to you about. Josie and Finley were asking why I wore a lot of dresses and skirts. They weren't making fun of me, they just thought it was different."

"Don't worry about it, Miriam. If they say something just let them know that not everyone is going to dress like them. You dress a lot like your mom does, and I think that is wonderful. We shouldn't feel pressured to dress like others, just because. Each of us is unique and it is OK to show it in how we dress. Don't let others make you feel bad for being you. I love you for you, not for who I think you should be."

"Thanks, Mom. They did mention that I did dress a lot like you and that Aunt Lauren said you were always different growing up."

"Well, I may be the different one but I have a ranch and she doesn't so there!"

They both just laughed.

Grandma entered and was also dressed and ready to go.

"Glad to see that you two are dressed. They picked up Kristen and are on their way here."

A few minutes later, Lauren and the girls pulled up out front and everyone got in. Luckily, she had a seven-passenger SUV, so she could accommodate everyone in one vehicle. Grandma was upfront with Laurent, which let Emily and Kristen sit together, and the three girls were in the back. Their first stop was for breakfast, which they had at a local diner. They talked quite a bit about what everyone wanted to see that day, so they could make a plan. Luckily, everyone wanted to shop, which is why they were there, and the guys were back home.

Once they were done with breakfast, they were on the road, for the two-hour drive. They were about thirty minutes out when they could tell they were getting close, as they began to see a few horses and buggies on the streets. Miriam was excited to see the horses, and Emily said they should look at some kind of buggy for the ranch, so they could ride around. Miriam loved that idea, and the girls were a little jealous, which is why Emily mentioned it. She wanted the girls to realize that even though Miriam might be different, she was still an awesome person.

The main outlet stores had opened just before they arrived, which was their plan. They spent most of the morning and into the afternoon checking out all the stores. When they were done, they headed to a restaurant down the street that was known for their country, home-cooked meals. For most of them, this was a special treat, but for Emily and Miriam, this was pretty standard for Oklahoma food. After lunch, they decided to check out some of the shops, many of which sold Amish-made goods, including food and things around the house.

By this time, it was well into the afternoon, so they decided to head back for the night. Emily told the girls that she would pick them up tomorrow for breakfast and they would spend the day together. It was another great day for Emily and Miriam, and they loved the time spent with the family. After a quiet evening together, they headed to bed, to be ready for another day.

Emily awoke on Sunday morning at six. She headed off to the kitchen for her coffee and to wait for Miriam. It would just be her with three girls for the day. She wasn't worried about Miriam, it was Josie and Finley that concerned her. While they had been fine with their mom, she was unsure how they would act when it was just her. She was hoping that they would not complain too much about stuff, or she was worried that Miriam might say something to them, and it may not be pretty. She shouldn't worry though, as the girls and Miriam had gotten along pretty well these past few days, except for a few questions that they asked.

It was about 45 minutes later that Miriam woke up and joined her mom on the couch.

"Ready for an exciting day with your cousins?"

"I'm ready for an exciting day of breakfast."

"Oh, Miriam! Well, go get dressed and we can go pick them up and go find some breakfast."

They headed off to get dressed, then left to go pick up the cousins. When Emily picked them up, she asked where they wanted to go for breakfast, and they both wanted pancakes, which was fine with her and she knew Miriam would never turn down pancakes.

While at breakfast she asked the girls about what they were interested in, to see what they may have in common with Miriam. The girls were in fourth grade, so there were many differences in what they were interested in, but still many things in common. They asked her and Miriam about the ranch and wanted to hear more about it and the types of animals that were there. They had never ridden a horse and Miriam got to tell them how much fun it had been in Colorado, and how she was looking forward to buying a horse soon for the ranch.

Once they had finished breakfast, they headed towards Philly. This route took them over the Delaware River into Philly, and through downtown along the Schuylkill River for a while. It was a very scenic route. They passed by the art museum and its famous steps, the zoo, and many parks as they continued to follow the river out of the city and into the suburbs. They finally exited at their first destination, Valley Forge.

The girls were a little surprised that they would be stopping here first. It was something that Emily wanted Miriam to see and try and understand the importance of what happened here, so long ago. They drove around for a bit and saw some of the major sites. After a little bit, the girls asked if this is what they would be doing all day, as they were beginning to think that their aunt was a little odd. She replied that this was something that she wanted Miriam to see, also the large mall in neighboring King of Prussia would be opening shortly, and that was their next destination. All of the girls were excited to hear that.

Emily asked the girls to show her some of the popular stores for girls their age. She was curious about what was popular, compared to when she was their age. Most of the stores were a little young for Miriam, but she enjoyed seeing what her cousins liked. They took a lunch break and checked out some more stores. Emily let the girls purchase some clothing, after clearing it with their mom in advance. Miriam then showed the girls some of her favorite places, which they enjoyed, since it was where they would be buying clothes soon enough.

After a great day of shopping, Emily took them out for dinner at a neighboring restaurant that was known for their cheesecake, which would make a great dessert. She made sure she brought some cheesecakes back with her, to share with the family. All of the girls had a great time, and Josie and Finley enjoyed spending time with Miriam and their aunt. Once the girls had been dropped off, Emily and Miriam headed back to enjoy a quiet evening with the grandparents.

Monday morning and Emily was up at six. Today was their last full day in NJ with her parents. It had been a very filling time, and she was beyond thrilled with the quality time that Miriam had with everyone, from her parents to her two cousins. They had done so much and seen so much. She knew that Miriam was excited to have a family, beyond just a mother. She now had two cousins she could keep in contact with, as they had already been texting her. The family didn't have any plans for today, except they were coming over for dinner tonight, so she should have some quality time with just Miriam and her parents, which sounded great to her.

Shortly after she got on the couch, Miriam joined her. This time she was laying on her mom like she usually does at home. Emily placed her hand on Miriam's face and brushed her hair away, so she could see her beautiful smile.

"Good morning, Miriam. Are we a little tired today?"

"Spending time with Josie and Finley while shopping is fun but tiring."

"Today should be a quieter day. I don't think they are coming over till dinner, so it should just be the four of us for a while."

"Good. Grandma doesn't wear me out like they do."

They sat on the couch for a bit until Grandma got up and started on breakfast. Once breakfast was ready, the four of them gathered around the table to enjoy some time together. Grandma asked them if they had any plans for the day, and they let her know that they didn't have anything planned yet. Grandma let them know that she was hoping to spend some quiet time with them today before dinner when the rest of the family was coming over for one final meal together.

After breakfast, Grandpa took Miriam for a walk, so they could spend some time together. This gave Emily and her mom a chance to be alone. Her mom started by telling her how much fun they had with both Emily and Miriam these past few days. Everyone had nothing but good things to say about Miriam. They all loved her and were so thrilled that she would be a permanent part of the family. Lauren also had mentioned to her mom how much the girls enjoyed having a cousin to spend time with. Though they initially thought Miriam was a little odd, with how she dressed sometimes, they learned that she was pretty cool, and enjoyed her.

Her mom also began to express some concern about her raising Miriam by herself. It wasn't that she thought that her daughter was incapable, it was more concern if something happened to her. She let her mom know not to worry and that she would make arrangements once the adoption was final in case something happened to her. She also let her mom know not to worry, as she didn't need to work anymore, and she had plenty of time to take care of Miriam. She just worked while Miriam was in school. That made her mom feel a little better, she just hated the idea of Emily alone so far away from the family raising Miriam on her own.

They spent a quiet day with the grandparents, alternating between watching TV, talking about stuff, and taking walks on this nice warm day. After the past few busy days, it was nice to take it slow for a day and just enjoy each other.

    The rest of the family came over for dinner, where they enjoyed meatloaf, mashed potatoes, and lots more food, plus some of the cheesecakes that Emily had brought back. Everyone let Miriam know how much they enjoyed spending time with her and hoped to see her again soon. Miriam let them know how much she had enjoyed them and was glad to be a part of the family. They all stayed till after dark, so they could enjoy a little more time with Emily and Miriam. After they had left, the two headed off to bed but feeling very loved. Tomorrow they would say goodbye to the grandparents and head to New York City for the last part of the trip.

Tuesday morning and Emily was up at six. As she was getting her coffee, she was feeling a little sad. In a few hours, she would say goodbye to her parents, and it would likely be a few months, at the least, till she would see them again. They wouldn't need to leave till around lunchtime, so she had some time. She didn't have much planned with Miriam for today in New York, except check into the hotel and have dinner. They just wanted to relax some after quite a few busy days and some more busy days to come.

It was about 30 minutes later that Miriam joined her on the couch. She just leaned against her mom. After a few minutes, she decided to talk.

"Mom, these past few days have been wonderful. I love having a family and cousins, but I miss having time with just the two of us."

"I know how you feel, Miriam. I love spending time with my parents, my two sisters as well as their families, but I do miss spending time with just you. I'm not worried about what I need to say or what I need to do. I feel so relaxed when I am with you. I feel like we can both be ourselves, which I love."

"You're the best, Mom. That's why I love you so much!"

"I love you, Miriam because you are you!"

As they hug, Grandma enters the room.

"Grandma wants to join in!"

"There's always room for Grandma hugs!"

The three of them hug for a moment, then Grandma decides to head to the kitchen to make a wonderful breakfast for her girls. After some time, she has prepared pancakes, eggs, sausage, bacon, and some biscuits. She knew it was their last meal there, and she wanted it to be special. Miriam loved it and made sure there were no leftovers, which made Grandma happy. After breakfast, they spent some time in the living room, just talking with the grandparents about every topic they could think of.

When it turned into the afternoon, Emily decided it was time to head out. All of their bags were already packed, and her dad insisted on helping them load the SUV. They gave their final hugs, and the grandparents told Miriam that they were so happy to have her in the family, and they hoped she could come to visit again soon. They told Emily that they were so proud of her, and she turned out to be a wonderful lady. Both of them got into the SUV and wiped the tears from their eyes, as they drove off.

To get to the turnpike that would take them to NYC, they first had to drive almost to Philly. When Miriam asked why all Emily could think of is "it's a Jersey thing". They finally got to the turnpike and headed to NYC, though their hotel was outside the city. Emily didn't like to drive in the city, so she stayed outside and took the train or subway into town, depending on their destination. If they wanted to see something a little farther away, they could drive, without dealing with the traffic.

After what seemed like a few hours, they arrived at their hotel. It was in Newark, NJ, and was connected to the train station with a walkway, so they could easily start their day without much effort. Emily had booked a two-bedroom suite, which gave each of them their own room, plus they shared a living room. The room had a fantastic view of the skyline, and Emily pointed a few of the highlights.

They decided to get cleaned up and dressed up to head downstairs to the restaurant for dinner. While it was not quite ladies' night, it was nice anyway. After dinner, they headed back to the room to relax, before heading to bed, ready to explore the Big Apple in the morning.

Emily woke up at six on Wednesday morning. As she was preparing her morning cup of coffee, she was having mixed feelings. She was glad to be this close to NYC, and she was looking forward to showing Miriam around for the next few days. She was also wishing she had spent more time with her family. She was also starting to miss her life in Tulsa. While this had been a very enjoyable trip, she was longing to be back home again. She has a wonderful life in Tulsa, and she couldn't wait to be back.

Shortly after she had gotten up, Miriam came out to the living room and joined her on the couch. She was excited to see the city. She had heard so much about it, that she couldn't wait to get started. After getting dressed, they headed down for a nice breakfast, though it wasn't quite as nice as what Grandma had made the day before.

When they were done with breakfast, they headed out, taking the walkway to the station. After purchasing their tickets, they waited for the train, which came pretty quickly. Miriam had never been on a train like this before. They took their seats for the approximate twenty-minute trip. Miriam was surprised to see that much of the last part of the trip was underground. Her mom told her that the station they were going to was underground, and actually underneath an arena.

When the train arrived at the station, Emily told Miriam to hold her hand, as the crowds could get a little crazy at times, and she didn't want her to get separated as they left the station. It took them a few minutes to exit the station, which seemed more like a mall at times than a train station.

When they exited the station, Emily let her know that they were in midtown. They headed over to the Empire State Building first, to try and beat the long lines that inevitably formed. Their wait wasn't too bad, and Miriam loved the views. She saw so many interesting buildings that she wanted to explore.

When they had finished with the Empire State Building, they walked the few blocks over to Macy's. Miriam could not believe that most of the building was shopping, and she said she could spend all day there looking around. Emily explained to her that this was the store with the Santa Claus that was in the Christmas movie that they had watched with her grandparents.

After looking around for a few, they headed north to Times Square. Miriam loved seeing all the lights and signs. She had never seen anything like it before. Emily showed her where the ball was set up to drop tomorrow night to ring in the new year. She also let her know that they didn't want to be anywhere near this place tomorrow night.

Emily asked if she was ready for some serious shopping, and Miriam got excited. They walked a few blocks over to 5th Avenue, and Miriam couldn't believe all the stores. They explored a few of them, and many were multiple stories tall, of nothing but clothes. Miriam said she would need a week, just to get through this. Her mom just laughed, as they headed for lunch.

After lunch, they headed to the subway for the ride downtown to the Financial District. Miriam had never been on the subway before, and it was quite an adventure for her. She wanted to know how people could figure out which route they wanted and what direction. She did enjoy the ride on the subway. She had decided to stand up and hold the railing, which resulted in her being moved all over the place. Luckily, it was not a busy time and the car was relatively empty.

Being a business major, Emily loved the Financial District, and she showed Miriam the World Trade Center and told her more about what happened that day, and where she was, and what she was doing. Miriam had seen information on TV about it, but this was something different, especially when they viewed the memorial. They also passed by the stock exchange and Miriam wanted her picture with the bull.

After seeing some of the Financial District they headed south where Miriam could see the Statue of Liberty and wanted a closer look. They headed over to where they could catch a boat over to the island. Emily explained what the statue meant to those that came here for a better life, and the process they went through when they came here. She knew Miriam would love to hear the story, as that is what her family did a few years ago. It had a special meaning to Miriam, and she was glad that her mom had brought her out here. She was glad that her mom embraced her background and didn't try to pretend it didn't happen. She remembers when her family made the decision to come here, and how it soon changed everything.

After getting back from the island, they found a local restaurant. After dinner, they walked over to the Financial District and took the direct train back to Newark. When they got back to the hotel, they wanted to relax for the rest of the night. It had been a busy day with lots of walking and so many things to see. Emily let Miriam know that they had only seen a fraction of what there was to see in Manhattan, and that was only one of the five boroughs that made up New York City. Miriam laughed and said they would need a month to see it all, and her mom said that was probably right.

They spent the rest of the evening relaxing on the couch, looking for something to watch. They finally found a movie and watched it till it was time to head to bed for the night. It felt great to be just the two of them again, exploring the world. Tomorrow would bring more adventure for the two of them, and possibly a few surprises as well. It would be New Year's Eve, and they were in the Big Apple. Anything was possible.

New Year's Eve morning and Emily was up at six. As she got her coffee, she reflected on the year, since it was the last day of the year. It had been an incredible year for her, and one she could not have even imagined happening, just a few months ago. In a matter of days, she would legally become the mother of a beautiful fourteen-year-old girl. She had hoped to have kids someday, but this was completely unexpected. She also had more success professionally than she could have imagined. She was thankful for the success she had seen this year.

Miriam joined her on the couch about thirty minutes later. She had enjoyed yesterday and was looking forward to seeing more of the city. Once they had gotten ready, they headed to the restaurant for breakfast. Miriam enjoyed the food, but she missed the large selection that her Grandma had cooked for them.

After breakfast, they headed to the station and took the train back to Penn Station, this time they stayed at the station and took the subway uptown for a while. When they emerged from the subway, Emily let Miriam know that today they were in a different borough, the Bronx. Up ahead was the Bronx Zoo, and that was their destination for the day.

This was quite a zoo, and it took them most of the day to see what they wanted to see. Miriam not only loved seeing the animals, but she also wanted to learn more about them, such as where they are from and the types of places that they live in. There were quite a few animals that she had not seen before in person, so she was excited. For lunch, they had some pizza slices, which they didn't eat that often back home.

Once they had seen everything they wanted to see, they took the subway back to Penn Station and the train back to the hotel. While it had been a busy day, they decided that they were not quite ready to head to bed, especially since it was New Year's Eve. They got cleaned up and changed into something a little dressier and headed out to check out the town. Their first stop was a restaurant for dinner. They were quite hungry from all the walking around they did. After a nice dinner, they headed out to check out some of the shopping in the area. They found a few outlet stores in the area and picked up a few things.

After the stores began to close, they headed back to the hotel for their New Year's Eve party. It was not just for hotel guests and was quite the place to be that night, as it one of the few family-friendly events in the area. While they did have adult beverages, they had plenty of other options.

They alternated between dancing for a few songs, getting a snack, or just sitting next to each other, with Emily placing her arm around Miriam. As it got closer to midnight, they headed back to the dance floor to ring in the new year together. The last song ended shortly before midnight and everyone began the countdown. As the clock struck midnight, and other couples were kissing, Emily wrapped her arms around Miriam and held her close, kissed her on the cheek, and told her that more than anything this coming she wanted Miriam to be her daughter and spend as much time with her as she could. Miriam responded that it was what she wanted more than anything as well for the coming year.

After dancing together for one more song, they decided to head upstairs to bed. Not only had it been an incredible day, but it had been an incredible couple of months together, and they now had a whole new year to spend with each other. They could hardly wait to see what wonderful memories the coming year was going to bring them. They knew that as long as they had each other, it would be a wonderful year for each of them.

New Year's Day Emily didn't wake up till close to eight. It was rare for her to get up this late, and it was also rare for her to stay up to midnight, but she and Miriam had a great time last night, so it was worth it to her. She had the feeling, though, that she would need two cups of coffee to get going this morning. She hadn't yet thought of any plans for today, and she knew she didn't have the energy to do the amount of activity that she had done the previous two days. She did want to do something as this was their last full day to see New York, and tomorrow morning they would be back on their way home to Tulsa.

Miriam was up shortly after and laid on her mom on the couch.

"Well, good morning and happy new year, Miriam!"

"Good morning, Mom, and happy new year too!"

"Feeling a little tired this morning?"

"Oh yeah. Feel like I could use some of your coffee."

"I bet. How about we get dressed and go get some breakfast?"

"You had me at breakfast."

They headed off to get ready and down to the restaurant for breakfast. While at breakfast they talked about what they wanted to do today. Miriam also said she didn't have the energy to do the amount of stuff that they had done the past two days. Emily said they could drive around and see a few things, and if they wanted to stop somewhere, they could. Miriam liked that idea, as she did want to see some things, but didn't want to be running around like they had.

After breakfast, they headed out. Since it was a holiday, Emily decided that it would be OK to try driving in New York City, so they got in the car and headed out. They took the Holland Tunnel into the city. They explored the SOHO and Tribeca neighborhoods first, checking out some of the unique areas and stores, before taking the Brooklyn Bridge into Brooklyn. In Brooklyn, they drove around a bit, before stopping at Prospect Park and the Zoo. This was a much smaller zoo than they had seen yesterday, so it was perfect for today.

Their next stop was the borough of Queens, where they found a mall and walked around for a bit. For some reason, they always had the energy to walk around and explore a mall. While at the mall, they found some lunch, which they took with them to nearby Corona Park, where they enjoyed a picnic lunch together since it was a surprisingly warm and beautiful day. After lunch, they walked around for a bit enjoying the nice day and each other's company.

When they finished at the park, they headed south towards the JFK airport. They stopped for a few and watched some of the large aircraft takeoff and land heading to and from many international destinations. Emily told Miriam that in a few months they would be on one of those planes heading out together. Miriam said she couldn't wait.

They headed out west from the airport, which let them follow the shore for a bit, which let them pass by many of the beaches in the area, along with Coney Island. They would need to come back sometime to visit there. They then crossed the Verrazzano-Narrows Bridge, heading to the last borough of Staten Island. They drove around for a bit, grabbing some dinner, before heading back to the hotel.

They spent the rest of the evening packing and getting ready to head home in the morning. It had been another wonderful day to end an incredibly wonderful trip. Tomorrow, they would head home, which was OK, as it brought them one day closer to Miriam being adopted and becoming a permanent member of the family. It was worth it to head home if it meant that Miriam could become a permanent member of the family.

Saturday morning and Emily was up at six. While she had wanted to sleep in a little, they had a plane to catch in a few hours. The plane was scheduled to depart around 10, so they would need to leave the hotel in a little bit. While this had been a wonderfully memorable trip, she was glad to be heading home. She had just invested in a ranch that she was looking forward to learning more about and trying some new things with. The most important reason to head home was happening in two days, and she could barely wait any longer.

It was about 6:30 that Miriam came out and sat beside her mom. She had also greatly enjoyed the trip, but she was also ready to get back home to her new life.

"Well, Miriam, we better get some breakfast so we can get to the airport."

"Sounds good to me, Mom, both the breakfast and heading to the airport."

They headed down to the restaurant for their last breakfast at the hotel. After breakfast, they gathered their bags and loaded up the car, for the short trip to the Newark Airport. They got the rental car returned and loaded up their bags on the shuttle for the trip back to the airport. Once they checked the majority of their bags, they headed through security. It didn't take them long to get through, as it was still early in the morning.

By the time they got through security, they had ample time to get to their gate, without rushing through. As they were walking to their gate, they noticed that this airport was not quite as nice as some of the other airports they had been to recently. Just as they were arriving at the gate, an announcement was being made that due to needing an aircraft repositioned, they were switching aircraft types, so they would need all new boarding passes. Luckily, Emily was able to pull it up on her phone and was able to avoid the lines.

A few minutes later, they saw a much larger plane approach their gate than they had been flying. Emily let Miriam know that this was like one of the larger planes they were watching yesterday, heading to various international destinations, though today it would be flying them to Houston. When they boarded, they were pleased and surprised that this plane had the lie-flat seats, and each seat was like its own little area. This would be flying like neither of them had experienced before.

Once the plane was in the air, they laid their seats flat and enjoyed a movie on their screen. Since it was a longer flight, they were also served a brunch. They could definitely get used to traveling this way, and Emily told Miriam that this is what flying overseas was like, but with nicer meals. Miriam couldn't wait to travel overseas.

After about a four-hour flight, they arrived in Houston, TX. They had a little over an hour to get to their next gate. It was a longer walk, but it felt good to stretch their legs after a long flight. When they got to the gate, they were disappointed to see that the plane was much smaller and only sat fifty people. There would be no lie-flat seats or meals on this plane, but it was only going to be a ninety-minute flight back to Tulsa.

They arrived in Tulsa, just before 4 PM. They collected their bags and headed out to get their SUV. On the way home, they stopped to pick up some dinner. Emily was too tired to cook when they got home, and it was getting late. After two weeks away, it felt great to be at home and sitting on their couch again. Miriam even had to lay on her mom's lap again and said it felt good to be home. They both just laughed.

Not wanting to do laundry tonight, they opted to relax on the couch together. They caught up on a few of their shows and enjoyed some quiet time with just the two of them. It really did feel good to be home.

Sunday morning and Emily felt like she slept in but still woke up at six, though this time it was six Central time and not Eastern time. As she was getting her coffee, she thought how great it was to wake up in her own bed in her own house. Both of the hotels had been wonderful, but there was something about being in the familiar and comfortable. She also enjoyed the week with her parents, as well as other family members, but there are times when one doesn't need to worry about what others are doing in their home when you are visiting them. Breakfast this morning would be when she wanted it, and what she wanted, though she hadn't gotten groceries yet, so they were a little light on breakfast foods at the moment.

It was about thirty minutes later that Miriam joined her on the couch in her usual spot. She looked quite content to be there, and it was one of Emily's favorite moments in the morning.

"Well, good morning, Miriam! Did you sleep OK last night?"

"Yeah, it was good to be in my own bed again."

"I know the feeling. Well, I was going to make breakfast, but we haven't gotten groceries yet, so we don't have a ton of breakfast items. We can open presents first, then go get breakfast and groceries, or we can do those first."

"I'm hungry now."

"Why doesn't that surprise me. Well, let's go get dressed and find some food."

After getting dressed, they went to their favorite diner for a big country breakfast. The food felt like home, which was something they had missed while they had been away. There was something about a big country breakfast with biscuits & gravy and grits that said, "Welcome to the South". Once they had finished with breakfast, they headed to the grocery store for their weekly trip.

Once they got home and had the groceries put up, they headed to the living room for a late Christmas. Emily had spent some of her free time at work buying many of the gifts for Miriam since she was at school at the time. Miriam was excited to see the presents and was secretly hoping they were not all clothes. The first thing she got was a gift card to one of her favorite clothing stores. Her mom explained that this was for buying all the undergarments, so she could get exactly what she wanted. Miriam had a look of gratitude that her mom hadn't tried to buy all those things for her.

While she did get some clothes, she was excited for many of them. Her mom found her another skirt and jacket suit but in a different color, so she had more to wear if she wanted to dress like her mom. There were also many dresses that she loved as well. She also received many books and DVDs, many of which her mom also liked, so it gave them something for them to watch together.

The last gift that Miriam opened was a necklace with a gold heart pendant.

"Once the adoption is finalized, they will add your initials to it. I would have had it done already, but you mentioned that you wanted to change your middle name, but never told me what you wanted to change it to."

"I know, and I want it to be a surprise. I will tell you tomorrow when we are at court. I think you will like it."

"If that is what you want to do, then I guess I'll wait till then." She crossed her eyes, stuck out her tongue, just like Miriam loves to do. They both laughed, then Miriam came over and gave her mom a big hug and kiss on the cheek, thanking her for the wonderful presents, as well as the trip that they had just been on. Her mom let her know how glad she was that she enjoyed everything.

With all the major activities done for the day, Emily asked Miriam what she felt like doing for the rest of the day. Miriam said she wanted to relax some, but she had some gift cards to use, not only the one she had just received but others from her new family, that way she wouldn't have to travel back with a lot of presents.

They headed off to their favorite shopping center to spend a couple of hours spending all the gift cards. Miriam wanted to buy some more shoes, as a young lady cannot have enough shoes. She wanted another pair to wear to school that looked good with her dresses and skirts but was not overly dressy. She also bought another pair of heels, for when she dressed up like her mom, for looking at houses or for their ladies' night out.

At another store, she finally bought herself a purse. She didn't have a lot to carry with her but wanted something that made her look like she was grown up. The final place she went to was the store that her mom got her the gift card. She was able to a few items that she needed, and thankfully was able to buy what she wanted and was comfortable with, and not what her mom liked. She was a teen girl, and her mom had to be clueless on what she liked, especially when it came to that type of clothing.

After an adventurous time of shopping, they headed home to relax for the rest of the day. They watched a few of the DVDs that Miriam had gotten for Christmas, taking a break to make dinner together. It was a great girls' night in, and after the hustle and bustle of the past two weeks, it was the perfect way to relax and spend time together. Normally, today would also mark the end of the weekend, but this one still had one more day left in it. One more extra special day that would forever change the two of them.

Adoption day and Emily was up at 5:30. As she was getting her coffee, she was feeling a little anxious about today, yet incredibly excited. In a few hours, she would stand before a judge and formally adopt Miriam. Until everything was final, she was still worried that something would happen, even though there was no logical basis for it. All she knew is that the finalization couldn't come fast enough. She was ready to know that Miriam was her daughter for the rest of their lives.

It was shortly after six that Miriam joined her on the couch, laying in her favorite position, so she could look up at her mom.

"Well, good morning, Miriam. Are you ready for today?"

"More than anything! I really want you to be my mom!"

"I really love to hear that, since more than anything I want you to be my daughter!"

"I'm also feeling sad, as I feel like I'm saying goodbye to my mom again."

"You're not saying goodbye to her. If she couldn't raise you herself, she would want someone to love you and raise you the way that she would have. She started you on the journey, and I'm going to finish what she started. Does that make sense?"

"I think so. It just feels confusing at times."

"Don't let it confuse you. You can still love her and me. Many kids when their parents get divorced end up with several parents in their lives, and they can love all of them. It's something like that. Would you feel less confused if I made breakfast?"

"I'm already starting to feel less confused."

"Somehow I knew that would help."

Emily got up and headed to the kitchen to cook breakfast. There was one thing she knew she had to cook today, and that was biscuits and gravy. It had been over two weeks since Miriam had proper biscuits and gravy, and today was a special day. In addition to the biscuits and gravy, she also prepared some eggs and bacon. She wanted today to be special for Miriam and memorable as well, so she had a few things planned for the day. Miriam greatly enjoyed breakfast, just as Emily knew that she would.

Now that breakfast was over, she had Miriam get dressed, and they headed out for a little surprise before the big appointment. Emily had booked some mother-daughter time at the spa. They were both getting their hair trimmed and washed, facials, and Miriam was getting her nails done as well. It was a surprise that Miriam greatly enjoyed. She loved the attention that she got, and it made her feel very special. She also enjoyed spending some quality time with her mom.

Once they were done at the spa, they headed back home for a bit to get properly dressed for the hearing. Emily wore her usual work attire, while Miriam wore a nice dress and heels, which made her look like she was ready for senior pictures. Emily told her she was beautiful but quit growing up so fast. She wanted to enjoy the time that she had with her. Miriam gave her a hug and they headed out to the hearing.

When they arrived outside the courtroom, Rachel was there to greet them, along with the attorney that had overseen the process and was there to make sure everything was taken care of. Alexis and Kelli had come as well to show their support as they had grown quite fond of Miriam, and they were glad that Emily had found someone that made her so happy. They both noticed a difference when Miriam entered the picture.

A few minutes later, the bailiff came out and let them know that they could come in. Alexis and Kelli sat where the audience would sit, while the others proceeded to the front and sat at the tables that were usually for the attorneys in a case. Once everyone was seated, the bailiff left momentarily to let the judge know that everyone was ready.

A few moments later he reappeared with the command to "All rise for the honorable Judge Wilber". Once the judge had taken his seat, he let everyone else sit, while the clerk handed him the paperwork. He briefly looked through it to make sure everything was there and ready.

The judge had Emily and Miriam step forward in front of the bench. He then swore them in and told them that they were under oath.

Once they were sworn in, he started the hearing.

"Emily Gardner, I understand it is your desire to adopt Miriam today. Is that correct?"

"Yes, it is your honor."

"Miriam, is it your desire to be adopted by Emily today?"

"More than anything, your honor."

"Glad to hear it. I understand that you had a surprise for your soon-to-be adopted mom, and you had desired to change your name. Is that correct?"

"Yes, it is, your honor. Today, I want my name to be Miriam Hope Gardner. When my family died, someone told me I needed to have hope that things would improve and that I get adopted someday and have a new family. When I first met my mom, she gave me a hoodie that had the word hope on it. Somehow I knew that she would be the one that would adopt me."

By this time, Emily is practically in tears.

"That is a wonderful name, young lady. I think your mom approves of it."

"It is such a beautiful name for a beautiful young lady."

"I agree. Let me ask you one final question. Do you promise under oath that you will love and raise Miriam as if she were your own biological daughter? That will receive the same benefits, such as an inheritance that a biological child would receive."

"I do your honey."

"Then it is my honor to pronounce the child to be Miriam Hope Gardner, daughter of Emily Gardner. He picked up the gavel and handed it to Miriam and had her bang it."

Miriam ran to her mom and they both hugged, while Alexis and Kelli stood up and cheered and clapped. Once Miriam and Emily were done hugging, the judge shook their hands and congratulated them. The next few minutes were spent taking pictures and having the judge sign the decree and giving a copy to Emily. Miriam had told Rachel in advance what she wanted her name to be, so it was already part of the decree.

As they walked out of the courthouse, hand in hand, they were ready to officially start the rest of their lives as mother and daughter. Miriam said there was only one way to celebrate, and it was a ladies' night out to which Emily agreed. They both felt a sense of relief that this process was over, and they could look forward to spending as much time as they wanted together, which is what they both wanted, more than anything.

Made in the USA
Middletown, DE
17 March 2021